Protector

ELAINE GONZALES

for Jay
love you brother
♡ Eli Gonz.

Protector is a work of fiction. Names, characters, businesses, organizations, places, events, and incidents either are the product of the author's imagination or are used fictitiously. Any resemblance to actual persons, living or dead, events, or locales is entirely coincidental.

Edited by:
Nicole Wayland / Ford Editing
Penny Walker
Gabrielle Fimbres

Cover design by Audrey Tate / audreytate.com

ISBN: 0692653031
ISBN: 978-0-692-65303-6
eBook ISBN: 978-0-692-65388-3
Library of Congress Control Number: 2016903661
Elaine Gonzales, Scottsdale, AZ

For Nicolas

ACKNOWLEDGMENTS

Time to spread some love. Big thanks to some special people: My sister, Carole Agajanian, and her family—Aaron, Erica and Audrey. I couldn't have done this without you guys. My soul sister, Audrey Tate. You are my rock. #ilk forever! The Gonzales Clans of Tucson, every single one of you. Scott Craven, for showing me the way. A shout out to those of you who took the time to offer critiques and advice—Penny, Jill, Adrienne, Stephanie, Alana, Gabrielle, Becki, Allison, Serina. Your support has been invaluable. Finally, to my little man, Nic Slade, thank you for being such a cool kid and allowing me to do this. I hope it inspires you to follow your dreams.

The inferiority of women is man-made.
American author, activist and lecturer Helen Keller
June 11, 1916

PROLOGUE

The pain was acute. She'd never felt anything like it.

The weight of the world lay heavy in her heart now. All she had done, everything she had sacrificed—would it be enough?

She had no way of knowing, but there was no going back now. She was sure he would come after her. She knew his arrogance and distorted sense of justice wouldn't allow for anyone else to retaliate. He would track her down.

1

THURSDAY—BRISTOL, ENGLAND

I'm eighty-nine years old and I still get butterflies in my stomach.

Veronica couldn't help but laugh. It was ridiculous how nervous she felt. She stepped out onto the balcony and tapped a cigarette from the box. She glided it under her nose and breathed in its scent. Her wicked senses picked up the rich spices, and they tickled her throat. She lit her smoke and inhaled.

Why did it have to be like this?

Her work rarely made her anxious. She was skilled at keeping her emotions in check, but this was different. There was so much at stake.

A cool gust blew across the terrace. Veronica tilted her head back, allowing her long hair to billow in its current. She closed her eyes, and an image immediately appeared. It was always there, like an old photograph, and she treasured it.

She took a long, last drag off her cigarette, then disposed of it. She went back inside and upstairs to the bathroom, where she washed away the remnants of her habit and tended her hair. She leaned in close to the mirror and searched for a wrinkle, an age spot, or even a gray hair. Nope. Nothing. She could still pass for twenty-nine.

Eat your heart out, Angela Lansbury.

Veronica laughed and went back downstairs. Soon she grew impatient waiting for the call. She contemplated downing a few shots of bourbon but then thought better of it. The business at hand called for a clear mind. Lucky for her, a pure heart wasn't as essential.

Her phone vibrated on the glass counter and she quickly snapped it up.

"Yes. I'm ready. Tell Benedict to bring the car around. I'm on my way."

2

THURSDAY—BRISTOL

Charlie wouldn't shut up about it. Jude knew when his friend came home that morning he'd spend the rest of the day hearing, in great detail, about the incredible lay he had experienced. Charlie wasn't classically good-looking, but he wasn't unattractive. He was an average English bloke. Jude would tease him and call him Shaun because he reminded him of Simon Pegg in the movie *Shaun of the Dead*, complete with goatee and strawberry blond hair. He was also clumsily awkward around women, so when Charlie would get some, it was a big deal. And, apparently, the previous night's coup was the stuff of dreams. The jury was out on whether the facts were true or if Charlie's imagination was in full gear, but either way Jude had nothing better to do. Therefore, a day of free pints while listening to Charlie extol his affair was better than not doing anything at all.

Charlie and Jude were regular patrons at a pub down the street from their flat in Bristol, but that morning the pipes had burst, shutting it down for the day. Charlie was in such a good mood he suggested they go to the city centre to watch the football match at one of the hotel lounges with the large flat-screen TVs. Jude didn't object.

Charlie was on his second pint and fourth retelling when Jude saw her. He took notice as soon as she entered the lounge. Because of her, brunettes always caught his eye.

He had spent the past forty years yearning to see those blue eyes again. The memory of her face was so familiar to him. When he thought back on that night—that moment—it was as clear and as powerful as if it had happened yesterday. He'd never felt anything like it, and he ached to feel it again. He spent many sleepless nights thinking about her: wondering who she was, where she was, if she was still alive. He hoped she was afflicted with the Condition so there would be a chance he'd see her again someday. Mostly, though, he thought about being intimate with her. He wanted to know her and talk to her. He wanted to love her.

Right away, he recognized something in her manner. Her raven hair was swept to the side and slightly tucked into her jacket except for a few strands falling along her cheek. He watched as she approached a man and greeted him courteously. She took a seat facing Jude's direction, but he still couldn't see her clearly. His stare was fixed and his body taut as he waited anxiously for a glimpse of her eyes.

She was focused on the man, making small talk while she settled in. Jude tapped his fingers nervously on the bar. At last, a waitress approached their table and she looked up. Jude's glass slipped from his hand and a splash of beer flew up and hit Charlie on the chin.

"Bloody hell!" Charlie said with a laugh.

Jude didn't acknowledge the slight, which made Charlie notice his fixation.

"What is it?"

Charlie looked around to see what had captured his friend's attention. He didn't see her at first but then caught Jude's line of sight.

"Who is she?" he asked. Jude didn't answer.

"I don't know—she may be a bit out of your league, my friend," he razzed.

Jude remained silent. He couldn't take his eyes off her.

"Hey," Charlie elbowed him in the arm.

"It's her," Jude said.

"Who?"

"France."

Charlie furrowed his brow as he put it together. "No," he said skeptically.

"Yes, it's her," Jude confirmed. "There's no doubt."

Charlie glanced over at her again. She was deep in conversation with the man now.

"What in the world is she doing *here*?" Charlie asked.

"I don't think it's personal. They're talking about some property on Ashton Road."

"What I'd give to have your hearing," Charlie shook his head. "You have to go talk to her."

"What am I going to say—remember me from that shithole forty years ago?"

"Well, obviously she has the Condition. You don't think she'll remember you?"

"I don't know. I'd hope so, but I don't know," Jude said as he continued to admire her. "Man, she is pretty, exactly how I remember her."

"She is quite fetching," Charlie observed. "But, as you know, I prefer blondes or redheads. I mean, not that I would pass up someone like her, but she's definitely more your type. Actually," he said upon closer examination, "she's exactly your type. I don't think I've ever seen you with a blonde or a redhead."

Jude put his finger to his lips. "Shhh."

They both sat there watching her. Eventually, Charlie began talking to the bartender again while Jude kept his eyes squarely on her. He never wavered. He tried to be cool about it but his thoughts were on rapid-fire.

Would she remember me? Would she be scared? Would she try to kill me? Where are her companions? Did I put deodorant on today?

It was difficult for him to just sit there. He wanted to run up to her, take her in his arms, and show her how much he'd longed to see her, but the little Irish boy inside him kept him perched. If she didn't remember him, or worse yet, if she dismissed him, he'd lose his precious obsession.

It wasn't long before Jude noticed they were gathering their belongings.

"She's leaving," he said to Charlie.

"Well, go on then. You can't let her leave without speaking to her."

"No, I need her to see me first. I want to see her reaction."

Jude watched her put on her jacket.

"What are you doing?" Charlie asked in surprise as his friend remained stoic.

"Wait," Jude said and stood up.

She was making her way to the door when he realized she was scanning the room. She knew she was being watched. He saw her curiously survey the crowd, scrutinizing each face, until she reached him, and there it was. It was instantaneous, just like that night. Her mouth slightly opened but then quickly shut as she composed herself.

Jude deliberately held her gaze for a few seconds as he delighted in the moment. Then, he stepped away from the bar and walked toward her. Charlie, who was watching the scene unfold, guzzled the last of his pint and followed his friend. He wasn't about to miss this. He wanted a first-hand account since he had heard the story numerous times over the years.

3

1972—SOUTHERN FRANCE

It was cold, severely cold. The sun was setting, and the temperature was dropping. Veronica waited outside a dilapidated building on the outskirts of Grenoble, quivering underneath a thin trench coat and knit cap and scarf. She was pissed she forgot her gloves and cigarettes in the van. She thought about running back to get them, but then Noah came around the corner.

"We're pretty sure he's inside," he said before blowing into his hands. "Marshall and Colin are going in the back. We're going in the front, but I want you to stay by the door in case he tries to come out this way."

"Got it," she said confidently. She wanted to salute him like a soldier, but she didn't think he would appreciate the humor.

He broke the bottom pane of the glass door and unlatched the lock. They stepped into the dark and dusty lobby.

"Stay here," he said. "If you see him, don't hesitate, all right?"

"Okay."

After he disappeared into the blackened hallway, she looked around and inspected the dingy foyer. She imagined what it might have resembled when it was new. She skimmed the walls, peering up near the ceiling where she could see the wallpaper flaking off. It was too dark for a regular human to notice such a thing, but she could see it as if it were lit midday.

The smell permeating the hallway was a disagreeable array of odors that was hard for her to repel. She could detect traces of leather, ink, and men's cologne.

Brut, yuck.

She deduced it might have been an office building or a factory, most likely occupied by a company of misogynists, smoking cigars and blowing shit up each other's asses. She snickered at the thought. She had the urge to explore, but she knew she had to stay put. There was a man lurking around who could possibly be heading her way, and she couldn't let him pass. So, she waited and listened. Her acute hearing allowed her to keep track of the boys. She could hear them rustling around the back of the building.

Jude was fucked. They had caught up with him and now he was cornered—in an abandoned building, no less. He had to think. He wasn't sure how many of them there were. He saw three of them earlier at the house, maybe more on the road. He knew who they were and why they were chasing him. He knew he might not make it out alive.

He walked carefully through the dimly lit hallways, passing dank, barren rooms. He could hear them outside. They weren't in the building yet, but he knew they weren't going to leave until they scoured the place.

He had to find somewhere to hide, at least until he could figure out what to do next. He came upon a room crammed with discarded furniture and quickly decided to shield himself among the furnishings. He was maneuvering through a maze of cabinets and desks when he noticed a door at the rear. He peeked in. It was dark and hollow. He stepped inside and shut the door behind him. It went pitch black; not even a sliver of light seeped in from below the door. He moved through the darkness, feeling his way along the wall. There were shelves, lots of them, mostly ceiling-to-floor units. It was a storage room. He frantically felt around until he touched a cold metal rack along the back wall. He bent down and reached below it to gauge the space. He knew it would have to do. He squeezed underneath it, burrowed against the wall, and then listened carefully for his pursuers. He heard them enter the building. He tried not to move, but he was so cold. His clothes were wet, and a shiver ran through him.

It didn't take long before he heard someone enter the adjoining room. It was obvious they weren't trying to sneak up on him. Whoever it was made a point of shoving furniture around and knocking items over. Jude lay terror-stricken beneath the shelf.

The racket continued for a few more seconds before an unnerving pause, and then the door creaked open. Jude inhaled slowly and held it in. The beam from a flashlight moved around the space. He was sure he would be caught, but then the door closed and the room was black again. He laid his head on the cold ground and exhaled.

He waited until he could tell they were a good distance away before slipping out from under the shelf. He opened the door and peered ahead, looking for a path out of the room. He moved gingerly through the clutter, well aware that their hearing was as keen as his own. When he reached the hallway, he heard them again, shuffling around upstairs and in the back. This was it, he thought. He hustled toward the front entrance. When he felt cool air wafting ahead of him, he sped up with anticipation. Then, suddenly, one of the floorboards beneath him broke and he fell through. The crash echoed throughout the building, followed by a resounding hush as everyone came to a halt. Jude lay frozen on the busted surface. Immediately, he heard them scrambling overhead. He pulled himself up and bolted down the corridor. He knew he was close.

Veronica stood very still with her gun pointed in the direction of the hallway. She wasn't sure what it was she heard, but she knew it wasn't one of the boys. She stepped carefully toward the daunting entry and heard someone running toward her. She took a defensive stance a few feet back and prepared herself.

Without regard for what may lay ahead, Jude ran into the lobby at full speed but abruptly pulled up when he saw her. She stood at an angle with her right arm extended out in front of her, her left arm behind her back, and a gun aimed directly at him.

As soon as she saw him, her eyes opened wide and bore into him. The light from the street lamp was enough for him to see their vibrant blue color. She glared at him so fiercely he lost all sense of his surroundings.

Veronica was shocked at the sight of him. He was dripping wet, his black curly hair dangling around his face. His eyes were blacker still and full of emotion. They seared through her.

Holy hell!

She kept her gun pointed at him and tried not to appear affected. He looked frantic but not dangerous, almost childlike as he trembled before her. She did not feel threatened. She wasn't sure what she was feeling, but she knew it wasn't fear.

The last thing Jude expected to see was an attractive woman with a gun blocking his only way out. Her dark hair was partially pulled back under a knit cap, exposing her fair skin and exaggerated features. She was strong and powerful in her stance, holding him in her sight with a confidence that assured him she was in control. He was so entranced by her appearance it paralyzed him.

They stood mesmerized for only a moment, until they heard the others closing in on them. The panic returned and Jude looked away, hoping for another way out, but he knew there was only one way for him to go. He turned back to her.

"Please," was all he could muster.

His plea nearly knocked her over. It was heartbreaking and sad, and yet unbelievably sexy. She stepped back as if trying to distance herself from the surge of emotions that were beginning to overwhelm her.

Jude's affliction gave him a hypersensitive ability to perceive emotions in people, even when they were unaware of it themselves, and he sensed her yielding just before her stern expression began to soften. Veronica realized she wasn't going to hurt him. She lowered her gun and stepped away from the door.

What the hell am I doing?

Jude couldn't believe it. He walked up to her and soaked in as much of her as he could. There was a tenderness in her expression that told him she was just as affected by their encounter.

Veronica was crushed by the depth and anguish in his eyes. He stared at her with such intensity that she felt naked before him. She could feel herself slipping away; then she heard Noah holler and she snapped out of it, but it was too late. Jude ran past her and out the door.

Oh my God, what did I just do?

She pointed her gun in the air, pulled the trigger, and dropped to the ground. The boys came running out from the hallway and through the open door. Noah stopped to help her.

"What happened?"

"He came running around the corner. He had a gun," she feigned.

"Are you okay? Are you shot?" he asked as he pulled her up.

"No. I'm all right."

"Damn it, we had him!"

They stepped outside but didn't see anyone. Noah went farther out into the deserted street and surveyed the area. There wasn't any sign of him.

The freezing air had enveloped Jude's wet body the moment he hit the pavement. The industrial area was desolate. He had no idea which way to go. He sprinted ahead toward a row of darkened buildings and slipped through a narrow alleyway. The back lot was filled with empty crates and metal shipping containers. He quickly mounted one of the containers that was up against a building and scaled precariously up toward the roof. He almost fell from an unsecured railing but managed to reach the top. He ducked down and peeked over just as one of the men ran through the alleyway and into the lot. He watched as the man continued on.

Jude knelt down and tried to catch his breath. He was about to settle back when he heard voices. He crawled to the front of the building and looked over. There she was, standing outside the factory. She paced nervously while another man scoped out the area. Moments later, two other men showed up.

"He's gone," Colin said, out of breath and looking directly at her. "How the hell did he get past you?"

She didn't say anything.

"What the fuck happened?" Marshall chided as he joined them.

"He had a gun," she said.

"So did you! Did you shoot him?" Marshall retorted.

"I missed."

Marshall squinted his eyes at her. He knew she was an expert shot.

She sensed his doubt and glared back at him with arched eyebrows.

"What?" she growled with attitude.

"I just think it's odd that both of you had a gun and no one was shot," he said.

"Maybe he didn't shoot because I'm a woman. Believe me, I know how you guys lose your shit when a woman is involved."

"Did he say anything?" Colin asked, dodging her insinuation.

"We didn't chat. He came around the corner. I took a shot and missed. He shoved me aside and ran out the door. End of story."

She wasn't sure if she was selling it, but she knew these boys very well.

"Look, I'm sorry. Maybe next time I should stay in the van," she said.

She pulled her coat collar up, shoved her hands in her pockets, and walked away, leaving the three of them surprised by her unexpected resignation.

"Shit. Come on, V. It's okay," Marshall called out. "We should've realized he might be armed."

She kept walking.

I'd like to thank the Academy.

When she reached the van, she climbed in and found a cozy spot in the back. She put on her gloves, lit a cigarette, and took a lengthy drag. She closed her eyes and pictured him.

Damn.

After they left, Jude slid down against the icy brick and sighed. He was relieved but also surprised. He knew he had made an impression on her and it thrilled him. The past twenty-four hours had been traumatic and devastating, yet as he sat there numb from it, all he could think about was *her* and those blue eyes.

4

THURSDAY—BRISTOL

What the fuck is that smell?

Veronica noticed it when she arrived, but the scent lingered as she sat in the lounge with the Realtor. It was subtle yet distinct, drifting enticingly over the stench of stale beer and various appetizers.

"Is something wrong?" the Realtor asked.

Can't you fucking smell it? No, of course you can't.

"I'm fine," she said. "About the property—we require absolute discretion. Will that be a problem?"

"I guarantee you no one will know the identity of the purchaser." He placed his hand on hers and leaned in, "You have my word."

She smiled then lifted his hand and placed it on the table. "Your word will be sufficient. May we go see the property now?"

"Certainly."

She stood up and slipped into her black jacket, cinching the belt with a terse tug. Her gifted sense of smell was often bothersome, but she had learned to control it. That's what made this particular aroma so vexing. She tried to ignore it, yet it was baiting her to find its source.

"I'll fetch your car, miss," the Realtor said. He picked up his briefcase and walked on.

She gathered her things, left some cash on the table to cover the bill, and proceeded toward the door. She was making her way through the tightly placed tables when a familiar sensation came over her, one that gave her cause for alarm.

Someone was watching her.

Cautiously, she glanced around the room, slowing her pace as she meticulously scanned the anonymous faces mingling around her. For a brief second, she wondered if her senses had deceived her, but when she reached the door she saw him. He was standing by the bar, staring intently at her.

As soon as their eyes met, she recognized him. He looked exactly the same—his face and those eyes. She caught her breath.

For the past forty years, this man had lived in her memory, haunting her with hopes and dreams of seeing him again someday. Now that day had finally come. He stood across the room from her in a crowded hotel lounge.

Immediately, all her senses heightened and honed in on him, as they were prone to do due to her affliction. She was sure she could hear his heart beating as rapidly as her own, and when he stepped away from the bar and moved toward her, the scent became stronger.

Good Lord, it's him.

There was no mistaking it now. It was fragrant and tempting, and there was something else. An undeniable heat was emanating from him, or at least she thought it was coming from him. The closer he got, the hotter she felt. It was like walking up to a fire, except he was the fire and she could feel the heat building as he approached.

When he stood before her, she was amazed at how perfectly his dark features and wavy black hair matched the image she had always carried with her. She often wondered if she had embellished him over the years, making him out to be more attractive than he actually was that night. She was pleased to know that was not the case.

"Hello," he said.

She didn't answer right away, still struck by his presence.

"Is it really you?" she said softly.

He nodded. "You remember?"

Seriously?

"Yes, of course," she said with a nervous smile.

Their eyes locked in on each other, neither willing to breach the moment. The heat coming off them was strong and sexual, and it was deeply affecting both of them.

"Excuse me, miss, your car is waiting," the Realtor interrupted.

"One second," she said, holding up her index finger at him.

She took a step closer to Jude.

"I can't believe it's you," she said. "After all this time."

"What are you doing here?"

The Realtor cleared his throat, but it went unnoticed.

"We need to talk," she stated.

"Yeah, we do."

"Will you meet me tonight?"

Jude's face lit up with a smile that made her gasp.

"Absolutely," he said.

She was floored.

"Um, all right then," she stuttered. "I'm staying at the Radisson BLU." She checked her phone. "Let's say, seven?"

"I'll be there."

A few more seconds passed while they stood captivated.

"Miss?"

"I have to go," she said, motioning to the door.

He held her eyes. "One more thing," he said. "What's your name?"

She grinned, realizing they had never actually been introduced.

"Veronica." She put out her hand. "Room 1702."

"Hello, Veronica. I'm Jude."

Jude.

He finally knew her name. He could barely contain himself. He took her hand.

"Did this just happen?" he said. He gently pulled her close. "I've dreamt about this moment," he whispered in her ear.

Holy shit.

He moved back slowly, softly brushing his cheek against hers. She was sure she had stopped breathing.

He didn't want to let go of her. He worried something might happen and he'd spend another forty years searching for her again. As she backed away from him, his heart filled with hope at the thought of finally knowing her.

Reluctantly, she retreated, but she kept her eyes on him. She paused at the door, and then walked out.

Jude didn't move. He was completely blown away.

When Veronica slipped into the backseat of the town car, she tried to regain her composure but was altogether unsteady, almost faint. She collapsed into the cool leather upholstery. She took a deep breath and slowly exhaled. She could still smell him.

"What the hell was that?" Charlie blurted.

"What?" Jude said, not realizing Charlie was standing behind him.

"If I hadn't seen it, I wouldn't have believed it. It was like in a movie. You both just stood there, ogling each other. It was rather impressive, not to mention slightly disturbing."

Charlie headed back to the bar and Jude followed, still feeling dazed.

"It was, wasn't it?" he said. "Impressive, that is."

"Undoubtedly," Charlie agreed. He waved to the bartender for another round. "So, what are you going to do now?"

Jude leaned back against the bar and smiled.

"I'm going to the Radisson BLU at seven."

5

1942—PENNSYLVANIA

This can't be true.

She couldn't believe what she was hearing. It made no sense.

Her mother knelt down in front of her. "Do you understand what we're saying, Veronica?"

She stared blankly at the ground.

"I want you to try. It's really quite simple," said her father, who was standing by the window.

She closed her eyes tight and tried to wish them away.

"What you're saying is, I'm never going to die?" She opened her eyes and glared at them.

"No," they both said simultaneously.

"This has nothing to do with death," her mother explained. "It has to do with living. If you are fully affected by the Condition, then you may end up living an exceedingly long life."

This was how Veronica first learned about their affliction. She was seventeen years old.

Her parents had stopped aging when they were in their twenties, and they believed they had passed this trait on to her. She tried to grasp what they were telling her, but she couldn't wrap her head around the idea that she may never grow old.

"Are we the only ones?" she asked.

"No, most of the Clan have the Condition," her father stated.

Her heart sank.

She never thought her life was extraordinary. She grew up surrounded by a close-knit group of people her parents referred to as their Clan. They lived discreetly on several acres of private property north of Philadelphia. The children were home-schooled, and they didn't interact much with anyone outside of the Clan. She thought it was a normal life. They never struggled or wanted for anything, and she always felt safe. There was never any reason for her to be troubled. But now, it seemed, there was.

Her head was spinning. She wanted to know everything. Her parents were hesitant to delve into the specifics of how they came to be afflicted, but Veronica was adamant. Eventually, they told her the whole story.

It happened when her parents were students at Cambridge in 1922. Their social circle consisted of like-minded scientists and mathematicians who gathered frequently to exchange ideas on various topics. They were an affluent group of young adults who exulted in their social standing. They were passionate and full of self-confidence that, on occasion, teetered on arrogance.

The men were industrious scholars at the top of their respective classes, while their female counterparts were equally studious, despite being denied full membership at university during that time. They were the *crème de la crème* of their generation, and once a month they would gather to celebrate their wealth and vitality with an elaborate dinner party, flush with expensive spirits and a sumptuous feast. It was during one of these affairs that the effects of aging and talk of the Fountain of Youth were first broached. They debated scientific approaches to extending life expectancy. At first, it seemed implausible, but the more they discussed it, the more they convinced themselves, with tremendous audacity, that if it could be done they were the ones who could do it. They soon became preoccupied with the possibility of producing an antidote similar to the legendary elixir.

Since their families' wealth and station afforded them the ability to travel the world at their leisure, they went in search of modern and ancient remedies used to preserve youth. It was on one such trip that two of their Irish friends, Eliot Turner and Scott McNair, came back from India with a vile of what they believed could be the breakthrough they were seeking. They were confident they could break it down and use it as a baseline for their own research. Several of them, including Veronica's father, worked on it for more than a year until, finally, they came up with a formula they believed could ease the aging process. They discussed who would test it, whether only a few should dose it or more. They agreed that in order to verify its true effectiveness, it would have to be a large sample. Therefore, they all decided to take the serum, as well as several close friends and family members who had been following their quest and wanted to participate. In all, twenty-five people willingly chose to tempt fate.

Within a few months, the participants reported significant changes. They could feel something was happening. Their senses were enhanced, they healed from injuries faster, and they were unnaturally healthy. They never got sick, not even a sniffle, but they couldn't yet determine if the aging process had slowed. Since they were young, the effect wasn't noticeable.

However, the physiological developments were unexpected and confusing. They weren't sure how or why those symptoms were taking place or if they would last. The purpose of the experiment was to prolong their youthful appearance and, maybe, live a bit longer than normal. They weren't prepared to deal with the issues the side effects created. They continued to document everything and test regularly; they knew they had to be patient. They hoped time would give them the answers.

The group attempted to live their lives normally during this period. They graduated and moved away, some back to America, others to Ireland and France. Many married and started families. They all kept in touch and continued to monitor their progress. They kept their symptoms a secret, but it became more difficult as the years passed. Eventually, rumors began circulating within the group that the aging process had, indeed, been affected.

In 1931, Eliot called a meeting of the original twenty-five participants. Communication was slow at that time, so he wanted everyone to come together to discuss the situation in person. When they gathered in London, they were shocked to discover they all looked exactly the same, as if they were still students at Cambridge. No one had physically changed in any manner. Initially, some of them were ecstatic that the experiment was a success, but that was short-lived. They had hoped to slow down the process, not stop it altogether, and, at that point, that's what they feared may have happened.

Many members of the group panicked. They had severely altered their physiology and didn't understand the consequences. They had no way of knowing if they would begin aging again, or if they would remain in the same condition, and for how long. Their abnormal symptoms were distressing and difficult to hide. Would they have to deal with them for the rest of their lives? The questions were endless, and no one had any answers.

Scott suggested they get the medical community involved, but Eliot quickly shot that down. He believed it was in their best interest to keep it a secret. They had hoped to create an antidote they could share with the world, but now the outcome was far more serious than they expected and Eliot saw only the negative impact it could have on them and the human race. He argued that World War I was still fresh in their memories and it could be dangerous if their serum fell into the wrong hands.

A larger—and graver—issue became apparent when they questioned whether their children could be affected. By this time, there were forty-four kids between them. Birth control was limited and large families were the norm, so it wasn't unusual for there to be that many offspring already. Unfortunately, all the children were born after they had taken the serum. The oldest child was seven years old.

They started testing the children and quickly concluded they were all afflicted. They were aging normally, but they were experiencing the side effects. They never got sick and recovered rapidly from injuries. Everyone had thought they were fortunate to have such healthy children and never made the connection. That is, until they came together and realized that every child had the same characteristics. They were developing heightened senses of sight, hearing, and smell. Similar to the early days of their experience, the symptoms were there, but they didn't yet know if the children would stop aging as well.

The Originals, as they became known, decided to form into Clans once the children were diagnosed. They realized they had to begin living inconspicuously, for the sake of the children. It was a daunting predicament, especially since they didn't know how long they would have to live like that. They brought in their immediate families to help keep their secret, and this created an organized society of Clan members who lived in the United Kingdom, Ireland, France and America. They communicated as often as possible through letters and telegraphs, making sure everyone was informed on the progress of the children as well as their own developments.

Veronica was part of this first generation born into the Clans, who became known as the Elders. They grew up within the Clans, but most weren't told about the Condition until they reached adulthood. It was then that testing showed their aging process was slowing down and the Originals knew they could no longer keep it from them. Because it wasn't known yet just how much their physiology had been altered, the Elders spent most of their early adulthood sheltered within the Clans. It wasn't until they reached their thirties that it was determined they were no longer aging.

When it became clear that the children were entirely affected by the Condition, the Originals were devastated. They had spent years trying to come to terms with the enormity of the situation and the possible societal backlash that could occur if it was ever discovered what they had done. But once they realized their children were also going to have to live with the consequences, their paranoia consumed them and they immediately closed ranks. They unanimously decided to never disclose their predicament and to stay hidden for as long as possible. Once they agreed to this, they formed a governing body within the Clans to help maintain their anonymity, the first and foremost objective being to protect the Clans and keep the Condition a secret.

The wealth and education of the Originals made it easy for them to establish their own communities and become self-reliant. The majority believed that if the Condition became known, the ramifications could be catastrophic. By the 1950s, regular society was frightened by its own shadow, not to mention the threat of nuclear war, beings from outer space, and gigantic mutant insects. It terrified the Originals to think what would happen to them and their children if their secret was revealed, and they knew as the years passed it was going to become harder to conceal it.

Eliot's eldest son, Marshall, didn't hesitate to take up the cause in Ireland. His father had been very open with him from a young age, so he understood the dangers involved with the Condition. With his father's help, he distributed cryptic newsletters in the mail to all the Clans, encouraging them to live anonymously and keep their families small. He stressed the importance of it in no uncertain terms, emphasizing it was vital to their existence. Marshall organized a group of Elders he called the Protectors, and when the Governing Order was formed, they officially acknowledged Marshall's men and gave them the authority to monitor Clan members and help keep them hidden and under control.

By midcentury, there were well over one hundred members living with the Condition. Over time, some heeded Marshall's advice and abstained from having children, but many did not. Because the Condition kept them young and healthy, childbearing years extended far longer than normal. Fear and guilt kept the Originals in line, but first- and second-generation Clan members continued to have children well into their fifties and sixties. Consequently, the Clans grew exponentially, and by 2014 there were more than three thousand Clan members throughout the world.

6

THURSDAY—BRISTOL

Jude lingered by a water fountain across the street from the Radisson BLU, smoking a cigarette and replaying the events of that afternoon. Finally, he thought, he found those blue eyes again and they were as stunning as he remembered. What really surprised him, though, was how she still took his breath away. It was as if she stepped right out of his dreams. Her presence was imposing, just like that night when she stood her ground without any trepidation. That was what turned him on, and he was pleased she still had that air about her.

He kept an eye on the time and grew anxious to see her. There was so much he wanted to know, particularly about that fateful night. He wasn't ignorant about her possible involvement in the deadly events that had taken place, but he hoped there was a reasonable explanation. So much time had passed; he refused to consider any potential risk. He shook his head and flicked his cigarette into the street.

She didn't hurt me then; why would she hurt me now?

He had spent decades away from the Clans and avoiding anyone with the Condition. But this was different; she was different. He knew he was meant to see her again. He zipped up his jacket and crossed the street.

Veronica was calm as she waited for him to arrive. She tried not to let her excitement get the best of her. She thought about what she would say to him, but as she sipped her bourbon, she realized more than anything that she wanted to kiss him. She really, really wanted to kiss him. She had fantasized about it hundreds of times, along with what he might taste like and how he smelled. She wanted to touch his hair. It was wet and curly that night, and she always wondered what it would feel like to run her fingers through it. There wasn't any part of him that she hadn't thought about in great detail. He lived quite vividly in her memory.

Unfortunately, she did harbor some concern over her desire for him. Frankly, it freaked her out. She had no idea what kind of man he was and yet she wanted him so badly. But it wasn't just a physical attraction. The moment she laid eyes on him, she felt a connection. She was instantly drawn to him. She'd never felt anything like that before or since, and it only manifested over the years. The memory of him flourished and he became the love of her life, a forty-year affair in her mind. And it was enough for her. If she needed affection, she found it. She had had relationships over the years, but most were superficial. It never bothered her because she just didn't care, but with Jude it was different. She definitely cared. Now, seeing him in the flesh and still looking so damn good, it was like winning the lottery. She was thrilled but didn't know how the hell to handle it. She poured herself another shot of bourbon.

God, I hope he's not an asshole.

She caught a glimpse of herself in the mirror behind the bar and wondered if she should pull her hair back. She lifted her long mane up over her head and noticed her necklace that fell beneath her blouse. She pulled it out and cupped the silver Irish trinity-knot pendant at the end of it. Running her thumb along the cool metal, she drifted off as the memories it held filled her mind. She stayed fixed on her reflection until a knock at the door brought her back. Without hesitating, she unclasped the necklace and put it in her pocket.

When she opened the door, his scent poured over her like water bursting through the doors in *Titanic*. She sometimes hated her superhuman sense of smell, but not today. He filled her up and she loved it.

Jude was taken aback when she appeared. She looked even better than she did at the lounge. She was barefoot and wore faded jeans and a pale mauve cotton shirt. Her hair was tousled and fell down along her chest. He always thought of her with stately features, but seeing her now, it was obvious there was much more character in her face. Her eyes were bold underneath straight-layered brows that made them appear narrower than they actually were. Her lips were full, framed by subtle smile lines that he found especially appealing.

A few seconds passed as they looked each other over.

"Hey," he finally said.

"Yes, hi!" She laughed. She stepped back and allowed him to enter. "Come in."

She closed the door and leaned back against it, gripping the handle behind her for support.

Jude walked in then turned back to her. When their eyes met, the energy surged between them. It was a confluence of desire, excitement, curiosity and nerves, and it was more intense than the first time they stood before each other.

"I've often wondered what I would say to you if I saw you again." She smiled. "My thoughts are a bit muddled at the moment but I think it was along the lines of—where the hell have you been all this time?"

Jude laughed. "Aye, many times I've wondered the same about you. Although, I don't think I ever imagined running into you in a hotel pub in Bristol."

"Funny how the universe works," she said softly.

"You look beautiful," he said. "Exactly how I remember."

"The Condition does have its benefits. You aren't as wet as I remember, but definitely the same."

Veronica finally released the door handle and walked up to him. The heat radiating from their bodies was both soothing and erotic. She couldn't help herself. She reached up and took hold of a black curl that was lying along his temple. She wrapped her finger around it.

Yes!

"You have no idea how much I've wanted to see you again," she whispered.

Jude gently stroked her cheek with his fingers.

"I think I do."

He took her face in his hands and gazed into her eyes. He had always wanted to hold her close enough to see every speck of blue.

Spectacular.

Veronica's heart was beating so fast it hurt, and then he kissed her. His warm lips tenderly caressed her mouth. She put her hands on his waist to hold herself steady, but touching him made her tremble even more.

Jude eased back and put his forehead against hers. "I've wanted to do that for some time now."

She brought her hands up to his neck and held firmly against him.

"I can't believe you're here. Tell me I'm not dreaming," she said.

Jude put his arm around her and pulled her in. He kissed her deeply this time as she maneuvered her hands into his hair. They had waited decades for this moment, and it was exactly what they wanted to do.

"I don't care if we're dreaming. This is fucking incredible," Jude whispered in her ear.

He felt her slightly wilt in his arms. She pulled back from him, flushed and teary.

"Shit," she said and turned away. She took a deep breath then laughed it out. She wiped her eyes and turned back.

"Would you like a drink? I need a drink." She grinned.

She went over to the bar and Jude followed her. He stood close to her as she served up a couple shots of bourbon.

He held up his glass. "To my flatmate, Charlie, for suggesting we go to that pub today."

Veronica tapped his glass with hers. "To Charlie."

Jude winked at her and downed his drink.

Veronica immediately poured another round then led him into the living area where they sat next to each other on the couch. Whatever it was they felt that night in France, they were both aware it had endured the test of time. Jude was ecstatic. Veronica was dazed.

"I have to say, I'm a little surprised you never forgot what happened between us," she said coyly.

"Why? It was a powerful moment. I remember it as if it happened yesterday."

"I suppose I didn't want to let myself imagine you felt the same way. Forty years is a long time to carry something like that around."

"It wasn't a burden, believe me." Jude took her hand. "I never forgot you. So many times I wanted to search for you, but I had no idea where to even begin. I went back to France once, but I knew you weren't there."

His touch electrified Veronica's senses. Like a flutter, it coursed through her veins until it reached every part of her body. She looked into his eyes and suddenly every ache she'd ever felt for him came rushing back. She put her head down and clutched his hand.

"I searched for you, but it was like you never existed. Where have you been?"

"It took a long time for me to settle down after what happened, and I steered clear of the Clans so I didn't stay in one place for very long."

"What are you saying, you've been living underground?"

Jude leaned back into the couch and finished his drink. "I've lived most of my life away from the Clans."

"But how? I've heard that's terribly difficult."

"It's not easy, but it's manageable. And then you become accustomed to it."

"I don't know how you could. I can't even imagine it."

"It's not that bad," Jude said under his breath.

"No, I suppose not."

He sat up and placed his glass on the coffee table. "May I ask you a question?"

"Of course."

"That night, why did you let me go?"

Veronica felt a tug in her heart. She didn't want to say something silly and cheapen the moment. Before that night in Grenoble, she didn't believe it was possible to be touched so deeply and so suddenly by a complete stranger. For the longest time, she couldn't even admit to herself what actually happened. She never trivialized it by calling it love at first sight.

"It was your eyes. There was so much emotion in them, and the way you looked at me. I was paralyzed by my feelings."

Jude took her hand again and kissed it. "You saved me. I can't thank you enough."

Veronica gulped.

"I was struck as well," he said. "The warmth you exuded overwhelmed me. I'd never been so drawn to someone." He leaned in close to her. "I'm still drawn to you."

He smelled so good she began to feel woozy.

What the hell is going on?

"It's a little stuffy in here," she said and abruptly stood up. "I'll open the balcony doors."

Jude reached into his jacket pocket and pulled out his cigarettes.

"Do you mind?" he said, holding one up.

"Not at all."

They stepped out into the cool night air and Veronica quietly inhaled as much of it as she could. She was especially sensitive to fresh oxygen and breathing it in had a calming effect on her.

Jude kept his eyes on her as he lit his cigarette, and she indulged him. She remained silent while he canvassed every inch of her.

In his dreams, she was a diminutive figure, petite and powerful. As he looked her over, he realized she was taller than he remembered. She was still several inches shorter than his six foot self, but the way she carried herself made her seem statuesque. And despite her casual attire, her hourglass figure was unmistakable. Her curves and ample breasts cast a provocative silhouette.

"I swear I didn't do you justice," he said. "My memory of you pales in comparison."

Veronica blushed, which surprised her. She was not the blushing type.

"Are you trying to sweep me off my feet?"

"If that's the effect it's having then yes."

Veronica laughed and looked out over the Bristol skyline that had faded into darkness. She was so happy, almost giddy, and her nerves began to wane. When she looked back at Jude, though, his expression had changed.

He took a drag off his cigarette. "Why were you there with those blokes?" he asked grudgingly.

Veronica returned to her view. She knew he was going to ask about them, and although she had prepared herself for it, she immediately tensed up.

"I was involved with one of them. We had been together for some time. He worked with the Protectors and I went along with him on occasion. It was foolish, I know that now, but it was such a turbulent time back then."

"Are you still involved?" he asked.

She turned around. "With him?"

"With all of it."

"No." She smiled and raised her eyebrows. "Everything changed for me that night."

She wanted to tell him everything. How he's been in her heart all this time. How she hasn't been able to give herself completely to anyone because of how she felt about him. How she always hoped they would find each other. She wanted to tell him exactly how she felt, but she didn't. She knew she shouldn't. Not yet.

Jude searched for the faintest sign of deception. He could tell there was more to it, but her explanation sounded plausible, and he wanted to believe it.

"I shouldn't have been there either. It was stupid, and I paid dearly for it. Everything changed for me that night, too, in more ways than I care to say, but that was a long time ago. I just had to know why you were there. Now I know."

He leaned over and kissed her on the cheek.

Well, that was easy.

Veronica held his hand as they stood in the shadows. They didn't speak. They just stared at each other, both contented in the moment. Veronica studied his face. His features were undeniably masculine—dark, full eyebrows, a prominent chin and the reddest lips. His black hair was out of control, curly in some places, wavy in others. It was shorter than when she saw him last, laying along the nape of his neck, with long sideburns that blended into a smattering of light stubble along his jawline and upper lip. Without question, he was the sexiest man she'd ever laid eyes on. That's what she thought of him forty years ago, and that's how she saw him still.

When he finished his cigarette, she went in for another hug. It was her new favorite place—in his arms.

They returned to the living area a bit more relaxed. Jude settled back on the couch, but Veronica sat across from him this time. She thought a little distance would help her stay focused. They eased into a conversation about what they had been up to and were surprised by some of the similarities.

Neither had ever married, nor had children. Both had moved around quite a bit—to be fair, a common characteristic among Clan members— but they both stayed predominantly on the British Isles and, unknowingly, somewhat near each other most of the time. They both resented the Originals for what they had done, and for insisting they be grateful for it. Neither considered their affliction to be a blessing. However, when it came to their views of the Clans and the Governing Order, known widely as the G.O., the similarities stopped there.

"I take it you're still bound within the Clans," Jude said.

"You could say that. I handle real estate affairs for the G.O. That's why I'm in Bristol. I'm closing a deal on a major acquisition south of here."

"You work for the G.O.?" He appeared bothered by this news.

"Is that a problem?"

He didn't answer.

"What's wrong? Why does that upset you?"

"I would prefer you didn't tell anyone about me. If they know I'm here, they might try to bring me back in, and I don't want that."

"I don't think they would do that. You've stayed out of trouble all these years, right? What other reason would they have to be interested in you?"

Jude shrugged.

"What happened in Grenoble was ages ago," she said. "If they wanted to find you, they would've done so by now. Besides, I wouldn't tell anyone. I've waited this long to see you again. I wouldn't do anything to ruin that."

He smiled, feeling somewhat relieved.

"Why have you stayed away from the Clans?" she asked.

"Well, back then, the Protectors were after me. After that night, I knew I would never be part of it again." He rested his elbows on his knees and put his head down. "There was always something sinister about the Clans. I knew that even when I was young. It was stifling. I couldn't breathe whenever I was around them. I remember they wanted to control every part of my life." He looked up at her. "Didn't you ever feel that way? Like you wanted to abandon all of it and be free of it?"

"No, not at all. I never imagined running away from it. I suspect it was different in your Clan, but in mine I was safe and sheltered. I didn't feel repressed by it. It wasn't until I ventured out and began interacting with Regulars and other Clan members that I noticed the disparity, but I adapted to it. I accepted the necessity for the rules and guidelines."

He shook his head. "It was too much."

"You're Irish. Where are you from?" She hadn't picked up on his accent at the lounge. It was a proper East Coast Irish dialect, one with which she was very familiar.

"Dublin."

"I lived near Dublin back in the late sixties. I wonder if we ever saw each other."

"I was gone by then."

"Is your family still there?"

"Mostly," he replied, without elaborating. He did not like talking about his family.

She felt his apprehension. "Oh, not close, huh?"

"Is your family in America?" he asked, trying to steer the topic away from him.

"No. My parents passed away a long time ago."

"I'm so sorry. How did they die, if you don't mind me asking?"

"It was a car accident about twenty years ago. They'd been alive for almost a hundred years before a pathetic drunk driver snuffed it all out."

"Your parents were Originals?"

"Yes."

Jude paused. "I'm an Elder as well."

"So, our parents knew each other."

"I guess so. That's a wee bit strange to think about. I forget sometimes what a small world the Clans are. I wonder if we ever met as children."

"Did you ever visit the States?"

"No."

"My parents brought me to London when I was six. I think it was when the Originals realized what they had done, but I don't remember much, and I didn't return here until I was in my forties," she said.

"I would've been three at that time." He laughed at the thought. "Maybe we did meet and we just don't remember."

"Maybe."

Veronica thought hard about that. What if they *had* met as children? Would it be possible they felt a connection back then but were, obviously, too young to notice? She never once considered the possibility that they may have met when they were young.

Interesting.

"I'm surprised you've managed to stay under the radar," she said. "The Elders are pretty closely monitored. Do you have any siblings?"

Jude balked, clearly befuddled that the subject came back around to his family.

"I had two brothers, but they're no longer around."

"I'm sorry. I don't mean to pry." Veronica got up and picked up their glasses then went back to the bar.

"No, please don't apologize. I just don't like to discuss my family."

Jude knew he should be wary of anyone with the Condition, a lesson he learned the hard way a long time ago, but he simply didn't want to think of her in any other way than what she was to him right then. He had always had this vision of her in his mind, and she was slipping easily into what he wanted her to be. He didn't want to spoil it by being too cautious. He'd spent the past forty years living prudently. He had finally found her and wanted to enjoy every second of it.

When she returned, she sat next to him this time. She leaned in and touched his curls.

"I love your hair," she said. "It's exactly as I hoped it would be."

"This mess? It's shit."

"You're crazy."

She put her hand through his hair and pulled him close to her. Jude leaned her back against the couch and didn't hold back. Veronica breathed him in as she tasted him, and the combination was exquisite. She could feel herself slipping away.

Hang on now!

After a few seconds, Jude sat back and grinned.

She took in the full scope of his eyes. They were wildly expressive and touched something inside of her, just like the first time. She knew she could lose herself in them.

"Are you freaking out?" he asked.

"Yes. Is it obvious?"

"Everything is obvious to me."

"So, I needn't bother trying to be mysterious?" She batted her eyelashes.

He chuckled. "No, not like that. I can't read your mind, but I can sense what you're feeling."

"Just me or everybody?"

"Everybody."

"Oh Jude, that can't be easy."

"It's not."

"Wait, so you know what I'm feeling right now?"

A sly grin lit up his face.

"Oh my God." Veronica laughed. She stood up and moved away from the couch. "That's not fair."

Jude got a kick out of her reaction. "There are perks."

He walked over to her and came up close, putting his hands on her waist.

"It's not invasive. I promise. It's like a vibe—a sensation. But let me say, what I'm picking up from you is so different from anything I've ever felt before. It's feels extraordinary."

Veronica didn't know what to say. She was wholly unprepared for the physical and emotional attraction she felt for him. As much as it frightened her, the passion stirring inside of her felt so incredible it overpowered any uncertainty. She placed her hands on his chest and felt her way up and over his shoulders, and then she nuzzled into his neck.

"It is extraordinary," she whispered.

Hours passed, but they didn't notice. They fell into an intimate rapport as they delved deeper into their histories. They ordered dinner, listened to music, talked about movies and their favorite places to live, all the while failing miserably to keep their hands off each other. Except for Jude's occasional smoke break, they spent most of the evening comfortably entangled on the couch. In between long, sensual kisses, they shared details about themselves in such a way it felt like they were old friends catching up, not new lovers who were hearing these revelations for the first time.

It didn't take long for Jude to begin noticing the little peculiarities of her personality. He loved how she trailed off into her own thoughts when she spoke of something especially dear to her, like her favorite band, Stereophonics. When she described how much she loved the singer's voice and how it physically affected her, Jude was moved. Her passionate nature was further evident when he dared to trivialize her favorite movie, *The Way We Were*. She considered herself a film connoisseur and enjoyed lively discussions on the topic. Jude discovered how much it meant to her when after some good-natured teasing, at the expense of Robert Redford, she held her own and playfully put him in his place. He laughed more that night than he had in a long time. He knew right away they were going to get along. She didn't take herself too seriously, which was exactly the type of person he always wanted to be with.

Jude was gentle—definitely *not* an asshole. Veronica couldn't read people as well as he could, but it was apparent to her he was the type of Clan member who suffered greatly from their circumstance. But he was a survivor. He was eighty-six years old and still thriving. She admired him, and felt a little sorry for him. She was so taken by him she allowed herself to open up in a way she only did with her closest companions. She knew he was infinitely more special than she ever imagined.

Jude took her hand and massaged it. He stroked her fingers all the way down to her fingertips. Veronica watched him and was amazed at how erotic such a simple act could be. He seemed enthralled, as if he were studying every aspect of her fingers. Then, he brought her hand up to his lips and kissed it. He looked up with a sensuous gaze and kissed it again, this time keeping his eyes riveted on hers. Her insides stirred, and she was drenched.

She couldn't take it any longer. She stood up and brought him with her. She moved her hands up to his neck and kissed him ardently, fully expressing her desire. She wanted him now more than ever. She took his hands and walked backward, guiding him with her toward the bedroom upstairs. Jude was so aroused he wasn't sure if he was going to make it to the bed.

Veronica set the pace, slowly unbuttoning his shirt as she kissed him. He ran his fingers through her hair, supporting her head, and eagerly accepting her. He felt his way down her back and reached underneath her blouse. The touch of her soft skin almost sent him over, but he controlled himself. He released his mouth from hers, and pulled her shirt up over her head.

Methodically, they undressed each other while kissing every newly exposed area. They tried to be serious about it, but it turned into a light-hearted romp as they attempted not to tickle each other or get tangled while peeling off each other's garments. The heat between them grew stronger with every touch, every kiss, until every last stitch was removed. Jude placed his forehead on hers, then kissed her softly on the lips. He opened his mouth to speak, but no words came out. Veronica put her finger on his red lips and kissed him. He knew he was ready to give himself completely to her. She moved fluently onto the bed and opened her arms, beckoning him to come to her.

Jude held back for a moment. He wanted to remember her exactly as she lay before him. He was overcome by how irresistible he found her. Nothing existed outside of that bedroom, and he wanted to cherish it. Gently, he climbed onto the bed and into her arms. She embraced him and he nestled his warm body next to hers, which made the heat between them flare even stronger.

Veronica moved his hands along her body, allowing him to touch every part of her. She deliberately took her time so she could savor every sensation. He tenderly kissed her skin as she guided him. At first, he had to concentrate so as not to lose control, but then he realized he didn't need to—she knew exactly what to do to keep him tempered. He found it incredibly easy to follow her lead. Soon, he was moving with her, anticipating where she wanted him next.

As his hands and lips perused her body, she breathed in slowly, filling herself up with his scent. She could practically taste it as it consumed her. It was a hot, earthy aroma—distinctly virile and unmistakably sexual. It was intoxicating. She felt warm and wet and strangely high from it. She was at his mercy. She raised her arms up overhead and stretched while he kissed and suckled her between her thighs.

The moonlight shone through the sheer curtains and Jude caught a glimpse of her in the warm glow. Her skin glistened from the torrid foreplay. She tried to stay still, but he was closing in, and as her body tensed, she knew she was on the verge, and so did he. He inched his way back up to her, kissing her body along the way, and then he entered her, and she cried out. He pulled himself up so he could see her. Her eyes were dark and seductive, enticing him with every soft gasp from her mouth. He couldn't help but smile, and neither could she. It was perfect. He came down and sucked on her bottom lip, then nibbled his way down to her neck. They moved effortlessly in rhythm until they erupted together.

Fuck yeah!

Depleted and fabulously content, they lay next to each other in awe. Clearly, the bond they shared was stronger than they both anticipated. The ease in which the evening progressed, without it being the slightest bit awkward or uncomfortable, was anything but ordinary, and they were both mindful of it. They knew their lives were about to change.

It was still dark outside when Veronica woke up. She didn't sleep much. She never did. When she was younger, she would stay up all night reading, then rise at dawn feeling refreshed. She was sure it was due to the Condition, but it never bothered her.

She rolled over on her side and watched him sleep. He had always been so striking when she thought back on that night so long ago, and now he was lying next to her looking gorgeous in the muted light. She managed to wrangle a strand of curls along his neck without disturbing him. She had a habit of playing with her own hair, but the texture of his had a weirdly pacifying effect on her. She was both curious and delighted with it.

She didn't anticipate her affection for him would be so immediate and profound, and she wasn't sure how to deal with it. This could get complicated, she thought. She moved closer and smelled his skin.

Damn.

She laid her head on his shoulder and cuddled up next to him. She softly ran her fingers through the thin layer of black hair on his chest and traced it down his abdomen. She thought about her life away from that hotel room. She was keenly aware of how impossible their situation was, and she wished everything were different. She had a feeling she could love him, *truly* love him.

Unbelievable.

This sudden turn of events kept her awake the rest of the night

7

1942—DUBLIN, IRELAND

Jude never liked to socialize. He preferred the company of his brothers and family. It's not that he was shy or insecure—he wasn't. He knew he was personable like his siblings; he just had no interest in interacting with other people. Because of this, he was rarely seen without one of his brothers. Mark, the oldest, was seventeen, Kelly was sixteen, and Jude was fourteen. They lived in a Clan of twenty-two people southwest of Dublin. It was made up mostly of their father's family and some of his college friends and their families. The Clan was a self-reliant community that lived on the earnings of the Originals, who did business in Dublin. They had strict rules about staying close to home, but occasionally, the Elders were allowed to take day trips into the city.

Jude loved visiting Dublin. He and Kelly would get lost in the museums and library. Sometimes they would sit for hours outside watching people bustle about and tracking the trams and cars that moved around like insects through the winding streets. They both dreamed of living in a big city someday, either there or somewhere else in Europe. They couldn't wait to grow up and travel the world.

Living in a private community with their Clan was never bothersome to Jude, but it was to his brothers. They often complained about not being able to keep company with anyone outside the Clans. Except for the day trips to Dublin, they were only allowed to interact with Clan members. Occasionally, they would have social gatherings with the other Clans from Ireland and the U.K., but that was more like a family reunion than an opportunity to meet new people. As Mark grew older he became more suspicious of it. He would often gripe about all the rules that didn't make sense to him. Kelly usually agreed with him, but for different reasons. He was the heartbreaker of the boys. He and Jude resembled each other. They were both lean with dark hair and soulful eyes, whereas Mark was fair-haired and thick, more like their father. But, unlike Jude, Kelly was an extrovert, charming and charismatic, which made him very popular among the female Elders. He loved the attention he received from them, but he preferred the girls in the city, and many day trips consisted of Jude following him around as he pursued a young lady. For Kelly, his complaints about the Clans had more to do with the limited dating pool.

When Mark turned seventeen, World War II was raging. Ireland had stayed neutral despite the Germans bombing Dublin in 1941. After that, Mark became obsessed with news of the war and the Allies' involvement. He talked incessantly about joining the British military to fight the Nazis. His parents kept his interests at bay, siding with the Irish sentiment to stay out of it, but Mark would not let up. He monopolized the radio, listening to news reports and propaganda, and in Dublin he would hang out at pubs to discuss the war with like-minded young men.

Finally, after one evening in which the discussion became more heated than normal, his parents knew it was time for their boys to know the real reason why Mark could not leave to join the war. It wasn't because of Ireland's neutrality or the risk of losing their firstborn. It was because the Elders were extraordinary and unlike the regular humans who lived outside of the Clans.

When Jude's parents explained the Condition to the boys, Mark did not take it well. He was angry they had kept it secret, but then he realized what they were actually saying.

"We're captives. Are you saying I can never leave here?"

"I know it's difficult to understand, son, but this is how we have to live in order to protect ourselves," their father explained.

"Protect ourselves from what? Who are we afraid of?" Mark argued.

"That's just it—we don't know. We don't know how the Regulars would view this. We're not aging, and we're not sure how long it will go on. We may end up living longer than normal humans, and that's a frightening notion."

"Are we going to live forever?" Jude interrupted, trying to comprehend what he was being told.

"Possibly," his mother answered. "We can die an unnatural death, but it appears we won't suffer the same maladies as regular humans. Do you understand what that means?"

His parents were both highly educated so the boys had received an exceptional education directly from them. Jude knew exactly what she was saying.

"I can be killed, but I won't get sick and die," he answered.

"Yes, we believe you boys have the Condition," his mother said.

"How could you do this to us?" Mark yelled. "I don't want to stay here for the rest of my life. I want to see the world. I want to fight in this war."

"Mark, calm down," his father tried to reason with him. "We don't know what will happen in the future. A time may come where we can move about freely, but right now we can't take that chance. There's too many of us living with this. If we expose ourselves, we could endanger everyone's lives. You may not want to live your life here in this community, but who's to say they wouldn't lock us all up in some godforsaken place? You've read about those camps the Americans are forcing the Japanese into. Who's to say that couldn't happen to us? We don't know what would happen, and for that reason we have to keep this secret."

"What *do* you know? All I'm hearing is we don't know, we don't know. This is unacceptable!"

Jude and Kelly kept quiet as Mark and their father continued the discussion back and forth. His parents had hoped that explaining their situation would subdue Mark's desire to leave, but it had the opposite effect. He was inconsolable and even more determined to leave. His father pleaded with him not to do anything rash, to be reasonable for the sake of their family. It took some coaxing from their mother but, eventually, Mark relented. He looked over at his younger brothers and knew whatever he did would affect them. He decided to let it lie—for now.

That night, when the boys were in their room alone, Mark told them he wasn't going to stay home for much longer.

"I have to leave. I can't stay here. There's too much going on in the world. There's a war being fought across the sea. How can we sit idly by and do nothing?"

"Mark, our entire country is staying out of the war. Why do you have to get involved?" Kelly asked.

"Because I want to kick some German ass and stop Hitler. I want to fight like those before us who fought in the first war. Jesus, don't you feel any obligation to this world we live in?"

Jude and Kelly looked at each other, knowing they did not.

"Well, at least it explains what we've been wondering all this time, why the hell we're not allowed to make friends outside of the Clan or invite anyone home," Kelly said.

"I don't believe it," Mark said, refusing to accept it. "How do we know they aren't making this up just to keep us here?"

"You think they would lie to us?" Jude asked innocently.

"Hell yes," Mark blurted out.

"No," Kelly objected. "It's true. I heard Marshall talking about something similar about a month ago. I was standing behind him and his father at the market, and I don't think they knew I was there. I remember his father saying something about aging and protection. I had no idea what they were discussing, but it sounded interesting. I think it's true, Mark."

"I don't feel any different," Jude muttered.

"Actually," Kelly said, thinking hard about something.

"What?" Jude asked.

"Remember when we were at the library a few weeks ago and I told you I could hear that girl whispering from across the room?"

"Aye, I could hear her, too. So?" Jude answered.

"I don't think everyone could hear her."

"What do you mean?"

"I think we can hear better," Kelly explained. "Father said some of our senses might become more acute as we get older. I think that might be one of them."

Jude's eyes widened as the notion became clear. They *were* different.

Mark fell back on his bed. "It doesn't matter. They can't keep me here."

"Please, Mark, don't leave," Kelly begged.

"I'm already gone."

A week went by without any further mention of leaving. Mark seemed to acquiesce to his parents' wishes but, actually, his intentions had not changed. He secretly planned his getaway and kept it from his brothers.

It was a cold autumn day, and Jude and Kelly were in their room fussing about when they heard their father come home and immediately head up the stairs to their room.

He burst in. "Where's Mark? Have you seen him?"

Kelly thought about it. "I saw him this morning."

Their father eyeballed him, then left the room. Jude and Kelly raced downstairs to find out what was happening.

Their mother came out of the kitchen as their father returned to the living room and began pacing.

"He's gone," he said with a solemn expression they had never seen before.

Their mother stood still, realizing what her husband meant.

"Do they know?" she asked.

The boys weren't sure who "they" were, but it was apparent this worried her.

"I don't know," their father answered.

Just then, the telephone rang. It was a loud, obnoxious ring that made everyone jump. Their father went over to it and appeared unsure whether to answer it, but he did.

"Hello ... Yes ... We suspect so ... I understand."

Their father glanced over at their mother.

They know.

Jude had a knack for reading people, and he sensed their dread at once.

Their father hung up the phone and noticed Jude and Kelly lingering near the staircase.

"Your brother has run away," he said evenly. "Did you know of his plans?"

"No," Kelly answered. Jude shook his head.

Their father didn't know whether to believe them, but it made no difference. Mark had run off with another Elder named Liam. Liam had shared their plans with his younger brother, who quickly caved when his father questioned him as to their whereabouts. The Clan leaders were now aware that two Elders had left the community without permission. Everyone panicked.

It was a long night that first evening. Clan leaders and other members were in and out of their home. It was obviously a tense situation. Their main concern was that their secret could be revealed if the boys were hurt in any way. One of the side effects of the Condition is regeneration. Wounds, bruising, and even broken bones healed at an incredible rate. It would certainly raise red flags. The boys had to be found and brought back straight away.

Marshall Turner, one of the Elders from their Clan, volunteered to go after them. The Clan leaders agreed and allowed him and a few other Elders to hunt for the boys and bring them back.

Jude and Kelly listened from the hallway. The thought of Marshall pursuing Mark made the hair on Jude's neck stand up. Marshall wasn't much older than Mark, but he was mean and he scared the crap out of Jude.

"He wouldn't hurt Mark, would he?" Jude said in a low voice.

Kelly didn't answer right away. "I hope not."

"I can't believe he left us," Jude lamented. "He didn't even say good-bye."

"He did."

Kelly motioned to Jude to follow him back to his room. Once there, he closed the door and locked it. He went to his bed and pulled out a letter from underneath the mattress and handed it to Jude.

It was from Mark. He had left it in Kelly's dresser drawer, where he found it that morning.

I know you're both going to be upset with me for leaving you behind, but I know in my heart when the time comes you, too, will leave the Clan and we will all be together again. Keep your heads down and follow the rules until you are older. Then, find a way out and we will meet again. I'm going to help defeat the Nazis, then travel the world and experience everything it has to offer. I can't wait to share it with you. I love you both very much and I am proud to be your brother.

I will see you soon.
Mark

Jude put the letter down, feeling worse than before. It made the situation real and painful. He loved his brother dearly. He looked up to him and admired him, and now he was gone. Even worse, he knew his brother was in danger. Marshall was after him, and Mark had no way of knowing.

Word swiftly spread around the community, especially after a few days turned into a week. Because of Mark's actions, all the Elders were told of the Condition, no matter how old they were. It was out there now, and the Clan leaders wasted no time assembling the members to make sure everyone understood the situation and the consequences. There were daily gatherings in the meeting hall where the Originals laid out, in very specific terms, the rules of the Clan and how serious the punishment would be for any violation. They were graphic in describing what could happen if their secret were to be discovered. Fear was their tactic, and it worked.

There weren't any updates on Mark and Liam during that week. Jude and Kelly suspected Marshall was keeping the leaders informed, but they were not privy to that information. As far as they knew, Mark was still on his way to England to join the military. They kept their hopes up that he would make it, but they soon found out that he did not.

It was the middle of the night on the seventh evening when Jude and Kelly were woken by a commotion coming from downstairs. They recognized Marshall's voice among those shouting and snuck into the hallway to find out what was happening.

Mark was there, and he was in pain. He was sobbing and trying to speak, but Marshall wouldn't let him talk. Jude's mother tried to help him. Marshall kept her at bay, saying he wasn't done with him yet. Jude's father put his arms around his wife and pulled her back, but she couldn't take it. She ran upstairs past the boys.

Jude and Kelly slowly inched their way down the staircase until they had a better view into the living room. Marshall's father was there, as well as two other Originals. Mark was on the floor. There was blood on his face, and his clothes were tattered. The boys were horrified. Kelly wanted to run down there and protect Mark, but Jude held him back. They sat tight-lipped and listened.

Marshall was acting like a taskmaster. He stood above Mark, barking at him.

"You're never going to leave again, right?" he snarled.

"Yes," Mark whimpered.

"You're never going to put the Clans in danger again, right?"

"Yes."

Kelly couldn't hold back. He tore away from Jude and bolted downstairs toward Mark. Jude's father intercepted him before he could reach his brother and snatched him back.

"No, wait!" shouted Marshall. "Let him see this. Let this be a lesson to him and all the Clan members. This is what will happen if you threaten the Clan's existence. It can't happen. I won't let it."

Marshall's words stung. Hearing him indicate they were forbidden to leave left an indelible mark on Jude. He suddenly felt as if he was being held captive, much like Mark had said.

Marshall declared himself a Protector of the Clans that night and made it known that if anyone posed any threat to the Clans, they would have to answer to him.

Mark was never the same after that. He never attempted to leave again, and he never spoke about what happened while he was gone. It was as if the fire that burned so bright inside of him had been extinguished. He never mentioned the outside world, or traveling, or the war. He stayed close to his parents, like a child who had been lost and then reunited with them. He became a sedate and passive man.

For Jude and Kelly, it was a hard lesson. Seeing their older brother beat down like that was difficult. Even when they were alone, he was different. Something had died inside of him. He never opened up to them and forbade them from talking about the things they used to enjoy discussing. The Mark they knew and loved was gone, and they missed him.

Everything changed in their community as well. Day-to-day routines stayed the same, but beneath it there was anxiety and uncertainty. Their day trips were limited, and talk of Regular society became hushed. Jude and Kelly kept a low profile. They didn't want to cause any trouble or give their parents cause for worry. The fire still burned inside of them, but they didn't dare attempt to leave or even discuss it. They were afraid, as were the rest of the Elders. For the next decade, they lived obediently, hoping that someday things would change.

That day eventually came in 1955.

When it came time for the Elders to continue their education, they were permitted to attend nearby universities as long as they followed strict rules set by their Clan leaders. Most continued to live at home, but some were allowed to live on campus. When the Governing Order was established, they had Marshall assign Protectors to keep an eye on the Elders who were living away from their communities. They were carefully supervised because it wasn't known yet if they were afflicted with the full extent of the Condition.

When it was determined the Elders were no longer aging, those who had previously lived away while they were in school began to request permission to travel and live beyond their communities. This led to heated debates between the G.O. and the Clans. What initially seemed to be an appeal for more freedom became a major shift in the lives of Clan members once word spread that many of the Clans were experiencing the same issue—as the Elders grew older, it became difficult to distinguish them from their parents. They appeared to be the same age, some even older. It had become harder for them to be inconspicuous. Many of the smaller Clans had moved around to dispel suspicion. But for the larger ones, such as the one near Dublin, that wasn't an option. After much deliberation, it made sense that eventually the Elders would have to branch out and create their own communities. They couldn't be expected to thrive and prosper within the confines of their individual Clans. The Originals had raised the Elders to be cautious of the Regulars and to live discreetly and anonymously. They had to trust that it was enough.

Jude and Kelly were in their late twenties and had lived a peaceful life. When they heard about the requests from the other Elders, they jumped at the chance to formally petition their leaders for that same privilege. They argued that they understood the gravity of the Condition. They knew the consequences and would take every precaution to not call attention to themselves and to stay out of harm's way.

The petition was the talk of the community. All the Elders knew that if Jude and Kelly were given permission to leave the Clan, it would open the door for the rest of them. Marshall knew this as well, which is why he opposed it. By this time, his Protectors were based everywhere the Clans existed, but he knew that if the Elders were allowed to roam freely, he would have to figure out a way to track and monitor them to make sure they stayed in line. Marshall saw it as a dangerous move, but even he knew it was inevitable.

Permission was granted.

Jude and Kelly were ecstatic. Their patience and conformity had paid off. They tried to convince Mark to come with them, but they knew that was impossible. He had married a Clan member years earlier and had three small children already. Even though he was thrilled for his brothers, Mark was heartbroken when they left him.

For Jude and Kelly, it was equally devastating. They wanted Mark to go with them. It was his dream to see the world. They decided he would be their inspiration to see and do as much as possible. They wanted to bring back a piece of everywhere they went and share it with him.

Unbeknownst to them, neither would ever return home.

8

FRIDAY—BRISTOL

When Jude woke up, he knew exactly where he was. She was lying on his chest, sleeping peacefully. It wasn't a dream; it had really happened. He had found her. He closed his eyes and pictured her in a whole new way. He'd lived all those years with only one image of her; now he had many. He thought about her laughing and smiling, twirling her hair in her fingers, how her eyes fluctuated between light blue and blue-gray, how they lit up when she spoke about her favorite band and movies, and how delicious she tasted.

He remembered making love to her. He never imagined it would be so effortless, and he had imagined a lot. She was everything he'd hoped she would be, and the best part was that he knew she felt the same way. He was sure of it.

He touched her hair and stroked it down her back, which caused her to stir. She burrowed into his neck and breathed him in. Smoothly, she moved herself up onto him and began kissing his face.

"Good morning," he said, amused by her enthusiasm. He ran his hands up her bare back.

"Yes, it is," Veronica sighed and continued to pepper him with kisses.

He moved one of his hands up through her hair and brought her to his mouth.

Good morning, indeed.

They lounged in bed the rest of the morning, ordering room service, and making love. Jude was instantly in tune with her. He knew where to touch her, how to kiss her, and how far to take her to make her explode. He loved how it made him feel when she reached that place.

He wanted to stay with her as long as possible, but unfortunately, the day was cut short when Veronica received a text message from the Realtor she had met with the day before.

"Damn, I have to meet this guy," she said, annoyed. "It's Friday. Some of the paperwork needs to be processed before the weekend."

She buried her face in his neck again and kissed him.

"Do you want to wait here?" she said. "It should only be a few hours. I had planned to drive back to London for the weekend, but I can stay."

He couldn't imagine not spending the weekend with her. Of course he wanted her to stay in Bristol.

"Maybe I'll run home," he suggested. "Pick up a few things and meet you back here. How's that sound?"

"It sounds perfect."

Veronica couldn't keep her thoughts together as she was driven from the hotel. She was astonished at what had transpired—and excited beyond belief. Little details about him kept popping into her head, which made the smile on her face permanently etched. It was far more than what she had expected, far more. She adored everything about him. He was thoughtful and affectionate, an attentive listener and well-spoken, and the way he looked at her was hypnotizing. She knew this was dangerous. She wasn't accustomed to feeling so ... normal. She knew she had to hold it together and finish what she came there to do. She slipped on her ear buds and closed her eyes.

Jude couldn't keep still on the train ride home. He gleefully tapped his fingers on the seat in front of him, making no effort to hide his mood. He was immensely satisfied. He texted Charlie to see if he was home, but he wasn't. Charlie asked how the night went and Jude simply replied, "Incredible!"

When he arrived at his flat, he threw himself on his bed and thought about her. It had been such a long time since he was this worked up about a woman. He had avoided serious relationships with Regulars because of all the ridiculous issues that would arise, and he didn't associate with Clan members. This was different. He believed the possibilities were endless with her, and he was elated.

He closed his eyes and thought about touching her and kissing her lips. He could still smell her. He became aroused, but decided he'd better take a shower and save it for later. Unfortunately, the cold water did nothing to hinder his excitement. The memories of her were too vivid to ignore, and he ended up spending more time in the shower than he had intended. When he finally emerged, he was impressed at how refreshed and reenergized he felt. For the first time in a long time, he was happy to be alive.

He wrapped a towel around his waist, peered in the mirror and debated whether to shave. He was a hairy bugger, always had been. He was able to grow a full beard in no time, much to the envy of his brother Kelly, who had the face of a prepubescent girl, but Jude preferred to keep himself groomed. He had done just that before meeting up with Veronica the day before, but his perpetual five o'clock shadow already needed trimming.

Back in his room, he wasn't sure what he should bring with him to the hotel. He didn't want to assume they'd be staying in the entire weekend, even though that's what he hoped for, but as he picked through a vast array of T-shirts and plaid oxford button-downs, he realized he didn't have many options. He had never moved past the casual look of the seventies.

Before heading downstairs, he phoned into work and said he had to leave town for a family emergency and didn't know when he'd be back. He wanted to make sure he was available to spend as much time with her as possible. He had nowhere to be but back at the hotel waiting for her.

Jude was in the kitchen when he heard his phone ring upstairs. He ran back to his room and picked up just in time.

"There you are," Veronica said.

He felt an ache in his heart when he heard her voice.

"Miss me?" she cooed.

"You have no idea, especially now," he said on his way back downstairs.

"Good. I wanted to hear your voice. Are you home?"

"Yeah, just grabbing a bite to eat before heading back. How much longer?"

"I should be done in about an hour and a half, two max. I can't wait to see you."

He gave in to his blush since no one was watching. He was thrilled she rang.

Veronica couldn't put the card in the door fast enough. All she could think about was kissing him. When she walked in, Jude was standing by the couch waiting for her. She dropped her bag and ran to him. He snatched her up as she leapt into his arms, and she thrust her fingers into his soft curls. He seized her open mouth and kissed her vigorously.

"God, I missed you," she exclaimed. "What have you done to me?"

He backed up to the couch and sat down, placing her on his lap while sucking gently on her neck.

"I was thinking the same thing. You've bewitched me."

Veronica breathed into his ear, "Have I? Are you under my spell now?"

Jude bent his head back in utter delight.

"I am," he confessed.

He came back up and nibbled on her lower lip, then slipped down to her chin and jawline until he was back to her neck. Veronica closed her eyes and leaned to the side for him to kiss her there. She tilted her head back and guided him to the other side. His lips were hot and moist as he made his way down to her chest where he started to unbutton her blouse.

He gently laid her down on the couch then went back to her blouse, kissing her body after each button. When he reached her stomach, he came upon a scar about two inches long near her belly button. He kissed it.

"What happened here?" he asked.

The man who killed your brother did that to me.

"A kitchen mishap between me, a large knife and an onion," she said.

He kissed it again.

"Maybe you should stay out of the kitchen," he mused.

"Good idea."

"Let's get you out of these clothes."

The afternoon sky merged into dusk while they lay across from each other in bed. The dream-like ambience didn't go unnoticed by Veronica. She was still coping with her unexpected emotions, and the mood lighting wasn't helping.

"This is really happening, isn't it?" she said as she stared into his eyes.

"Yeah, it is."

"You don't seem surprised."

"I'm not. I think I've been in love with the thought of you for so long that it doesn't feel out of sorts. Does that make sense?"

She nodded. "I guess I'm just surprised at how liberating it feels. It's been a long time since I've been so at ease with someone."

She propped her head up on her elbow and reached over to play with his hair.

"What's really strange," she said, "is that I've managed to live all these years with just one memory of you, then after one evening together, I can't bear to be away from you. It just doesn't seem real."

"It's real," he said. He took her hand and put it on his face. "See, I'm really here."

"I thought you said you shaved this morning," she said, grinning.

"I did. Very funny."

She laughed, then leaned over and kissed him. "You are very real and I'm so grateful for it."

He moved her long bangs so he could see into her eyes.

"When do you think you'll be finished with your work here?" he asked.

"I'm hoping I can drag it out a few more days, but I should be done by the middle of next week."

Jude fell back onto the bed. "A few more days, huh?"

"Don't do that. Don't think about the time."

She scooted over and draped herself on top of him. She folded her hands on his chest and rested her chin on them.

"I have a feeling we're going to be seeing a lot of each other," she said.
"Promise?"

"Yes."

"Good," he said, then smiled. "I'd like that."

She eased herself up to his face, purposefully rubbing her body against him. He let out a soft, gratifying moan.

"Thank you," she said. "For not turning out to be an asshole."

He rolled her over onto the bed.

"You're welcome."

They spent the next two days falling in love. Despite acknowledging how fast it was happening, it didn't deter them in the least. They wanted to love each other.

By Sunday evening, Jude was certain his life was never going to be the same. No matter what happened between them, the time with her was so special he knew he would carry it with him forever.

Veronica tried not to think about her feelings. She didn't want to over-analyze what was happening, but it was a difficult task. She tried to focus on just enjoying every moment with him.

Jude relaxed against the headboard of the bed as she sat cross-legged next to him. They had just finished off a large pizza while watching an episode of *The X-Files* online. They were pleasantly exhausted after spending the weekend having sex pretty much everywhere possible. They were now intimately acquainted with the nooks and crannies of the shower, living area, and staircase.

"I shouldn't have had that last piece," Veronica whined as she stretched out on the bed. "I'm so full."

"We'll work it off later." He laughed.

"I'm sure."

She rolled onto her side and leaned up on her elbow.

"Do you ever wish you weren't afflicted?" she asked while picking off the sausages from the last piece of pizza.

"Sometimes, but then I'd probably be dead."

"Why would you think that? You're only eighty-six. You could still be alive."

"No, I'm sure I wouldn't be," he groaned.

"You don't know that. It's true our lives would be different without the Condition, but Regulars live to be quite old these days." She lay back. "I can't imagine what it would be like to live as a Regular and have death hanging over you like that."

"Why do you ask?" he said.

"I was wondering if you ever think about it. Immortality isn't for everyone, you know."

"We're not really immortal, but I understand what you're saying. I used to think about it a lot." He sat up. "I wondered how long I was going to be around. I don't put myself in precarious situations anymore, so, realistically, how many years could I continue to exist? I do think about *that* sometimes."

"Immortal or not, the Originals are well over a hundred and ten, so you could conceivably live that long, or even longer."

He smiled bashfully. "If someone had told me that a week ago, I probably would've been pissed at the thought of living that long, but now, not so much."

"Oh, I see. Now you *want* to live forever?"

"Absolutely."

He put his hand out for her, which Veronica readily accepted. He brought her over and she nestled onto his lap. He ran his fingers along her face, tracing her lips with his thumb.

"As long as I can spend it with you," he whispered. "I can't believe how different I feel—about everything."

The next morning, Jude put his sunglasses on and lifted his jacket collar as he stepped out of the hotel. It was a typical damp morning in Bristol, but he didn't notice. He couldn't hide his pure joy and contentment while he set out for the train station. He was, undoubtedly, a changed man, and nothing could hamper his lively disposition, not even the two men watching him from across the street.

9

MONDAY—BRISTOL

Veronica stood in the shower and let the hot water pour over her. She bent her neck from side to side, feeling a gentle stretch down her shoulders. It had been years since she felt that good. She thought back over the weekend and wished he were still there with her, in the shower, holding her. She had to brace herself when she imagined his hands on her body.

Oh my God.

She looked up and let the deluge of water douse her lust. With a laugh, she shook it off. She ran a soapy loofah along her arms and chest, down to her belly and legs, and then closed her eyes as the water rinsed her body. She lingered in her serene state and sighed at the thought of having to face the real world.

When she finally felt ready to embrace it, she stepped out and dried herself off. She put on a cushy hotel robe and opened the bathroom door.

"I was starting to wonder if you were ever coming out of there."

"Fuck!" Veronica shrieked as she grabbed hold of the doorjamb.

Her friend Evie was sitting on the bed with a drink in her hand, appearing quite pleased with Veronica's reaction.

"Good God, Evie! What the hell are you doing here?"

"Just checking in to see how things are going, love," she said in her thick British accent.

Veronica gathered herself and walked over to the dresser.

"Aren't you happy to see me? It's been almost three months," Evie said.

"You could've knocked and told me you were here."

"Yes, but that wouldn't have been nearly as fun."

Veronica rolled her eyes. She pulled out a set of black undergarments from the top drawer.

"Ooh, black panties. What on earth is going on here, V?"

Veronica turned away from her friend, opened her robe, and slipped on her panties. Then, she dropped the robe and finished dressing.

"I said what are you doing here?"

Evie got up from the bed and sauntered over to her. "I'm here to see how the real estate deal is progressing. It's going well, isn't it?" She smiled mischievously while taking a sip from her drink.

Veronica huffed and stepped around her. "It's going fine. Everything is right on track."

"Good," replied Evie, and then followed Veronica downstairs to the living area.

Evie went straight for the bar and refilled her drink. She was a slender woman, not as shapely as Veronica but similar in stature. What made her stand out was her stunning natural hair color. It was a beautiful mix of sunset hues, orange and red with golden highlights. Women paid dearly to achieve a color like that, and Evie knew it was special, which is why she wore it long, well below her shoulders. All the more for women to envy, she would say. She had a vivacious personality that matched her crazy hair color and Veronica loved that about her, and Evie loved Veronica, as her mentor and best friend.

"Can you spare a cig, love?" Evie asked.

"I don't have any. I thought you quit?"

"Why would I quit? *It's not as if it can kill me*," she said, mimicking Veronica in an American accent. "Isn't that what you always say?"

Veronica laughed as Evie searched her bag.

"I hear the property is pretty spectacular," she said after finding a nearly empty pack at the bottom of her purse. "I haven't seen it yet, but I'd love to."

"That won't be necessary. Everything is in order."

"Aw, come on. Just a peek."

"No," Veronica said sternly.

"You certainly don't seem tickled to see me. That makes me sad, V."

"Stop it. You're doing it again."

"Doing what?" Evie said coyly.

"Being daft."

"Why are you being so bitchy? I would think you'd be in a better mood. I only came by to check in on you. The mother ship wanted a report since you haven't texted or called since Friday. They're counting on this *big real estate deal*," she said sarcastically while putting up her jazz hands.

Veronica walked over to her friend, took her drink from her hand, and drank from it. "Let me say this again—everything is fine. Nothing to worry about." She handed back her drink.

Evie squinted her eyes at her, which made Veronica realize she was, indeed, being a bitch.

"I'm sorry," Veronica caved. "You startled me. I was in such a happy place, and now you've brought me back to reality."

"Yes, I think that's what they wanted me to do. Apparently, this deal is quite important to the powers that be. I hope you realize that. Everyone's paying attention."

Veronica shrugged her shoulders, appearing indifferent again. "I'm working my end. That's all I can do."

"Good," Evie said as she placed her glass on the bar. "Ooh, guess who I got a call from? Manny from Cabo. You remember Manny. He ran that adorable seaside villa. He said it's open for tenants again. We should go down and spend a week there after you're finished here." She picked up her coat and put it on. "God, when was the last time we were there together, '98?"

"'94," Veronica corrected.

"Are you sure? I think it was '98."

"No, it was 1994. I remember because you kept singing that 'Shoop' song by Salt-N-Pepa the entire time. Holy hell, I thought I was going to strangle you." Veronica laughed.

"That's right! *Here I go, here I go, here I go again! Girls, what's my weakness? Men!*" Evie sang and started dancing.

"You still dance like a white girl in the '80s," Veronica giggled.

"You say that like it's a bad thing."

"Seriously, I'm going to throw something at you if you don't stop."

"You need to lighten up, love."

Evie settled down and walked up to Veronica. "I merely wanted to say hello and see how you were doing. All indications are everything is right on point. I'll get out of your hair." She gathered a small strand of Veronica's wet hair and trailed it down to the end. "I have missed you, though," she said softly, then kissed Veronica on the lips. She smiled and stepped away. Then she picked up her purse and strolled toward the door.

"Oh, and turn your phone back on. Otherwise, you'll be seeing me again." She winked and walked out.

Veronica sat down on the couch. She didn't even know where her phone was. She looked around but didn't see it.

"Fucking hell."

10

MONDAY—BRISTOL

When Jude arrived home, Charlie was in the kitchen making tea.

"He's alive!" Charlie exclaimed.

Jude was beaming. He took his jacket off and sat down at the table.

"Could you look any more pleased with yourself?" Charlie snickered as he sat across from him.

"It's unbelievable, man. She's lovely, really lovely."

"Of course she is. You've waited forty years to see her again. I can't imagine she would've been beastly. That's not how love stories are written," he said and then sipped his tea. "Unless you're a twat, then I guess it would be a comedy."

They both laughed.

"I'm completely falling for her. I can't even think straight," Jude admitted.

Charlie set his cup down. "It's only been four days, Jude."

"I know, I know." Jude walked over to the stove to pour himself a cup. "She's just so ... perfect."

"No one's perfect," Charlie rebutted.

"Yeah, but she's pretty damn close."

"Can she cook? Because if she can't cook, she's far from perfect in my book."

"Is that so? Join us in the twenty-first century, old chap."

"So, tell me about her," Charlie said.

"She's American."

"Shut up."

"But she's been living over here for some thirty years now."

"How old is she?"

Jude grinned. "She's eighty-nine."

"Fuck no!" Charlie sat back.

"Aye, she's older than I am."

"Man, that *is* unbelievable."

"She really is. She's intelligent and cultured, but not in a posh kind of way. She's down to earth and funny. She loves movies, even more than you, and she'll take the piss out of you if you don't agree with her."

Jude smiled, took a drink of his tea, and then gazed off as he thought about her.

"She's got this way of looking at me when I'm speaking to her, like she's truly listening. Her eyes, man—her eyes kill me."

"And I take it everything else is," Charlie motioned with his hands, "agreeable?"

"Yeah, more than agreeable. Fucking incredible."

"It sounds like your dreams have come true, my friend. So now what?"

Jude shrugged. "I don't know. I want to spend as much time with her as I can."

"Where does she live?"

"London."

"Well, that's a problem."

"Maybe."

"What? Don't tell me you're thinking of taking off for London after less than a week with this woman."

"I didn't say that. I'm just saying I'm open to whatever happens, as long as I can be with her."

"Bloody hell." Charlie walked over to the sink and dumped out what was left in his cup. "How long is she in town?"

"Indefinitely right now—until she finishes the real estate deal she's working on. Could be a week."

"Then settle yourself. Don't start planning the wedding. The last thing I need is for you to get all worked up over her, turn your life upside down, and then have it come crashing down on you. No, I've got no time for that."

"So, this is about *you*?" Jude said, laughing.

"Of course," Charlie quipped.

Jude wrinkled his nose at him. "Honestly, you want me all to yourself, don't you? Fess up."

"Bollocks! I just don't want to have to find another roommate. Not after that last bastard took all my CDs," he sneered jokingly.

Jude went over to Charlie and put his hands on his friend's shoulders.

"I appreciate the concern and I promise I won't make any hasty decisions. At least not without consulting you first." He smiled. He grabbed a Coke from the refrigerator and left for his room.

"There are some messages for you by the phone," Charlie called out. "Some bloke with an Irish accent thicker than yours left a couple of voicemails."

"Thanks," Jude said. He ignored the phone and went upstairs.

Across the street, the two men sat in a car. The man in the driver seat picked up his phone and dialed a number.

"No, nothing. All quiet over here. Okay."

"Well?" asked the other man.

"Sit tight and wait."

When Jude returned to the hotel, Veronica was waiting for him out on the balcony. She was leaning up against the railing with a drink in her hand. She was smartly dressed in a silk blouse, black skirt, and knee-high boots. Her hair was swept across her chest by the chilly breeze, with strands flying wildly around her face.

"Aren't you cold?" Jude asked. He gathered her hair and put it behind her, clearing the way for a kiss.

"Not anymore," she sighed when his warm lips met hers.

He put his arms around her waist and clutched her tight, then put his forehead on hers. "How was your day?"

"Routine, except I had a difficult time staying focused. Imagine that. Somehow your scent has infiltrated everything I own. I can smell you even when you're not around now."

"My scent? I have a scent?"

"Darling, you have the sexiest aroma I've ever come across. I noticed it in the lounge before I even saw you. It's delicious."

"Ah, yes, your superhuman ability. Too bad you can't fly. I'd love for you to lift me out over the city."

"If I could fly, we'd be so far away from here already." She fondled his curls then kissed him.

"Are you hungry?" she asked.

"I will be. What's your pleasure tonight?"

"Sushi. I've got such a craving. Are there any good restaurants around here?"

"Yes, actually. There's a wonderful place not far from here. I'd love to take you."

"Excellent."

Jude's favorite Japanese restaurant was an ideal setting for their first venture out in public together. They sat across from each other in a private booth softly lit by hanging red lanterns and traditional candles.

"This is a beautiful place, Jude. Well done. Do you come here often?"

"I do, but I usually sit at the bar. It's pretty romantic back here."

"This is nice—being out with you. It feels more real, not so much like a dream," Veronica said as she held his hand.

Jude brought her hand up and kissed it. She absolutely loved how affectionate he was, and, lucky for her, he wasn't self-conscious about it.

"Did you go into work today?" she asked.

"Nah."

"Aren't you worried about getting fired?"

"No, it's just a job. They're pretty flexible."

"What did you do all day?"

He appeared somewhat embarrassed.

"Tell me," she begged.

"I watched *The Way We Were.*"

"You did?" she said excitedly.

"I did."

Her exuberant expression showed how touched she was by the gesture. "So, what did you think?"

"It was good. I can see why you love it. There was something quite lovely about Streisand. I found her very appealing. She kind of, just sort of, reminded me of you."

"I'll take that as a compliment. Did you love the ending?"

She could tell he didn't.

"It was okay. I mean, they both moved on, so obviously, it wasn't an epic love."

"How can you say that? They truly loved each other. It just wasn't meant to be. You can tell by the way they look at each other before parting ways at the end. It's beautiful and emotional."

"It wasn't meant to be because he couldn't handle her activism, and then he cheated on her while she was pregnant. What a dick. Then, she moves back to New York and remarries, and he moves on as well. It really wasn't *that* romantic."

Veronica gasped.

"Can't you see that?" Jude said playfully.

"No." She pulled her hand from him and served herself some more sake. "Just so we're clear, what you're saying is, if she had fallen apart over losing him, say, fallen into despair or committed suicide, then it would've been romantic? Is that what you're saying?"

She was becoming noticeably agitated, but he couldn't help himself. He loved how passionate she was about her movies. He had purposefully provoked her just to see her get heated. He paused as he thought about how best to answer.

"I see your point, but you have to admit, it would've been more dramatic." He winked at her.

"Good Lord, Jude, that's typical. Are you aware that in a great deal of literature and film, men are always the reason women lose themselves and fall apart? You know what that says? It says that everything we are and everything we hope to become is dependent on a man. That's complete bullshit. It doesn't have to be that way. We are resilient. We can survive and move on. Which is exactly what she does."

"I agree, but let's be honest, all of the stories you're referring to were written by men, and as men we are self-centered and conceited. Therefore, it's hard to imagine women moving on successfully after we've finished with them," he said with a glint in his eye.

Veronica calmly sat back and leered at him. Then, she got up and leaned over the table, getting close to his face.

"I hope you'll be kind when you're finished with me," she whispered.

Even though Jude knew she was mocking him, he went in to kiss her. She pulled back.

He laughed. "Oh, I'll never be finished with you."

"How dare you," she smirked, then went back in and allowed him to kiss her, which he did very lovingly.

"It was thoughtful of you to watch it," she said when she sat back down. "Although, as a man, I don't think you're capable of comprehending the true nature of the story, but I'll give you credit for the effort."

Jude laughed again, this time more heartily. She cracked him up, and he adored that about her.

"Thank you, but I understand the story, and I can definitely relate to the era. My brother was fascinated with the McCarthy trials. He followed anything and everything to do with ..."

Veronica waited for him to finish, but he didn't.

"To do with what?" she asked.

He had lost his train of thought. "Um, he was consumed with the war and the Allies. It was all he talked about."

Veronica tried not to react. He never spoke about his family, and when she would inquire, he would always change the subject.

"Was this your older brother?" she asked delicately.

"I don't like talking about my family, love. It's too painful," he said abruptly.

She nodded and looked away. He knew he had opened the door and then slammed it shut. He set his chopsticks down.

"I'm sorry. I know you want to know more about my family."

"It's okay."

He could sense she was hurt by his refusal to share this part of his life with her. He picked up his sake and finished it off.

"All right. I'll tell you," he said.

"You don't have to. I didn't mean for you to feel obligated."

"I may never want to do this again. Go ahead, ask me."

"Are you sure?"

"Aye."

"Your brothers, you said they're not around anymore. Where are they?"

Jude took a deep breath. "They're both dead. One of them died in France, the other at home in Dublin."

"Please tell me he wasn't killed at the house in Grenoble."

"Not at the house, but right after."

"I'm so sorry, Jude."

"I'd rather not get into the details but, let me just say, both could've been prevented."

"Were they young?"

"For a Clan member, yes. My oldest brother was married with three young children. It was difficult for them after he died. I tried to help out, but I couldn't engage without exposing myself. I stayed in touch as much as I could."

"Do you still keep in touch with them?"

"Of course. They're my family. I just don't visit."

"Do any of them live near here?"

"Some of them are in London, I think."

A wave of paranoia suddenly washed over him. He was uncomfortable with where the conversation was headed. He didn't see any harm in discussing it with her but, despite that, he wanted to stop.

Veronica didn't press the matter. She was satisfied with the information he had shared. She knew it was hard for him to speak of it. The fact that he finally opened up a little excited her and had her feeling all tingly inside as they finished their dinner.

While they waited for the check, she sat quietly watching him. She was smoldering, and he knew it. She bit her lip seductively, then rubbed her shoe against his leg, extending it up into his lap.

His eyes widened and he tried not to squirm. "Really?" He laughed.

"Oh yes," she sassed.

He smiled broadly. He had one of those smiles that filled up his whole face. An ear-to-ear grin that made his almond-shaped eyes squint beneath his dark eyelashes.

Yum.

He took her hand and pulled her closer. "I'm not sure that was such a good idea. I'm about to make a scene here. We'd better get the check quick."

The heat between them was mounting rapidly. Luckily, the waitress came back with the check and they promptly left the table. Jude helped her with her jacket, then put on his coat as they stepped outside. They cuddled while they waited for her driver, Benedict, to pull up. He held her close, keeping her warm in the cold night as she burrowed into him and kissed his neck. He looked around anxiously for her car. He was about to burst.

As soon as they entered the backseat of the town car, he kissed her so deeply she felt it throughout her body. She reciprocated fervently while lifting her skirt and straddling him. He peeked over her shoulder to make sure the glass partition was still up.

He caressed her thighs and moved his hands under her skirt, reaching beneath her panties and behind her. He pulled her in tight, and she massaged her fingers through his hair as he kissed her chest. She inhaled slowly, taking in his insanely delicious scent. Everything melted inside of her. She unbuttoned his peacoat, pulled it open, and unfastened his belt.

Their passion had intensified during their time together. Now, when he was inside of her, it was challenging for each of them not to climax immediately. She had become insatiable. She couldn't get enough of him, and Jude felt the same way. His desire for her was immeasurable.

He held her face in his hands and kissed her. Then, deliberately, he tempered his movement. He wanted to savor the moment. Veronica moved in rhythm with him, staring earnestly into his eyes as he slowed down. He leaned back and watched her. The streetlights flickering on her body through the rear window made her appear ethereal. She tilted her head to the side, letting her hair fall over her shoulder. Soon, they were still, gazing upon each other in the shadowy light.

A sense of peace came over her, something she was as unfamiliar with as the love she felt for him. She ran her hands along his face and into his hair, and kissed him on the forehead. She nuzzled his nose and was about to place her lips on his when he pulled back slightly.

"I love you," he whispered.

Veronica didn't hesitate and kissed him madly.

"I'm never letting you go," she breathed. "Never." She put her forehead on his and began to move.

Jude closed his eyes and succumbed to the sensation that was building again. Her body pulsed over him, and she commanded the pace. He opened his eyes and tugged her hair from behind which made her breasts heave toward him beneath her lace bra. He released one and gently sucked on it. Veronica arched back and moaned. They reached a ferocious climax just as they arrived at the hotel.

They were collapsed in each other's arms when Veronica noticed the car wasn't moving.

"Oh, shit. I think we're here."

The car was parked in front of the hotel and Benedict was standing outside the door, waiting respectfully for his patrons to exit the vehicle.

"I guess we better get out." Jude laughed. "Benny might not appreciate another go of it."

"I'm sure he would stand there all night. He is diligent if he's anything at all."

Back in the hotel room, they lay peacefully in bed. It had only been four days, and the bond between them had grown even stronger. Jude loved her in a way he had never expected. She'd been in his heart for so long, but now she was in his soul. When he was with her everything made sense. He had lived his life in such discontent that he didn't know how to feel otherwise—until now. She filled him with love and laughter and desire, things he hadn't let himself feel for ages. He had found her and she opened up his heart. He knew he never wanted to be apart from her again.

Veronica's love for him was just as powerful, but it was difficult for her to accept it. She never gave herself to a man the way she already had with him, and never with such ease. She didn't think she was capable of it; now she knew she was and she knew why. She had saved it all for him. She knew the moment she saw him in the lounge. She loved him, and she knew she would for the rest of her life, no matter what happened.

"What's wrong?" Jude asked.

"Nothing's wrong. Why would you think something was wrong?"

"There's a sadness in your eyes. I see it sometimes. I'm curious what makes you sad."

She was surprised by this revelation.

What sadness?

"I could not be further from sad right now. I don't think I've ever been this happy."

"Okay," he said, feeling slightly disappointed. He knew what he saw in her eyes, but he was willing to wait until she was ready to tell him.

This scared the hell out of her—that he could read her so well. She wasn't sure if it said more about her vulnerability or his perception. The truth was, she *was* sad, because deep down she knew this was just a dream. She was now absolutely sure of how much she loved him. Unfortunately, it didn't change the fact that what they had there in that hotel room wasn't going to last much longer.

11

TUESDAY—LONDON

James McNair admired the view from his window. A stretch of ominous clouds hovered languidly over London. It wasn't raining yet, but he could smell the precipitation. He closed his eyes and breathed it in. The smell of rain always calmed his nerves.

McNair was an Irish businessman who lived in the Regulars' world as an investment broker. He had run various companies over the span of thirty years, starting back in 1982, as a means to build capital for his other, more significant pursuit. He was second in command of a movement that had begun in the 1990s. The Insurgents were Clan members who refused to tolerate the Protectors.

A tenacious Irish Elder took it upon himself to preserve the anonymity of the Clans by forming the Protectors in the 1940s. Marshall Turner had grown up under his father's strict tutelage and learned at a very young age about the Condition and its consequences. His father instilled in him a high degree of paranoia and taught him that their survival depended solely on their obscurity. For this reason, when the first encroachment occurred, Marshall was ready to take the reins and create his band of guardians.

In the beginning, he preached his dogma with veiled intimidation and threats, but when the Elders were granted permission to live among the

Regulars, he knew he'd have to establish a more organized and resolute company of Protectors.

Over the next twenty years, his Protectors kept a watchful eye on Clan members. They used force when necessary but relied mostly on fear tactics. But the times were changing, and by the late 1960s, the counterculture that was infringing on the Regulars' society was also influencing the Elders. A revolution was occurring, and the Clans were not immune to it.

There were approximately three hundred members around the world at this time. The Clans in America had maintained a low profile since the growing hippie subculture provided an ideal mask for them. In time, this spread to the U.K., Ireland, and Europe, and led to a period during which the Clans thrived. Everything was askew in the world, and that obscured their presence amid the changing norms. For those Elders who lived nomadic lifestyles beyond the rigid constraints of the Clan communities, the unconventional cultural trends began to influence their way of thinking. They started to question the reasons for hiding their true identity. They wanted to exist uninhibited and free from the anxiety and threats of the Protectors. They took on the antiestablishment sentiments their counterparts in the Regulars' society were outwardly expressing and, gradually, began to ignore the Protectors' warnings and step outside the boundaries of the Clans' rules.

This was a frantic time for Marshall and the Protectors. In the early days, the Clans stayed put and closed ranks. But as the years passed, it became difficult for them to hide their circumstance. It was impossible for them to stay in one place for too long. Because of this, the Governing Order developed a flawless system that created new identities for members, which allowed them to begin a new life in a new place without drawing attention to themselves. Relocating became a way of life for Clan members and, in turn, they became adept at it.

Keeping track of everyone was a laborious undertaking for the Protectors. They worked closely with the G.O., who, by this time, had begun to infiltrate various areas of the Regulars' society, including law enforcement and medical facilities. This allowed the Protectors to stay one step ahead of many disturbances, but it became a constant struggle.

When the authority-opposed movement of the sixties was in full swing, Marshall recruited more Protectors to help restrain Clan members who were following suit.

By the 1970s, the Elders' children were coming of age and they, too, got swept up in the turmoil of the times. This second generation, who were also afflicted, had grown up in a less restricted environment and were much more relaxed with their predicament and much less discreet about it. They believed they were entitled to be open and free about the Condition and didn't feel threatened by the consequences. Some tried to expose themselves to doctors and the authorities, but their outlandish assertions were never taken seriously. They were careless in their approach and were never able to convince the Regulars. In one case, a Clan member was deemed mentally unstable and confined to an institution. With the help of the G.O., Marshall was able to secure her release, but he used what happened to his advantage and made sure everyone knew the repercussions of attempting to expose the Clans.

"The Regulars are not capable of dealing with our fate," he preached. "They'll turn against us and treat us like a scourge of humanity."

"Fear the Regulars" was his constant mantra.

Not everyone heeded his message and, eventually, his Protectors had to take drastic measures. They began inflicting harsher punishments as more members became unmanageable.

Clan members did not take this lightly. They believed the Protectors were overstepping their authority. Formal complaints were made, but the G.O. backed the Protectors. They tolerated their tactics because after fifty years the Condition was still hidden. It was obvious to them that the Protectors' methods worked. And because of what happened to the Clan member who was institutionalized, the G.O. held firm that the Clans must remain unknown to the Regulars—at any cost.

Most Clan members accepted their argument, but they still resented the power the Protectors had over them and the Governing Order. There were those who continued to resist their unrelenting control, provoking the Protectors and attempting to influence other Clan members against them. This power struggle created a dangerous atmosphere that put everyone at risk and led to an inevitable outcome. In 1972, the Protectors began killing instigators. This included Clan members as well as Regulars who either suspected or found out about the Condition.

This violent counteraction neutralized the uprising that had barely begun. Once the Protectors started to kill, the fear set in again and order was restored—or so the Protectors thought.

From this point on, the Protectors guarded the Condition with a heavy hand. They killed Clan members who were defiant or made attempts to expose the Condition and punished others who skirted too close to that line.

Regulars suffered the same fate. If they were seen as a threat or became suspicious, they were eliminated. It wasn't a common occurrence, but if it needed to happen, the Protectors wouldn't hesitate. They were exceedingly careful and deliberate in the manner in which they carried out these murders. For one thing, they never left a body behind. If they took someone out, that person simply disappeared and would never be heard from again. Marshall had assembled an efficient and disciplined group of Protectors who were masters at concealing their actions.

The G.O. never wavered in their support of the Protectors. They believed their actions were justified. The Protectors were clear about what would happen if their authority was challenged. If Clan members broke the rules, then it was their own fault if they were killed because of it.

Marshall refused to be reasoned with on this matter. He believed if Clan members lived cautiously, they wouldn't have to worry about his Protectors. Those who refused to abide by the rules deserved to be constantly looking over their shoulders.

The second generation continued to take exception with the Protectors' disciplinary actions. Some protested by violating rules and playing cat and mouse with them; others kept their feelings private, letting their hatred and resentment deepen. They stayed out of trouble and under the radar, but secretly they began to organize.

It was around the mid-1980s when two second-generation Clan members began plotting against the Protectors. Martin Pitts and James McNair had reason to despise them. The Protectors had killed members of both their families.

Early on, both Pitts and McNair had tried to reason with the G.O. They made formal requests for official discussions about the Protectors, but the G.O. refused to hear their arguments. They maintained their steadfast belief that the Clans' survival was dependent on Marshall's efforts.

Pitts and McNair disagreed.

They decided to use their own resources to gather evidence so they could bring the matter out in the open within the Clans. They hoped an organized protest would, at the very least, persuade the G.O. to rein them in.

They began with covert operations in which they put every Protector under surveillance. It was a difficult task. The Protectors worked undercover to preserve the element of surprise. Many of them lived normally with regular jobs and families of their own, which helped them keep a watchful eye within the Clans. But Pitts and McNair soon discovered there were those who held more authority, a preeminent group. They were relentlessly devoted to protecting the Condition. These Protectors were the most dangerous agents and were the hardest to track down. It took years to attain information on them.

While they observed the Protectors, Pitts and McNair did not interfere. They simply documented everything with photos and meticulous notes. They built up a hefty mound of evidence showing how much the Protectors violated their civil rights. It was their contention that despite the fact they lived anonymously, they were still part of the same society as a whole and therefore should be afforded the same rights. Unfortunately, this argument was presented to the G.O. by other Clan members and was shot down on the grounds that the Condition overruled certain inalienable rights.

Pitts and McNair soon realized their clandestine efforts were futile. The G.O. was never going to budge. They knew they would have to take matters into their own hands if they wanted to change the way the Clans existed. Thus began the Insurgency, in which they continued to secretly monitor the Protectors and waited patiently for a time when they could intervene and alter their course.

By the 1990s, there were more than two thousand living with the Condition worldwide. The Protectors were present in the United States but mainly dominated over the British and Irish communities, which had the largest concentration of Clan members. The Governing Order had become a formidable association, similar to the Masons. They were secretive and hidden but had begun to manipulate and influence the Regulars' society, their main objective being, as always, to shield and protect the Condition. Their power was unmistakable within the Clans, and the Protectors continued to be their guardians. After seventy years, the secret society was a well-oiled machine.

The Insurgents, on the other hand, had also grown over the years but were still not positively known to the Protectors. Rumors persisted about a mysterious group of Clan members who were in opposition to them, but the Protectors could never find any solid proof of their existence. Even so, their paranoid tendencies could sense something was up. The Protectors had an unsettling awareness they were being watched. Several claimed they were being followed, but they could never track down any Insurgents.

Around this time, Marshall began to lose his grip on the Protectors— and his mental faculties. He began to focus his attention on other troubles outside the Clans. He became obsessively involved in the turmoil over Northern Ireland. The G.O. was appalled that he would participate in such a high profile movement. This led to Colin Hughes taking over the majority of leadership responsibilities within the Protectors. He was a British Elder who had been by Marshall's side from the beginning. Despite the differences in their personality and temperament, Colin maintained Marshall's objectives with the same vigor and determination.

In 1994, the crisis in Belfast became an issue for the Protectors. A number of Clan members, including Marshall, had taken up with the Irish Republican Army in their fight against British rule. The Protectors were adamant that the Clan members stay out of it, but they disregarded their warning, insisting it was their right as Irish citizens to staunchly support their cause. The Protectors didn't see it that way. They murdered two of them when they refused to leave.

The Insurgents, who were there monitoring the situation as well, ambushed the Protectors and assassinated some of them. It was the first time a Protector had been killed by a Clan member. The line had been drawn, and there was no going back. The Insurgents knew the time had come to openly defy the Protectors. The war had begun.

For the next twenty years, the Protectors and the Insurgents fought behind the scenes of both the Clans' and Regulars' society. The Insurgents attacked the higher-ranking Protectors, who were responsible for nearly all of the killings. They had been tracking them for years so it was easy in the beginning. But once the Protectors knew they had a target on their backs, they went into defensive mode. They continued to oversee the Clans; however, their methods became more deliberate and less obvious. They sought out the Insurgents and eliminated them when they found them, but it was tricky for everyone involved. Both these groups were skilled at blending in and lying low. It became a long, drawn-out conflict in which the Insurgents never got the upper hand on the Protectors.

For the Clans, it was like a secret, real-life game of Risk. They were aware of the war going on around them. There were those who supported the Protectors, believing they were necessary to keeping the Clans concealed. Others sided with the Insurgents and wanted the Protectors eradicated.

The G.O. did not anticipate a full-blown rebellion when it finally surfaced. They attempted to uncover who was behind it, but since the Insurgents had stayed undetected for so long they impeccably covered their tracks. No one knew who was officially in command. Their skills at living in obscurity were a valuable asset in remaining hidden from the Protectors. Nevertheless, the Protectors had boundless resources and they continued to search for the leaders. It became a deeply underground war in the shadows of the rest of the world.

By 2014, the conflict was at a standstill. The Insurgents had failed to wipe out the Protectors, and both factions were still surreptitiously attacking each other. The Insurgents had taken out a number of Protectors over the years, but the Protectors were still in control. They weren't killing as often, however, and the Insurgents saw that as a victory. Colin didn't see it that way. He knew it was because Clan members were being more careful. It had been more than ninety years and the Condition was still unknown to the Regulars.

McNair relished his role with the Insurgents. He grew up hating the Protectors—not only had they killed some of his family, but he believed they ruled with such malevolence that he saw the Insurgents' mission as justice in its purest form.

Pitts was a British attorney who had both the means and education to lead such an organization. He greatly admired McNair and trusted him completely. McNair had thrown the first stone at the Protectors' glass house. He was there when the first Protectors were killed in Northern Ireland. He was the mastermind behind the operations in which the Insurgents got the best of the Protectors. He was the brawn behind Pitts' brains. They respected each other and saw eye to eye on their objective.

Despite his unflinching devotion to their cause, the weight of McNair's responsibilities sometimes wore him down. He appeared to be a healthy and fit thirty-something, but at times he was a tired sixty-year-old man who had seen and done things that had damaged his soul. He was unprepared for the events that were about to take place.

As McNair was taking in the view from his window, his assistant, Daniel, interrupted his peaceful state.

"Sir, a photo was just posted onto several of our sites. It's tagged 'Attention: James McNair.'"

This alarmed him. Very few people knew his real name.

"What is it?" he asked.

"We're not sure."

Daniel placed the printout on the desk. McNair walked over and peered down at the document. It was a surveillance photo of Jude and Veronica in an intimate embrace. He froze.

"Who are they?" Daniel asked.

McNair was stunned. He put his finger on Veronica.

"She's a Protector. Get Pitts on the phone immediately."

12

Veronica never feared the Regulars. In truth, she never paid much attention to them. She didn't have to. She grew up isolated from the Regulars' world. The Clan her family created lived on an extensive, secluded plantation outside Philadelphia. Two large colonial-style homes sat at the center of the property. Originals Jonathan and Marie Cooper lived in one home, and Veronica and her parents, Christopher and Celine Farrell, lived in the other. Jonathan and Christopher worked in the city, but the rest of the Clan rarely left the property.

Veronica was an only child but she grew up around lots of kids. She and her parents shared their home with her father's family, which included her grandparents, two uncles, their wives and four cousins. The Cooper family was a large brood as well and included five children. Veronica enjoyed a normal upbringing and never gave much thought to what went on outside her Clan. That is, until she found out about the Condition.

Her world fell apart when her parents explained it to her. Everything she thought she knew and believed in didn't make sense anymore. Instead of seeing the benefits of it, which is what her parents had hoped for, she only saw the negative.

Up until then, she never doubted her parents' respect and trust in her. Since she didn't have any siblings, all their attention was focused on her and they raised her as an equal. They never treated her like a child. They had always been very open and honest with her about everything. So, when she found out they had kept something of this magnitude from her, she felt betrayed. It made her question everything around her. She grew angry and resentful, and immediately put the blame solely on her parents.

Her parents knew the revelation would be shocking and they attempted to break it to her gently, but once Veronica began to understand the scope of the situation, she insisted on knowing all the details of how it happened and why. At first, they indulged her, until she became hostile toward them, and then they refused to discuss it any further. They hoped her anger toward them would lessen with time. Veronica wasn't as optimistic. She told her parents that her trust in them was broken, perhaps irrevocably.

It was difficult for her in the beginning. She isolated herself and bottled everything up inside. She didn't want to be different. She was uncomfortable with the thought of having extraordinary abilities and the possibility that someday she would stop aging. It didn't matter to her that she wasn't the only one and that everyone in her Clan was afflicted. In fact, it fueled her anxiety. The Regulars' world suddenly became a frightening place, one that could someday swallow her up and destroy everyone she loved. She was scared to death of what could happen if they were ever discovered. And as her paranoia grew, it left her unable—and unwilling—to forgive her parents.

Shortly after the Elders were informed of the Condition, a newsletter began arriving from Dublin with information from the other Clans in the U.K., Ireland, and Europe. Veronica became even more infuriated when she found out the actual number of people who were *infected*, as she put it. To make matters worse, rules and limitations were now being forced upon them. She read Marshall's newsletters with disdain, but soon his words began to make sense to her. She agreed with his views about how they needed to live in obscurity, that it was vital to their survival. Her understanding of his convictions revived her self-confidence and gave her some comfort. She began corresponding with him for support and more clarity about their dilemma, and his long letters filled with preaching and encouragement had a lasting effect on her. He made her believe she could make a difference in their world and help protect the ones she loved.

Once she accepted Marshall's dogma, she made a point to spread his words. She passed around the newsletter, sometimes reading it herself to anyone who would listen. She became obsessed with the Clans' affairs and spoke of nothing else, much to the chagrin of her parents. Her father was not a supporter of Marshall's newsletters. He found them to be highfalutin, in his words, and bordering on dictatorial. World War II was at its height, and her parents worried Marshall was exhibiting Hitler-like tendencies. They knew how to live discreetly; they'd been doing it for almost twenty years. They didn't appreciate a snotty Irish Elder telling everyone how to live their lives. And now, their daughter was caught up in his teachings and she wouldn't shut up about it. They adamantly disapproved of her persistent support of Marshall and wouldn't allow her to discuss him or his opinions in their home. This caused the friction between them to deepen.

Veronica disregarded her parents' wishes and continued to communicate with Marshall via letters and occasional phone calls. She didn't speak of it as often at home but dedicated herself to his cause by contributing to his newsletter and making sure the Elders in her Clan knew all about it. Marshall was thrilled to have an American counterpart, which is how he viewed her. He tried to persuade her to come visit him, but her parents refused to allow it, which she didn't mind. The thought of a transatlantic trip by flight or ship did not appeal to her. Marshall had the same trepidation for overseas travel, but promised that someday they would meet.

Veronica was twenty years old when she decided to study at Temple University. She wanted to face her fears and gain an understanding about the Regulars. She was curious about their differences and knew the only way to find out was to live among them. Her parents argued against it, but to no avail. She knew she could handle it. She trusted herself. She'd had long discussions with Marshall about it and felt she was ready. Plus, she didn't want to be confined to the Clans for her entire life. She knew this was the best way to ease into it.

She spent seven years at Temple, extending her studies for as long as she could. She lived at home for the first five years but then moved closer to the campus when she felt more comfortable. She mostly kept to herself and didn't actively engage with the Regulars. Despite appearing confident, she worried someone would notice she was different. Instead, she watched and listened, learning as much as she could about them.

By her thirtieth birthday, she knew she was no longer aging. She had spent most of her life giving samples of blood, skin, hair, and anything else the Originals needed to verify what she always knew. She was completely stricken, and now she was of an age where she could put a stop to all the testing and move forward with her life. Once the Elders were given more freedom, she began traveling to the other Clans in New York and Virginia. She had become undaunted in the Regulars' world. She was cautious and had learned to blend in and hide her eccentricities.

She was still an ardent supporter of Marshall and his now-notorious Protectors. She and some of the Elders in the nearby Clans had let it be known they were proponents of his cause. The Clan members in America were much more compliant than in Europe so it wasn't as challenging to keep tabs on them. But once the Elders began leaving their communities, Veronica knew it was time to form an official faction of the Protectors, and she led them with tremendous zeal. Her unquestionable commitment to guarding the Clans' anonymity was the reason the U.S. Clans never posed a problem in the early days.

And yet, despite her unwavering dedication to their survival, her parents were livid with their daughter's decision to carry the Protectors' torch in their homeland. They had high hopes for their only child, and becoming a defender of the Condition was not one of them. They had brought in the best tutors from the East Coast when she was young, and she excelled beyond her peers. They knew early on she was exceptional, which is why they were extremely disappointed when she devoted all of her time and energy to Clan business. They were hopeful when she attended college and graduated with honors, but she never faltered in her devotion to Marshall. They tried to explain their reasons to her but she saw it as rejection, which fell right in line with their betrayal. She refused to comprehend why they were opposed to her being a Protector, and she grew to hate them for not supporting her.

When she assembled her group of Protectors, she moved to New York permanently. From there, they monitored the three Clans and kept an eye on the Elders who ventured out. Marshall was impressed with how she managed to keep her Clans in line. Albeit, they were a much smaller group than what he had to deal with, but the fact that she was a woman and held this kind of regard did not go unnoticed by him, his Irish Protectors and the G.O.

By the mid-1960s, Veronica had helped create a small but forceful band of Protectors. She oversaw the group while others handled the daily monitoring of Clan members. She spent most of her time working on additional degrees at Columbia University. She had a passion for learning and knew she could continue her education for as long as she wanted. She could simply change her name and enroll at a new university every six or seven years. This was the plan she laid out for herself.

It was in New York City that she began a relationship with a fellow Elder and Protector named Noah Green. He was originally from the New York Clan. She had met him a few times over the years when all the Clans would gather, but she didn't become truly acquainted with him until she started traveling to the city. At the time, he was involved with a Regular, which she found to be very unusual and dangerous, but they took an instant liking to each other and became friends. When she settled there, they began working together with the Protectors. He took her under his wing as she adjusted to living in the fast-paced, crowded metropolis. They spent a lot of time together, and it wasn't long before his feelings for her grew more intimate. He soon ended his relationship and began pursuing her.

At first, she resisted becoming romantically involved with him. She had taken a few lovers over the years but never let anyone get too close. Her relationship with her parents left a profound scar in her heart, and she was skeptical of anyone's affection. Noah was the first person she even remotely trusted. He was patient with her and waited until she came around, which she did once she realized how special he was. He understood her better than anyone ever had, and he supported her unconditionally, something to which she wasn't accustomed. And he loved her, very much. She was aware of it, but he never pressured her. He knew he wasn't her soul mate. He could see it in her eyes, but it didn't matter. The love she was able to give was enough for him. For her part, she cared about him more than she was willing to admit, and yet she was never able to fully accept his love.

Veronica was in constant contact with Marshall while she ran the New York Protectors, but it had been twenty-four years since she first reached out to him and they had yet to meet. He began insisting she come to Ireland. A lengthy journey across the ocean was never a consideration for her, but one of them was going to have to give in if they were ever going to meet.

"I don't understand why you won't even discuss traveling abroad," Noah said on one particular night when the topic arose.

"I either have to get in a metal tube or on a metal boat and travel thousands of miles over open water. No, thank you. Both options sound absolutely ridiculous," she contended.

"You're scared."

"Yes, I am. I'm scared to death to do either." She shrugged. "So, there's really nothing more to discuss."

He stared her down with his sultry hazel eyes and a flirtatious grin. He drove her crazy when he looked at her like that. It was irresistible, and she would usually surrender to him.

"What would you say if I went with you?" he said, coming up close to her. "I could hold your hand and keep your bourbon flowing."

"Why would you want to go with me?"

"Because you'll never make that trip on your own, and you shouldn't have to. Also, I've spent the last eight years waking up next to you. I'd miss you too much."

She ran her fingers along his forehead, brushing away his long brown hair. She kissed his full lips and breathed in his sweet scent. He was devoted to her and would do anything for her, and she loved him for it.

He softly touched her face. "I think we should go. You need to meet with Marshall. He could be a valuable ally for what we need to do here. We'll be back before you know it."

She knew he was right. She knew the time had come for her to go to Ireland.

It was 1966. She was forty-one years old.

Meeting Marshall was a critical point in her life. She always had the best intentions when it came to her role as a Protector. She never got any resistance from Clan members. They always revered her authority. But in Ireland, Marshall's situation was different. From the moment she arrived, she sensed apprehension in the Clan members. Marshall had used intimidation and the threat of violence to get his point across. She never had the need for those tactics in America, and yet she admired the respect that Marshall garnered. It was scary, but he was in control and she loved that.

"It's all in the way you deliver the message," he told her. "Fear is the greatest weapon against an inferior congregation."

Noah wasn't impressed. He thought Marshall was pompous and egotistical, but he could not deny his authority. It was palpable.

Marshall wasn't quite what Veronica had expected. The black-and-white photograph she had of him didn't capture his dominating presence. He was average height, but muscular, with dark blond hair that lay slickly down his neck. His fiendish eyes were an icy blue-gray that matched his cool demeanor, and his lips were tightly drawn, adding to his air of superiority. She didn't find him particularly attractive, but he was intense, especially when he spoke. The confidence and mannerisms in his voice commanded reverence. She assumed it came from his years of controlling the masses.

Marshall was delighted to meet his protégé at long last. She had sent him a photo of herself years ago that he kept on his desk, but when he met her in person, he was dazzled by her endless enthusiasm and found her to be incredibly intelligent, which intimidated him almost as much as her appearance. She was a believer, though, and he loved that. She ate up everything he fed her, and he knew right away there was something special about her. He quickly made up his mind that he was going to keep her close. The only wrinkle was Noah. Marshall didn't feel threatened by him, so he tried not to pay much attention to him.

Marshall was an eloquent host. He took the two of them on a tour of the communities in Ireland and entertained them with stories of his regime. He was careful not to exaggerate with self-importance. He was straightforward about his power and also his difficulties with the European Elders.

"They're a lively bunch," he cracked during supper in Dublin. "They've kept me on my toes all these years. They have a penchant for attention-grabbing predicaments, wouldn't you say, boys?" he said to his Protectors who were dining with them.

"They're a hapless group, if you ask me," grumbled Colin, Marshall's right-hand man. "You can count on them to find the most absurd situation and put themselves right in the middle of it. They're incorrigible."

They all laughed.

"What kinds of situations?" Veronica asked curiously.

"Typical rubbish, like showing off their strength. You know, moving a vehicle or throwing someone across a room," Colin explained. "Some of them have no control over their physical abilities, especially right after they've discovered them."

Physical abilities?

She glanced over at Noah, who shared the same bewilderment. Marshall noticed the exchange.

"Are you not aware of your physical capabilities?" he asked.

"I have no idea what you're talking about," Veronica admitted.

Colin and the other Protectors looked up from their dinner.

"Darling, the Condition is much more than just a fountain of youth," Marshall politely explained. "Besides our heightened senses, we can train our bodies to do incredible things. I'm not talking Superman-type strength, but definitely stronger than the average Regular."

"I know we're superior in genetics, but I didn't know you could build on that," Noah said.

"You can," Colin answered. "Our physiology is limitless."

Veronica was amazed. She had no idea. It had never dawned on her, and no one back home had ever mentioned such possibilities.

"Can you teach me?" she blurted out. She could barely contain her excitement. "This is unbelievable. I want to know more about this. Would you be willing to train me?" she said to Marshall.

By their expressions, Veronica could tell the men were shocked, either by her vivacity or because she was a woman interested in becoming physically stronger. It was probably both. Evidently, women were not part of the team. She had hardly spoken to any since she arrived, only the wives of some of the Protectors, but she wasn't like other female Clan members. She knew it, and Marshall knew it, too.

"Yes, we can train you. If that's what you want," he said.

"Wait, V, let's not be hasty," Noah interjected. "Maybe you should think about this first. You don't want to end up in a ridiculous predicament." He smiled, although he knew she could see he was serious.

"I want to learn more about this," she replied sternly. "Marshall, please, I'm very interested."

Marshall was impressed—and turned on. He offered to set them up in a flat in Dublin while they trained at their facility, but Colin objected straightaway.

"I don't think that's a good idea," he said to Marshall. "We've never trained a woman. We don't know her capabilities. What if there's an adverse effect?" He confronted Veronica. "I know this sounds exciting to you, but we have our hands full as it is. I don't have time to train a woman who has no need for these abilities. You're a lovely girl and you appear to be physically fit, but your body may not be able to handle it. And mentally, I'm not about to start something you may not finish."

Noah looked down, trying to hide his smirk. He knew the response Veronica was about to give. She stood up as all the men watched her.

"My body is no different than yours. If you're physically able to push yourselves, then there's absolutely no reason I wouldn't be able to do the same. And if you think my interest in this, all of this, is some kind of frivolous pursuit by a *lovely* American girl with no interests beyond titillating a group of arrogant Irish blokes, then you couldn't be more wrong. When I set my mind to do something, I always follow through. If you won't train me, I'll go back home and figure it out myself."

They were awestruck. Noah subtly covered his mouth to hide his amusement.

"Well then," Marshall got up and walked over to her. "I think you've stated your case. Colin?"

Colin had his arms folded, trying to ascertain how much of that speech was for real and how much was for show. He still doubted her.

"Fine. I'll take your word that you'll finish what you start," he said.

She didn't flinch but instead focused hard with a nod.

"Great!" Marshall declared. "Let's have another round of pints and we'll show our American friends we're not as arrogant as she seems to think we are."

"And by the way," Colin added, still staring at her. "I'm not Irish."

She smiled.

Back at their hotel, Veronica was overjoyed, but Noah fought to be the voice of reason.

"Have you gone mad?" he said. "I thought we were only going to be here a week. Now you're talking about a long-term arrangement. What's going on?"

"Don't tell me you aren't curious about what they were talking about?" she argued while undressing. "I want to be stronger. I want to see what I'm capable of. Who wouldn't want to try to be the best they can be?"

"You sound like an ad for Jack LaLanne. Honestly, how much stronger can you be?"

She didn't appreciate it when he was condescending and usually let it slide. He enjoyed pretending he had the upper hand in their relationship, but they both knew she was the dominant partner.

"Are you afraid I'll be able to kick your ass?" she said with a wink.

He went over to her and massaged her bare arms down to her wrists. Then, with a wicked smile, he put them behind her and gently backed her up against the wall.

"I'd love for you to kick my ass. Wanna try right now?" he whispered.

He pressed his tall, athletic body against her and began kissing her neck. Her body instantly reacted, succumbing inch by inch, all the way through. The thought of him holding her down and having his way with her sent her senses into a frenzy, but she resisted him and maneuvered from his tender grip and pushed him away.

"I'm serious. We traveled all the way here—we might as well get the most from it. What's the rush to get back to the States? Jeff and David have everything under control."

He laughed. "You didn't even want to come here in the first place, and now I'm going to have to drag you back."

Noah sat down on the bed knowing that wasn't true. He knew that if it came down to it she'd let him return home alone, and he absolutely did not want that.

Veronica went over to him, dressed only in her bra and jeans, and straddled him as he leaned back.

"I want to do this," she said. "And I want you to be here with me. It won't be for a long time, I promise."

He sat up and fondled the silver Irish trinity-knot pendant on the necklace dangling above her breasts.

"Do you really like it?" he asked.

"The pendant? I love it."

"I couldn't resist. It's such a cool design. I knew it would look beautiful on you."

"Tell me again what it means."

"Let's see, the woman said the three points can represent any three entities that are interconnected. The way I see it, it symbolizes you as a human, as a Clan member, and as a Protector."

"And the circle?"

"Eternity."

She put her hands in his hair and smoothed it back from his face. He gazed up at her.

"I just want you to be happy, V. Will staying here make you happy?" he asked.

"Yes," she said, kissing him softly.

He felt his way along her back and unclasped her bra. Deftly, he removed it as he laid her down on the bed.

"I don't know why I bother saying anything. You already had your mind made up. I might as well be mute," he said and kissed her hard. "I bet you'd like that."

"No, actually," she replied while he made his way down to her chest. "Then who would discuss movies with me?"

"Oh God." He stopped and looked up at her. "You're not going to start in again about *Doctor Zhivago*."

"No, maybe later," she joked as he continued down to her jeans.

Training was easier than what Veronica had expected. She had never done anything physical before—ever. She'd never even exercised. When she was a young girl on the plantation, the kids would play outside and run around, but there were never any organized activities. So, when she imagined training with the Protectors, she envisioned the type of things she'd seen on television: calisthenics, vibrating machines, pulleys and various elastic bands. In reality, the workout was much simpler. They jogged. A lot.

Marshall and Colin had built a private compound on the outskirts of Dublin that served as the main headquarters for the Protectors in Europe. On that property was a workout facility that consisted of a gym and outdoor track. They met there every morning and ran for what seemed like hours at times. Colin was a big believer in conditioning and endurance above all else, mainly because a Clan member's body responded in remarkable ways. Every benefit from running was greatly enhanced by the Condition, and the results were immediate.

Their afternoons were spent in the gym working with weights. While Noah trained with the other boys, Colin focused on Veronica and was very careful with her in the beginning. He didn't know what effect weight-lifting would have on her body. He showed her the correct techniques to increase her strength without building muscle. It wasn't about bulk; it was about potency. He taught her how to tap into that power within and then how to control it.

After a few weeks, Veronica and Noah were amazed at the contrast. It was different from the natural enhancements caused by the Condition.

These abilities had to be developed and maintained, and the end result was tangible. It wasn't superhuman strength, like Marshall had said, but it was well beyond the average capacity. Veronica noticed it most in her grip and forearm strength. She was able to hold Noah in a headlock with such force he would have to pick her up and flip her over to get out of it. She may have been stronger, but she still weighed less than the boys and therefore was easy to handle.

When this became obvious, Colin brought in a member of the Irish Army to teach her combat skills. He knew it would be essential for her to know how to deal with Clan members who were bigger and heavier. Learning ways to immobilize violators was a valuable asset for any Protector, but especially for her.

Veronica and Noah adapted easily to their new surroundings. They became as strong, if not stronger, than the rest of the Protectors. They would often all work out together and spar in the gym for fun. Veronica quickly became a fierce pugilist, never hesitating to kick someone's ass when egged on. The boys enjoyed her competitiveness and encouraged her in every way. They treated her like a sister, even though several of them would've preferred to be her lover, but Noah was always close by, and no one dared make a move while Marshall was around.

Inevitably, they were introduced to firearms. Veronica was apprehensive about it. She was confident in her physical skills, but all the boys carried a gun so she knew she had to at least learn to use one. The power it wielded frightened her, but, as with everything else, she was a natural and became quite comfortable with it. She spent a lot of time at target practice with Colin. She enjoyed training with him, and they eventually became good friends. Despite his initial reservations, he respected her for never giving up.

Veronica flourished in Ireland. She felt herself change both inside and out. The training had invigorated her, filling her with purpose once again. She soon realized this was always her one true calling. She was determined now to forever be a vital member of the Protectors.

Physically, she had proven herself to Marshall's men, but she wanted to be accepted as an equal on every level. She knew what she was capable of, and she never shied away from demonstrating it. It didn't take long for the Irish Protectors to recognize she was unlike any other woman they knew and that the gender disparity wasn't as rigid as they once thought.

Still, most of the violators they dealt with were men. Women were less likely to step outside the boundaries of the Clans, but Marshall and Colin knew this wasn't going to remain the norm. They knew it was only a matter of time before women became as much of an issue for the Protectors as the men. This is why they both agreed Veronica should stay with them and set the precedent for future female Protectors. She had become invaluable to their cause, and they weren't about to let her go.

Colin was the first to plant the notion in her that she should consider staying with them in Ireland.

"I'm proud of you, V," he said to her after one of their more strenuous workouts. They were relaxing on the gym floor across from where Noah and a few other boys were still sparring.

"I knew you would be," she said confidently.

"Now who's being arrogant?" He laughed. "Yes, you have put me in my place."

"That wasn't the intention."

"Of course it was," he said and winked.

"Okay, maybe it was, but thank you. That means a lot."

"Have you thought about when you're going to head back home?"

"No. I thought for sure Noah would be champing at the bit to return, but he hasn't mentioned it. Between you and me, I think he likes it here."

"He's a decent lad. Are you two planning on making it official at some point?"

She eyed him suspiciously.

"Sorry, I didn't mean to pry," he said, putting his hands up.

"Actually, we don't talk in those terms. It's not as if we're Regulars and have the pressure to fulfill certain obligations. That kind of commitment is unnecessary and unrealistic for us, don't you think?"

"I'm not sure what you mean. How could marrying someone you love be unnecessary and unrealistic?"

"Forever is infinite for us, unlike Regulars. It's unrealistic to promise someone you'll be with them forever when we don't know how long forever actually will be. Noah and I know how we feel about each other, and we know we'll be together for as long as we want. A piece of paper and the Regulars' laws are unnecessary."

"I never thought about it like that," he said. "But I see where you're coming from. You're not in love with him."

"Excuse me?"

"You're not in love with him. If you were in love with him, you'd feel differently." He leaned in. "My guess is you've never been in love, am I right?"

She tightened her lips, realizing he had hit the nail on the head.

"It's okay, I've never been in love either," he said. "But I've been around a lot of people who have been, and supposedly it changes you. You see things differently when you meet someone who rocks your world. Forever doesn't seem long enough."

Veronica shook her head. "Who knew you were such a romantic, Colin. I'm impressed."

"Don't be. I'm only repeating what I've been told. It doesn't mean that's what happens to everyone. But I have a feeling when that guy shows up, you'll know it, and you'll feel it more profoundly than the rest of us."

He got up and wiped himself off with a towel. "Hey, have you considered sticking around with us permanently? You've really inspired the lads. You could do some good here."

She cocked her head.

"And anyway, I'd miss you if you left." He said, smiling. "But don't tell anyone I said that."

Colin tossed the towel at her and walked away.

As she watched him leave, she thought about what he had said. The thought of staying in Ireland had crossed her mind. It was definitely a different vibe than in America, and she felt safe around the Irish Protectors. She already thought of them as family, even more than her own Clan. Being around like-minded people was comforting. She was beginning to realize she might have found a place to call home.

Within three months, Veronica and Noah were embedded in Marshall's group. They spent all their time with the boys, including joining them on assignments to check on Clan members. Noah actively participated, even though it was never his goal to be so involved with them. This was all about Veronica. He was there because of her, but he had become just as devoted to them as she had and they had accepted him.

The decision to stay in Ireland was not an easy one for him. Veronica had no issues with leaving her life and family behind in America, but Noah was conflicted about it. He tried to persuade her to return with him, at least for a while before deciding whether to stay, but she had made up her mind and he knew he wasn't going to leave her. In the end, they settled down in Dublin and became indispensable members of the Irish Protectors.

Time flies for those afflicted and before they knew it, five years had passed. Veronica had enrolled at University College Dublin and continued her beloved studies. Noah went back to the States on occasion to check in on the New York Protectors and to see his family. He also spent a lot of time traveling throughout Europe, keeping tabs on Clan members with Colin and the other boys. Veronica didn't roam around as much as Noah; she preferred working behind the scenes with Marshall, tracking Clan members, but she never passed up a trip to France, which is where they went in early 1972.

Word had reached Marshall about a group of Clan members in Nice who were posing a serious threat. They had sent an anonymous letter to the local newspaper, implying there was a secret society living in Europe. The editor at the paper didn't believe the claim, but he enjoyed the creative narrative and printed it anyway. Fortunately, it was received as an impressive work of fiction, and it circulated, eventually reaching Ireland.

Marshall was so outraged he insisted on leading the group to Nice to deal with the instigators. He brought Colin, Noah, and Veronica with him and made it clear there was going to be severe consequences for this tremendous violation.

By the time they arrived in France, the French Protectors had located the culprits. A French Elder and two second-generation members had been moving back and forth between Marseille and Nice trying to recruit Clan members to join them. They were not discreet, and because of this several Clan members in the area knew what they were doing. Even though they did not approve of their actions, they were still unwilling to help the Protectors. They tipped off the violators that Marshall and his team were hunting for them.

Despite that, the Protectors tracked the men to Grenoble in southeastern France. Colin tried to dissuade Marshall from an all-out attack on the men, but he wouldn't hear of it. Marshall insisted it was such a slap in the face to the Protectors and the Governing Order that it had to be dealt with in the harshest manner to prevent anyone else from attempting such an egregious offense.

"I want them dead," he said bitterly.

Colin, Noah, and Veronica looked at each other with sober expressions. They knew what that meant. A Protector had never killed a Clan member before. It would change everything, especially since Marshall had no intentions of covering it up. He was going to let it be known and use it as a lesson on what would happen if this type of breach were ever attempted again.

Veronica had concerns about it, but she stood by her mentor. She knew he was right. If word spread that the punishment for a violation this flagrant was not the most severe, then it could lead to other more dangerous transgressions.

It was evening when they found the men at an inn outside Grenoble. Noah went inside to identify them and saw they were at the bar drinking as if they hadn't a care in the world. He went back to the others, waiting in a van.

"There's five of them," he reported.

"Five?" Veronica said. "I thought there were only three."

"There's only supposed to be three," Colin answered. "Who are the other two?"

"I don't recognize them."

"So be it," Marshall stated decisively.

"Shit, we're going to kill five now?" Noah snapped.

"We don't know if the other two are Clan members," Veronica said.

"It doesn't matter. If they found others to participate, then they will all pay the consequences," Marshall declared.

It was a couple of hours before the men stumbled out together. Three of the men got in a car while the other two trailed close behind on a motorcycle. The Protectors followed them to an isolated house not far from the inn. As the men went in, the Protectors parked a short distance away.

Marshall was clear about what he wanted them to do. He instructed them to split up and surround the house. He and Colin would enter through the front, and Noah and Veronica were to cover the back.

"I don't want anyone getting out alive. Do you understand? They brought this upon themselves. It is an inevitable consequence we must now accept. We must be forthright in our convictions in order to protect our circumstance."

Noah glanced over at Veronica. He was obviously not moved by Marshall's self-righteous tone. She closed her eyes and breathed deeply. She readied herself for what she knew would be a decisive assault.

The cold air stung her lips as she moved carefully through the backyard and approached the house. One of the windows was slightly open with the curtains drawn. She could hear the men chatting. For a moment, she thought it sounded like more than five men, but before she could process it, the first shot rang out, and then all hell broke loose. There was a lot of gunfire, significantly more than what she expected. The instigators were firing back. As Veronica reached the back door, it flew open and a man ran out. She swung her leg around and hit him in the gut, causing him to fall to his knees. He was gasping for air when she kicked him again, this time in the back, and he fell face first into the grass. He rolled over and looked up at her.

"Are you a Protector?" he said in French, shuddering below her.

She pointed her revolver at his face. "Yes, I am."

13

TUESDAY—BRISTOL

Veronica abruptly opened her eyes and stared into the darkness. She wasn't quite sure where she was. She lay still and listened, then she heard it. She heard him breathing steadily next to her. She closed her eyes.

I'm safe.

The next morning, she awoke to the smell of coffee. She stretched her body as tall as she could make it, then curled up into a tight ball under the covers. She heard Jude enter the room and crawl back in bed.

"Can I tempt you with something warm and delicious?" he said, putting his arms around her covered body.

"Please," she moaned.

He let go of her and sat up. "There's coffee and toast and a few pastries—what's your pleasure?"

Veronica peered over at him from beneath the sheet as he poured her a cup.

"Coffee? Is that what you're offering me?"

"Aye, was there something else you wanted?" he teased.

"Nope. Not at all." She put her head back under the sheet and burrowed in.

Jude laughed and wrapped himself around her again. She had herself tightly swaddled in the sheet, but he managed to find an opening near her thigh where he reached in and unsheathed her from her lair.

"Good morning, my love," he said, kissing her cheek.

She loved his voice. It was deep and seductive, with a gentle Irish lilt that resonated inside of her.

"Good morning," she said lazily, while he continued kissing her lightly along her face.

She shoved the covers off with her legs and allowed him to traverse her body as she settled back on the pillow and closed her eyes. She felt happy and light-headed. Every time his lips made contact with her, she fell deeper still. She was blown away at how he affected her physically. It was all she could do not to pass out from it.

"I feel so high," she exhaled.

Jude made his way back up to her face. "What was that, love?"

She opened her eyes but went silent as he gazed upon her. His eyes filled her with so much emotion, she couldn't hold back. She began to tear up.

"What's wrong?"

"I've never felt this way before," she confided. "All of it. The way you touch me. The way you look at me. It's as though you can see right through me."

He lay down next to her. "I think that's what love is supposed to feel like," he said.

"Is it? You've experienced this before?"

"Well, no. This is definitely different."

"I've loved, but not like this," she said, wiping away her tears. "I didn't know *this* was possible, outside of a good book or a fucking movie. The way you make me feel scares me."

"Why?"

"It's too much. I don't know if I could ever give it up."

This puzzled him. "Why would you have to give it up?"

She looked over at him and touched his face. "This can't possibly last forever."

Jude didn't understand why she would say such a thing, and it showed on his face.

She kissed him.

"I'm sorry," she said. "I know I'm not making any sense."

She sat up and pulled her knees in, then glanced over at him. He was still lying on his side watching her.

"I love you," she said. "So much. How can that be?"

"Come here," he said. He brought her back down onto his chest. "I can't explain it, but I don't think you should be upset by it. We're very fortunate to have found each other again."

"Do you feel it as intensely as I do?" she asked.

"You know I do."

"Why doesn't it terrify you?"

He kissed her forehead. "Because I've waited all this time to love you," he said softly.

She closed her eyes tight, trying not to tear up again, then looked up at him. "I don't deserve you."

"You're too hard on yourself. Of course you deserve to be loved like this. Everyone does."

"If you say so."

She climbed on top of him and buried her face in his neck, breathing him in and kissing him. He gently pulled her down onto him and she gasped. She put her hands on his chest and pushed herself upright.

Everyone deserves to be loved like this.

Veronica knew she could get used to waking up with him. It was a glorious way to begin the day. She was already accustomed to having him around. He was very attentive and enjoyed looking after her. It had been a long time since someone spoiled her.

"Do you think if we hadn't run into each other in France we would've ever met?" Jude asked as he watched her get ready for work.

"I don't know. Would you have noticed me in the lounge?"

"I can't imagine I wouldn't have. What a fucking shame if our paths had never crossed."

"I know," she said from the vanity. "We're very lucky."

Jude got up out of bed and went over to where she was standing. He stood behind her and looked in the mirror with her.

"I'm wondering how much of this is luck and how much is fate," he said. "It could've been so easy for us to miss each other. What if you hadn't been there in France with Marshall, or if I hadn't seen you at the hotel? Then none of this would've happened. Is it luck or fate or something else? I wonder."

He went to the shower and turned it on. Veronica stood frozen, facing the mirror.

Did he just mention Marshall?

Jude came back over to her and kissed her on the shoulder. He moved her hair and kissed her neck but noticed she wasn't there with him.

"What's the matter?"

"Nothing," she said. She walked away from him and went to the bed to finish dressing.

Jude watched her from the vanity. His exceptional perception could be irritating at times. Even though there were definite benefits from it, it was difficult for him when he sensed every emotion. After five days with her, he thought he could read her pretty well. He knew when there was something she wasn't telling him. He got that feeling a lot, but he understood they were still getting to know each other and he couldn't expect her to be completely open with him all the time. He knew he would have to be patient, but already there were a few times when he knew it was more than that. It wasn't that she didn't feel ready to share something with him; it was that she was keeping something from him, and he hated that feeling.

"Why do you do that?" he asked.

"What?"

"Keep secrets."

She turned to him. "How do you know Marshall?"

He had to think about it. "Marshall?"

"You said, what if I hadn't been in France with Marshall. How did you know that?"

He was confused. "I didn't realize I said that. But you were there with Marshall. I saw you."

"You saw me, with Marshall."

"Yeah, after I ran out of there. I was on the roof of the building across the street. I saw you with them."

"And you knew it was Marshall?"

He wondered where this was coming from. "Marshall is from my Clan. I grew up with him."

Veronica was stunned. She tried her best to hide it, but it was no use. Jude shut off the shower, grabbed a towel, and wrapped it around himself.

"What's this about? Everybody knew who Marshall was, he made sure of that."

"Yes, you're right. Of course." She backed off, realizing she had started a conversation she did not want to have.

"Holy shit, was Marshall who you were involved with?"

"No, absolutely not."

"Then why are you upset?"

"I'm not upset. I'm late." She looked over at the clock. "Fuck, I'm really late."

She walked over to him and kissed him.

"I'm sorry," she said. "We hardly ever talk about the Clans. I forget you're a part of it all. I just hadn't heard his name in a long time. I didn't expect that."

She kissed him again. "Okay?"

He knew there was more to it but decided to let it go, for now.

"Okay," he said and kissed her. "Would you mind if I invited Charlie to join us for dinner tonight? He's dying to meet you."

"Sure."

She held his hand as he walked her to the door. When she got to it, she leaned back against it.

"I love you," she said.

"I know," he answered with a wily grin.

She started to giggle, but he pressed his naked chest against her and kissed her passionately. She ran her hands up along his warm back and into his hair.

Why am I leaving?

"All right, Han Solo," she joked. "I'll see you in a bit."

Jude shut the door and laughed as he headed back upstairs. He didn't know what to make of it. There were little things that were starting to add up to something, but he couldn't see it. That sadness in her eyes still bothered him, and now this weird reaction to Marshall's name. Being involved with a Clan member was exhausting, he thought.

By the time Veronica reached the car, her disposition had radically changed. She was reeling from the conversation with Jude.

Marshall knew him.

She was absolutely floored by this bit of news. She remembered grilling Marshall about that man in Grenoble and he had played dumb, saying he must've been someone the instigators had recruited from Marseille. She never believed that; she knew he was putting her off, but she never thought he actually knew him and that he was from his Clan. For years she sought him out, and Marshall knew him the whole time.

Bastard!

Later that evening, Jude and Veronica met up with Charlie at an ultra-cool piano bar and restaurant along Bristol's Harborside area, which was bustling for a Tuesday night. Charlie sat across from Veronica, and she could sense he was on edge.

"Are you okay, Charlie?" she asked gently and touched his hand.

"Yes, I'm sorry. I didn't know what to expect, what with the Condition and all. I've never met anyone with it besides Jude."

"As far as you know," she said, smiling. "We don't really go around telling everyone, and it's not like spotting a toupee."

Charlie perked up. "Hey, where have I heard that?"

"It's from *Seinfeld*."

"I love that show!" he beamed.

"I have a friend who's fanatical about it," she explained. "I think I've seen every episode."

This pleased Charlie and alleviated some of his anxiety. He drank his pint and watched Jude lovingly hold Veronica's hand on the table. He marveled at how happy his friend seemed.

"So, what did you think when Jude told you about the Condition?" she asked him. She appreciated that this was a unique situation for her. She wasn't used to openly discussing the Condition with a Regular.

"I didn't believe him. Not at all."

"How did he convince you?"

"He showed me photos of him and his brother back in the 1950s and '60s. He looked exactly the same."

"Yes, that would do it," she said and laughed. "You know, Charlie, you could be in a lot of danger for knowing about us. It's a very well-kept secret."

Charlie laughed nervously.

Jude grinned, knowing Veronica was teasing him.

Veronica smiled, knowing she wasn't.

"I can't imagine what it must be like, never changing, never growing older," Charlie said in awe. "Jude says he can't explain it because he doesn't know how it feels otherwise. Can you describe it?"

Veronica found his curiosity endearing. He reminded her of a child fascinated by tales of the unknown.

"It sounds exciting, I know, but it's not as dramatic when you deal with it every day. We live normally, just like you. For some of us, it's the same mundane day-to-day existence, except there isn't an end in sight. I'm sure you spend time thinking about your future and what you want from your life. A good job, good retirement, marriage, a family, all the normal wants and desires, but there's that ticking clock in the back of your mind. You only have a certain amount of time on this earth to accomplish those things."

Charlie nodded, thoroughly engrossed.

"That clock doesn't tick for us. There's no time limit. If we're careful, we can live longer than you can imagine. However, we each handle it in our own way. Some of us live as if any day could be our last; others live believing they're going to live forever."

"And you, how do you live your life?" Charlie asked sincerely but quickly backed off. "I'm sorry, that was presumptuous."

"It's okay. I'm comfortable talking about it with you. Jude trusts you, and I trust Jude."

Jude smiled and entwined his fingers in hers.

"I'm somewhere in between," she continued. "I try not to think too much about the future because it's so capricious. I travel a lot and therefore never know what's around the next corner. For instance, I was in Brussels three weeks ago preparing to come to Bristol to close a very important real estate deal. And now," she looked at Jude, "I'm on a totally different path."

Jude brought her hand up and kissed it.

"You see," she said with a shrug. "Our lives aren't that different. It can be ordinary or extraordinary. It's all in how we choose to deal with the cards we've been dealt."

"Wow." Charlie was riveted. "Is that how you see it?" he asked Jude.

"I agree everybody manages it differently," he answered. "There are some serious drawbacks, though, like never getting close to people because you have this enormous secret you can't share, or because you'll eventually have to watch the people you care about die. Other than that, yeah, she nailed it."

Charlie wasn't sure how to interpret that. He wanted to laugh, but it seemed sad and pessimistic.

"Well, yes," Veronica spoke up. "But that's more likely to happen when you live exclusively with Regulars. When you're surrounded by other Clan members you don't have to worry about those things as much."

"But then you open up a whole new set of concerns," Jude replied.

Veronica felt him tense up.

"See, Charlie," she said, squeezing Jude's hand. "We may have an affliction, but we are human. We feel the same pain and anxiety, the same happiness and joy. Right, my love?" she kissed his hand.

Jude nodded, feeling a bit embarrassed for being so morose.

"But you have incredible abilities—doesn't that make everyday life challenging?" Charlie asked.

"Not especially. You have to realize, we were born with these abilities. They enhanced gradually as we grew older, so it's not as if I woke up one day and could hear conversations a considerable distance away. I've learned to hear what I want to hear and block out everything else. Same with my sense of smell; I had to teach myself to expel certain odors and aromas. I have to say, though, that's the most difficult of the enhancements. Sometimes it's impossible not to smell something disagreeable."

"Fascinating, simply fascinating," Charlie said. "I bet your IQ is off the charts. Jude said you have several degrees. Do you retain everything?"

"Mostly." She laughed. "There was a period when I was obsessed with acquiring as much knowledge as I could, but that was when I was younger. I still read a lot, but for pleasure, not requirements."

"Whom do you read? I prefer the classics. I teach English literature."

"I read everything, when I have time. Although, I am partial to thrillers and crime novels."

Charlie sat back satisfied and impressed.

"Anything else?" Jude chimed in. "Her favorite color is blue, her favorite city is Rome, she prefers coffee to tea—*American*," he winked at her. "She loathes romantic comedies, and she has an irrational fear of the ocean."

"I wouldn't call it irrational," she mumbled.

They all laughed.

"I didn't mean to interrogate you," Charlie said kindly. "I'm just curious."

"It's quite all right, Charlie. I don't mind at all."

She quenched her parched palate with her favorite spirit.

"Tell me how you two met?" she asked.

"I was teaching at a secondary school up north, and Jude was the caretaker. We became friends rather quickly."

"You were a janitor at a school?" she said to Jude.

"Actually, I worked for a landscaping service. It was just a job."

"How many jobs have you had?" she asked.

"Hundreds," he said, smiling.

"He's a real Renaissance man," Charlie defended his friend. "There isn't anything he can't do or fix. He's the best flatmate I've ever had," he paused to take a sip of his beer, "and I'd like to keep it that way," he said slyly under his breath.

Veronica swallowed hard, trying not to choke as she held back a chuckle.

"Yes, but surely you don't plan on living with Jude for forever," she teased.

"No, but I'm quite content with the way things are."

"Okay, let's not get into this right now," Jude interrupted.

Veronica was enjoying herself. She could see how much Charlie cared for Jude. It was sweet and said a lot about both of them.

"Well, I couldn't ask for two better blokes to spend an evening with. Cheers," she said, raising her glass. They toasted and continued to revel in each other's company as the night went on.

Charlie was enchanted. He hung on Veronica's every word. By the time dessert was served, he was fawning over her like she was his prom date. Jude tried to hold back his laughter while watching Charlie make such a fuss. When Veronica eventually excused herself, Charlie expressed his approval.

"She's delightful, Jude. She's far more amiable than I anticipated."

"I told you she was lovely."

"Yes, but our tastes vary greatly."

"That's because you place too much importance on appearances," Jude ribbed.

"I do not."

"Yeah, you do."

"Maybe I do, but I require a little something up here, too," Charlie said, tapping on his temple.

"Oh, really?" Jude laughed loudly. "I do recall you proclaiming that you couldn't be with someone smarter than you."

"Never mind that. Veronica is perfect for you, and she makes you happy. That's all that matters."

Jude was relieved. He didn't think he needed validation, but he was thrilled he wasn't the only one who thought she was special.

After a few more drinks and several more requests to the piano man, Charlie reluctantly called it a night. Jude and Veronica walked him out to the street where Benedict was waiting. It was too late and he was too inebriated to let him take the train home. He gave Veronica an affectionate hug good-bye and kissed her on the cheek. Then, he placed his hands on Jude's shoulders.

"I want you to know, Jude, I love you like a brother, and I could not have parted with you to anyone less worthy."

He swung back to Veronica and went in to kiss her again, but Jude pulled him back by the arm.

"Okay, that's enough, brother."

She laughed as Jude loaded him in the car.

"He's hilarious," she said after the car pulled away. "Did he just quote Jane Austen?"

"Probably. I love him to death."

"That's obvious. You two are quite the pair."

Jude took her in his arms. "I think he fell in love with you a bit. That seems to be going around."

They kissed, and he put his forehead on hers. He loved doing that. It was as close as he could get to her eyes, but it had gotten harder to enjoy. The sadness was becoming more and more evident.

"Do you feel like a walk along the harbor before going back?" she suggested.

"Of course."

He took her arm in his and they made their way toward the waterfront. It wasn't as busy as when they first arrived, but there were still people milling around.

Jude was unusually quiet as they strolled the paved walkway. She held onto him, keeping warm and chatting about Charlie and the highlights of the evening. After a bit, she could tell something was up.

"What's going on in there?" she asked.

Jude didn't say anything.

"Come on, what is it?"

"I don't think you want to know."

"That's ridiculous. Why wouldn't I want to know?"

"I want to know why you're sad."

She stopped. "You're going to bring that up again?"

He shrugged. "I can't help it. I have to know. I see it every day now. It's kind of hard to ignore."

Veronica let go of his arm and started walking again, leaving him behind. He hung his head down in frustration and then followed her.

"Why won't you tell me?" he asked when he caught up to her.

"Because there's nothing to tell," she snapped. "Why do you have to keep on about it?"

She went over to the railing overlooking the harbor.

Jude didn't want to upset her, but what he saw was indisputable. That's why it bothered him so much. As each day passed, it had become more transparent. It was almost to the point where that's all he saw now. Something was wrong, and he wanted to know what it was.

He walked up behind her. "I know it's been less than a week, and I know you don't trust me entirely," he said, "but you have to know, this is purely out of love and concern for you. There's nothing malicious about me wanting to know what's hurting you."

She clenched the railing, astonished that he was broaching it so overtly. That's it, she thought; he's got superhuman perception.

Damn it.

She turned to face him. "I don't know what you're seeing. I'm not sad. Being with you these last few days has made me happier than I've ever been, so if you're seeing a sadness in my eyes, I don't know what it could be. Perhaps it's something from my past. If that's the case, then you're going to have to trust that someday I'll tell you everything. Just like someday you'll be able to tell me about your family and why it's so painful to talk about them."

She reached up and took his face in her hands.

"There's no doubt I've fallen in love with you, Jude. And as much as I want to tell you everything, there are some things I'm going to keep to myself for now. So, please, stop asking me about something I can't answer."

She ran her hand down to his chest then gently moved him aside. She stepped away from him and proceeded back to the hotel.

He didn't follow her. He watched her until she was out of his view. He went over to a bench, sat down, and lit a cigarette.

Fuck.

When he got back to the hotel, Veronica was in the shower and the bathroom door was shut. He went up to it and placed his head against it. He wished he could let it go. He wanted to let it go.

I have to try.

He got undressed and walked in. She was standing beneath the rush of water with her head down and arms extended, bracing herself against the tiled wall. He came up to the glass enclosure and watched her. She looked sullen beneath the stream. Her soaked hair veiled her face, but he could feel her anguish.

After a moment, she felt his presence. She tilted her head back and allowed the water to flush her hair from her face. She wiped her eyes and turned to him. They stared at each other in their usual way. All she could think of, as he stood naked before her, was that she wanted him to hold her. She wanted to forget the nonsense that was coming between them. She wanted to feel his body against hers.

She motioned for him to join her. He stepped inside and took her hand, and she pulled him close. The hot water surged over his shoulders and onto his body. He closed his eyes and let the warmth alleviate some of his tension. Veronica ran her hands along his torso, massaging the water over every inch. When Jude opened his eyes, he delved deep into hers. He tried hard to see past the sadness, further and further back. He didn't want it to matter anymore. He didn't want to make her feel worse than she already did. He wiped away the wet strands from her face and kissed her.

"I'm sorry," he said.

She pressed her body against his and laid her head on his shoulder. She felt relieved in his arms. She tasted his wet skin, all the way up to his neck and then to his mouth, and kissed him.

"I love you," she said. "Please let that be enough for now."

He smiled and nodded.

Later that night, after Jude fell asleep, Veronica sat up in bed. The light from the night sky shone in through the uncovered window and cast eerie shadows on the wall. She seemed mesmerized by them, but her mind was racing. She played with her hair, coiling strands in her fingers. She couldn't understand why she felt so disconnected from herself.

Why can't I control this?

She knew exactly what he saw when he looked into her eyes. She couldn't hide it. She trained herself long ago to be in control of her emotions, to be self-assured and confident in any situation, but it was pointless with Jude. He could see past her defenses as if they weren't even there. And although he couldn't possibly know what it was he was seeing, she knew he was never going to let it go. It was screaming and waving at him every time he looked into her eyes.

She wondered if it was because she was in love with him. She couldn't deny it. She'd never been in love like this. Maybe this is what happens when it's real, she thought. You open your heart and everything spills out, or maybe his super ability to read people is just that and nothing more. She was starting to panic. The fact was, she had allowed him in, way in, and now it was affecting everything.

She felt a cold sweat coming on, so she slipped out of bed and went over to the full-length window. The moonlight enveloped her naked body. She put her hand on the cool glass, hoping for some relief, and stared down at the waterfront below. It was empty now, sterile and serene. The amber lights from the walkway sparkled on the silhouette of the harbor, calling to mind her childhood home.

She had spent a lifetime keeping that young girl from Philadelphia hidden from everyone. She kept her locked her away, but she could feel her emerging. She hated feeling vulnerable; it reminded her of when she found out about the Condition. That's how Jude made her feel when he brought up her "sadness." She knew she was going to have to tell him something, and it had to be as close to the truth as she could possibly make it. It made her nervous to think how intuitive he was, and she realized she had to be more careful. She was nowhere near ready to open up to him about everything. She didn't know if she ever would be. She knew she had to find a way to appease his curiosity.

She went back to him and knelt down beside the bed. He looked flawless as he slept, so peaceful. Her heart throbbed knowing how much she loved him and how much she didn't want to lose him, and it terrified her because she knew it could be her downfall. She had to pull herself together if there was even the slightest chance they could be together forever.

When Jude woke up the next morning, he reached over but Veronica wasn't there. He pulled himself up on his elbows and scanned the room. She was sitting in a chair by the window, facing out into the morning light with her knees up against her body. He immediately picked up that something was wrong, but he didn't say anything. He liked to watch her when she was unaware. It was as if her guard was down and he was peeking into her true self.

"Hey," he breathed, not wanting to startle her out of her pensive state. She laid her head on her knees and looked over at him. "Hey."

"Are you all right?"

She got up from the chair and went back to the bed. She was wearing one of his white tank tops and nothing else. He hoped she would climb on top of him and take charge, but instead she sat on her knees next to him.

He suddenly noticed how drained she looked.

"Did you get any sleep?" he asked,

"No, not much. I have something to tell you."

She was visibly upset, and he knew it was because he had pushed her into disclosing something that was clearly painful. Her anxiety began to overwhelm him. He sat up and touched her face.

"I'm sorry. You don't have to say anything. I don't want you to share something if you're not ready. I know I can get mental about what I'm sensing, but I'll stop. I promise."

"It's okay. I want to tell you. It may not be what you're expecting, but I'm sure it's what you're seeing."

"Wait," he said. He gave her a kiss and put his forehead against hers. "I love you."

She waited for him to sit back.

"I could've prevented my parents' death, but I didn't," she said.

"You said it was a drunk driver."

"I know, but that wasn't the truth. They were causing problems with the G.O."

He thought about it for a second. "They were killed on purpose?"

"Yes, and I knew they would be."

"How could you have prevented it?"

"The G.O. contacted me and told me they were going to be eliminated unless I could persuade them to stop violating the rules."

"What were they doing?"

"It doesn't matter," she continued. "They didn't care anymore. They wanted to be exposed. I tried to explain how dire it was but they wouldn't listen. Afterward, the G.O. asked me if I was able to convince them and I told them I couldn't. I didn't say any more than that. I never saw them again."

Jude sat dumbstruck.

"Do you really think you could've stopped the G.O.?" he said.

"I could've done more. I know that now, but I didn't."

"Why?"

"I'm not sure. My feelings for them were ... strained. Our last conversation was contentious. I couldn't reason with them. I remember thinking it was hopeless. But now, I regret not making more of an effort, and I've had to learn to live with it."

The sorrow in her eyes was crushing. He took her by the hands and brought her over to him. He didn't know what to do other than to hold her. He could feel the pain she felt from it. He held her silently for a few moments.

"I'm so sorry," he finally said.

"I'm fine," she said and pulled away from him. She climbed out of bed and went back to the window. "It happened years ago, and I've dealt with it as best I can. I thought I had it in check, but I guess it's sitting right there in my eyes."

He sensed a bit of resentment in her tone, probably because he forced her to share this traumatic memory, but he didn't regret it. It all made sense now.

He went over to where she stood looking out the window. He put his warm body up against her back, gliding his hands down her side and then around into an embrace. He planted his chin on her shoulder and took in the view with her.

"I can't imagine how hard it was for you to tell me, but I'm glad you did," he whispered. "I want to know everything, even the awful stuff."

"You can't fix this, Jude. Whatever it is you see in my eyes, it will always be there. It'll never go away no matter how happy you make me, no matter how much time passes. It will always be there."

"I get it," he said. "And we don't have to talk about it again, unless you want to."

She nodded slightly and then turned around. He took her in his arms. She knew it was all better now. At least he'll stop with the sadness, she thought.

Jude doted on her the rest of the morning. He ordered breakfast, but not before he gave her a sumptuous treat while she lay back fully arched, accepting it enthusiastically. He was such a generous lover, and it was exactly what she needed to make everything wonderful again. Before she had a chance to descend from her rapturous orgasm, he took her and fulfilled his own needs, leading her back up again until they were both satiated.

Fucking incredible!

Breakfast arrived at the same time Veronica started receiving text messages from work. She skimmed through them while Jude sat on the bed and prepared their meal.

"Are they panicking?" he asked.

"Yes. I can't prolong this any longer. I have to finish this deal. It's pretty much done."

Jude didn't say anything. He kept on buttering his toast. Veronica leaned back and watched him trying not to react. His attempt at being coy was adorable.

"So, when do you have to go back to London?" he said, keeping his attention on his toast.

"I'm in no rush. I can stay through the weekend. How does that sound?"

He looked over at her draped along the pillows. She was on one elbow with the sheet lying across her abdomen, her hair falling to the front and concealing one of her breasts. She took his breath away, as usual.

"That would be lovely," he answered.

Later that morning, they walked out of the hotel together and waited at the curb for her car. He held her close as a brisk breeze blew over them. They kissed and nuzzled like newlyweds, oblivious to all the eyes on them.

When Benedict pulled up, Jude took a CD out from his jacket pocket.

"Here, I've got something for you."

Veronica lit up. "What is it?"

"It's a version of a song that reminds me of you." He kissed her. "It's grossly romantic, but I think you'll appreciate it."

"Aw. Grossly romantic, my favorite kind of romantic." She squeezed him tight. "Are you sure we can't drop you off?"

"No, I'll take the train." He gave her a long kiss good-bye.

She stepped toward the car and Benedict opened the door for her, but then she turned back to Jude.

"I love you," she said.

He smiled and winked at her.

As they drove off, she took the CD out of its sleeve and put it in the player. At first, she didn't recognize it, but as soon as the first note was sung she knew it was the Stereophonics. It was a version of the Roberta Flack song "First Time Ever I Saw Your Face." The singer's impassioned voice sent a sensation through her body, just as always, but this time it was all the more poignant. The words were significant; they were coming from Jude. It was beautiful and, yes, grossly romantic. She loved it. She sank into the seat and drifted away. It was the most romantic gesture she'd ever received. But as the song continued, her blissfulness began to fade. With every verse, with every ache in his voice, she realized how much Jude loved her.

Oh my God. What have I done?

14

1989—LONDON

When Veronica walked into Colin's house, she could hear Marshall yelling from the den.

"Who is he screaming at?" she asked Evie, who was at the dining table shuffling through a pile of scattered documents.

"Oh, you're not going to believe this one," she said mysteriously. "I'd get a drink if I were you."

"Great," Veronica sighed as she went to the bar.

She heard Marshall's voice more distinctly when the door opened, but it closed quickly and she wasn't able to make anything out. Seconds later, Noah emerged from the hallway.

"Was he yelling at you?" she asked.

"No, he's on the phone." He walked up to her and kissed her on the cheek. "Pour me one, will you?"

"What's going on?" she asked him.

"I think you need to hear it from him."

"What the hell."

The door opened again and Marshall came stomping out with Colin following behind.

"Good, you're here. Sit down," he said to her.

That wasn't a good sign. Marshall rarely gave you a chance to prepare yourself for any kind of news. He usually just threw it at you when you weren't looking. She stayed standing.

Colin walked by and touched her arm in a consoling manner.

She stepped aside as Marshall grazed by her and served himself a drink. He took a shot, then slammed the glass down. She was suddenly rigid with anticipation.

"We've got a problem with your parents," he said to her.

It didn't quite register. She glanced over at Evie and Noah, who were sitting at the table.

"What kind of problem?" she asked.

"First of all, this information stays here in this room," he said, pointing and making eye contact with all the others.

Veronica didn't say anything; she didn't have to. She was glaring at him in a way that said, "Fucking say it already."

"As you know, the G.O. has allowed the serum to be administered to specific Regulars over the years, including family members, those who have married into the Clans, and people with unique qualifications that would benefit our objectives. It has been carefully regulated. I believe somewhere around fifty-five individuals across all Clans have been given the serum in the past thirty years. Two years ago, though, the New York Protectors began encountering Clan members who weren't on file with the G.O. They investigated and discovered your parents had been doling out the serum pretty generously. It was determined they had dosed twenty-five people over a three year span."

"How the fuck do they have the serum?" Veronica asked, trying to make sense of what she was hearing.

"We think your father duplicated it with the doses he was given to officially administer," Colin explained. "He knew how to do it. He worked with Eliot and Scott when they created it."

She was ready to sit down now.

"The G.O. told them to stop and confiscated what they had left of it, or so they thought," Colin continued. "About a week ago, a woman was critically injured in a car accident in Virginia. The Protectors down there were notified because, apparently, she walked out of the hospital later that same day. They tracked her down and found out she was afflicted, but she wasn't on file. After some persuasive interrogation, her husband told them they were given the serum eight months ago by your parents."

Good God.

Colin paused to let Veronica digest the information. She didn't know what to make of it. It had been decades since she'd had contact with her parents. She didn't even know them anymore.

"So what now?" she asked. "I'm assuming the G.O. wants something done about it."

"Yes, they do," Marshall answered emphatically. "Your parents are over there infecting everybody they know. The situation is a mess. We're trying to figure out how many people have been affected so we can get them on file, but your parents are being defiant. Your father says he won't stop. He thinks it's time the world knew."

Her eyes widened. She knew exactly what that meant. Everyone did.

"Wait, they want us to take out two Originals?" Evie spoke up. "How can we do that?"

"It's all about the greater good, Evie, you know that," Marshall barked then pointed to Veronica. "And so do you. No one is beyond our reach when it comes to protecting the Clans, not even the Originals."

"And the G.O. approved this?" Veronica asked.

"Yes," Colin answered.

"The Protectors in New York are waiting for the go-ahead," Marshall added. "But I asked that they hold off until we told you about it. Do you want to go see your parents?"

"They're not going to listen to me. I haven't seen them in over twenty years."

Then, she realized what Marshall was actually saying. He wasn't asking whether she wanted to try to talk some sense into them, or even if she wanted to see them one last time to say good-bye. He was asking whether she wanted to carry out the order.

An uneasiness filled the room. Everyone understood the choice she was being given.

She got up and went over to the dining table. Noah was still her closest confidant. They had gone through so much together, and even though their relationship ended shortly after Grenoble, they remained devoted to each other. He stared at her for several seconds, then gave her a subtle nod. She knew he wouldn't let her deal with this on her own.

"Noah and I will go down there," she said decidedly, keeping her eyes on Noah.

Colin flashed a smug look over at Marshall. He knew she would go if given the opportunity. He was the one who insisted Marshall summon her and tell her in person.

"Veronica," Evie blurted. "You can't."

"Will the New York Protectors be there?" she asked Colin.

"Yes. They've already got surveillance on them."

"I'll go talk to my parents, but I know they're not going to stop. If I can't do it, I'll give the word to the Protectors."

Colin nodded.

"Fine," Marshall said. "I'm leaving for Edinburgh tomorrow. Colin, you stay on this and let me know when it's done." He poured another drink and left the room.

Colin walked over to her, "Are you sure about this?"

"Yes."

He moved her hair off her shoulder and followed it gently down her back. "Okay," he said then turned away and followed Marshall back to the den.

Veronica sat down next to Noah, feeling slightly shaken. She reached for a pack of cigarettes on the table and lit one. Evie went to the bar and grabbed the bottle of bourbon. She came back to the table and refilled Veronica's glass.

"Here," she said, handing it to her. "I don't know how you can do this, V."

"I don't know that I can." She swallowed the serving.

"Then why not let the New York guys do it? Why go there?"

"I have to see them. If I show up, they'll know how dire the situation is. Maybe they'll get a fucking clue, or not. I don't know. I just know I need to go."

Noah reached over and held her hand. "I understand. I do."

"I love you, V," Evie said. "I don't want this to mess you up."

"I know it'll be strange seeing them after all this time, but I don't think of them affectionately anymore. It's been years since I even thought about them." She laid her hand on Evie's arm. "I promise I won't do it if I feel even the slightest bit unsure about it."

She knew she needed to alleviate Evie's concern, but it was the truth. She had no idea what reaction she would have to seeing her parents after all these years.

The next morning, Veronica and Noah flew to Philadelphia on the G.O.'s private plane. Veronica sat quietly during the flight, trying to hide her trepidation, but it was pointless. Noah knew her too well and wouldn't let her dwell on it.

"I know you don't like to talk about Philadelphia, but maybe if we hash it out, it might make more sense," he said.

"I doubt it."

"V, you've never really explained to me what happened with your parents. I think I should know more if I'm going to walk in there with you."

"I know. I'm sorry. Thank you for coming with me. It means a lot. I don't know what I would do without you." She leaned over and stroked his leg.

Noah folded his arms. He knew what she was doing. "I'm not letting it go. It's a long flight, babe."

Veronica sat back and groaned.

"They hated that I became a Protector," she said begrudgingly. "They absolutely refused to support me."

"I know all that, but there must be more to it," he said.

"They're liars. They lied to me, and I never forgave them for it."

"What did they lie to you about?"

"About the Condition. They didn't tell me until I was seventeen." She got up and went to the mini fridge and picked out two small bottles of Jim Beam. "I know most Elders were told around the same time, but I always thought they trusted me. They led me to believe my world was normal and wonderful, all the while knowing someday they were going to rip it out from under me. How do you do that to a child? A child you supposedly love."

"I'm sure they loved you."

"I'm sure they did, but not enough to be honest with me and prepare me for this unusual existence. Marshall grew up aware of it. His parents never deceived him."

"Yes, and he turned out to be a very well-adjusted man," he said sarcastically.

"When I tried to deal with it in my own way, they fought me at every turn. They wanted me to be someone I wasn't. They wanted me to accept it, like they did. And believe me, it was devastating to see the disappointment in their eyes every time they looked at me."

"They probably had no clue how to deal with you. Maybe they didn't expect you to react that way. Not everyone took it as hard as you did. Did you ever think of that?"

"I wouldn't have reacted in this manner if they had told me when I was younger. If I had been allowed to grow up knowing the truth, things would've been different. *I* would be different."

She sat back and drank from one of the bottles. Noah reached over and took the other one from her.

"You need to be sharp for this," he said as he put it in his pocket. "Do you really believe that? How different do you think you would be? This is who you are. This is who you've always been. You're stubborn and willful and paranoid. I can't imagine you weren't any of those things before you found out."

"You're not helping."

"But I am—I'm being honest with you. You are all those things, as well as thoughtful and loving and funny and wicked smart. What I'm trying to say is, I don't think it would've mattered *when* they told you. I have a feeling you would've reacted the same way at any age."

A smile crept over her face. "Wicked smart, huh?"

Noah nodded.

"Thank you," she said. "I don't know what I'd do without you. I love you so much."

"Yeah, but not enough, eh?" he said with a cheeky twinkle in his eye.

Veronica finished off the bourbon and tossed the bottle onto his lap.

"Very funny." She put her head back and her mind began racing again.

"I don't feel right about this," she admitted. "I'm worried about what they're going to say. I have no idea what to expect, and I can't stand that."

"You know, they're probably going to have to be eliminated. You have to prepare yourself for that. I can't imagine we're going to be able to convince them to stop."

"They're not going to stop, but I want to know why they did it. I've been racking my brain trying to figure it out."

"Well, we'll find out here pretty soon."

When they arrived in Philadelphia, the smell in the air immediately took Veronica back. It was a woodsy scent mixed with a freshwater humidity that was different from the damp air in London. She began having flashbacks from her childhood. She recalled how she would sit for hours by the river on their plantation just breathing in the air. She used to love the fragrances that would emanate from the woods nearby. It was a pleasant memory, but she shrugged it off, not wanting anything to impede what she was there to do.

Two members of the New York Protectors picked them up. On the way out of town, they asked her questions about her parents, but she didn't have much information to share. She explained that they probably knew more about them than she did. She tried to remain calm, but driving though her former hometown made her anxious in a way she hadn't expected. As they continued on, she noticed they were going in the opposite direction of the plantation.

"They moved away from that property a while back," one of the Protectors explained. "They own a smaller piece of land closer to the city. They live alone now."

"Do they know we're coming?" she asked.

"They know we're watching them. They know the G.O. is fed up. So, yes, they probably know we're coming."

"But they may not know *you're* coming," the other Protector remarked.

Veronica grimaced and looked out the window.

It was dusk when they pulled up to her parents' modest home. It was such a contrast from the vast property where she grew up. When she stepped out of the car, the hues of the early night sky reminded her of her childhood again. She fought with herself not to jump back into the car and curl up in a fetal position in the backseat.

Veronica insisted the Protectors wait in the car, and she and Noah went up to the house alone. She was about to knock on the door when it opened and her father stood before her. She was surprised by his appearance. The Condition keeps you from aging, but it doesn't hide the effects of living. He resembled her father, except there were slight differences. He seemed tired and worn out.

"Well, look who it is, Celine," he called out. "Our long-lost daughter, the Protector, is here. We must surely be in trouble."

Yep, same man.

"May I come in?" Veronica asked.

Veronica's father opened the door farther and waved his hand across himself. "Oh, but of course."

When she stepped into the entryway, she saw her mother in the dining area. She, too, appeared weary, like her father.

The house was warm and smelled of cinnamon and freshly burnt hickory. It was exactly how she remembered it; however, it didn't *feel* the same, maybe because it was a smaller place. She recognized the furniture, the photographs neatly placed, and even the figurines on the mantel, but everything seemed a bit warped. It reminded her of the scene in *Willy Wonka and the Chocolate Factory* when Gene Wilder walks down the hallway to the tiny door. The whole lot gave off a distorted quality, including her parents.

"I knew it was only a matter of time until you showed up," her mother said.

"Is that all you have to say to me?" she asked.

"What do you want to hear?" her father replied. "How much we've missed you? How glad we are to see you? We know why you're here." He eyed Noah. "Who's this? Another Protector?"

"Yes, this is Noah. We've come to find out why you're causing all this trouble."

Veronica's mother casually entered the living room and took a seat on a dark green antique chair, the one she always sat in when she read to Veronica as child. Her father came up from behind and seated himself on the matching chair opposite her mother. The fireplace was between them, sparking with red-hot tinder that needed tending.

She followed them but didn't attempt to make herself comfortable. In fact, she felt so uncomfortable it was difficult for her to maintain her composure. She stood behind the couch in front of them while they sat watching her, as if they were on the witness stand and she was prosecuting them. Noah stayed back in the entryway, feeling the need to spectate. The tension was thick.

"And what trouble are you speaking of?" her father said arrogantly as he crossed his leg.

"I see. You want to play it like that. You need to stop giving out the serum. The G.O. is done tolerating you."

"Did you hear that, Celine? The Governing Order is done with us."

"Stop it!" Veronica raised her voice. "You need to understand this is over!"

"We understand, Veronica," her mother said.

Hearing her name come from her mother's lips nicked her heart in a way that made her stiffen up.

"We know exactly why you're here and what's going to happen," her mother conceded. "You must take us for fools if you think we wouldn't know."

"Of course I think you're fools. Why else would you be doing this? It's ridiculous."

"Is it?" her father said. "Do you even know why we're doing it? Do you even care?"

"I wouldn't be here if I didn't."

Her mother snickered and rolled her eyes.

Seriously?

Veronica sneered at her. "What happened? Why did you turn on the Clans?"

"Is that how you see it?" her father questioned. "That's not how we see it. We're strengthening the Clans. We're making them powerful."

"Powerful? Are you fucking kidding?" she huffed. "How are you making the Clans powerful by possibly exposing them to the Regulars?"

"Must you be so vulgar?" Her mother shook her head and sighed.

Her father leaned over. "She's been living in Ireland for the past twenty years, dear." Then, he turned back to Veronica. "We're increasing our numbers. We'll be a force to be reckoned with. They can't lock us all up."

"What does that even mean? Are you planning on starting a war?"

"No," her mother explained. "The more of us there are, the more likely they'll have to accept us."

Veronica turned around to Noah, who was still in the entryway. He was just as bewildered as she was.

She faced her parents again.

"Why would you think they'd accept us? I think twentieth-century humanity has shown acceptance is not one of its strong suits." She was getting angry. "Do you watch the news? All the hate spewed at homosexuals over the AIDS epidemic right now is evidence of that. I'm sure our affliction would certainly go over well. You don't think Christians, in this country especially, would see it as going against their God's will? You're fucking crazy if you think we'd be accepted without any consequences."

"Maybe so," her father said, "but at least there wouldn't be a need for Protectors anymore."

Veronica glared at her father. "What do you mean by that?"

She could hear Noah approaching behind her.

Her mother stood up. "If we're out in the open, then there would be no need for the Protectors. Wouldn't you say?"

Veronica staggered backward until she felt Noah's hand on her back. He braced her.

"What are you saying?" she said. "Are you telling me you're doing this to get rid of the Protectors?"

"We're saying it's time you moved on and made another life for yourself," her mother answered.

Veronica's mouth dropped open. She couldn't believe what she was hearing. She was speechless.

"You're not doing this on your own, are you?" Noah asked. "Who's helping you?"

Neither of her parents replied. They were resolute, keeping their eyes fixed on Veronica.

Noah had heard rumors of a subversive group trying to undermine the Protectors. This made him very suspicious.

"There's more going on here," he said. "You can't possibly think we'd believe you're doing all this for your daughter's sake."

"This is despicable," Veronica seethed. "Why would you think to do something as absurd as this? I don't believe you."

"We didn't think you would, but we wanted you to know before you do whatever it is you're here to do," her father said.

"I'm not going to do anything!" she yelled. "Fuck you!"

She turned away and headed toward the door.

"This isn't going to work," Noah said to them. "You must know it's over now."

Again, neither reacted. Their expressions appeared calm and self-assured, as if this all played out exactly how they expected. When Veronica reached the door, she looked back at them.

"I knew you wouldn't listen to me, but I didn't expect you to lay this on me. How could you?"

She opened the door.

"Veronica," her mother called out. "Remember, it is never too late to be what you might have been."

Veronica raised her eyebrows in disbelief.

"Is that what you want to leave me with, a quote from George Eliot? Thank you, Celine. I'll remember it always."

She and Noah walked silently to the car and got into the backseat.

When she shut the door, she noticed a storm moving in from the east. She closed her eyes and tried to smell the oncoming precipitation.

"Well?" said one of the Protectors.

Noah took hold of Veronica's hand.

She breathed in, then shot her eyes up at Noah.

The greater good.

15

WEDNESDAY—BRISTOL

The moon was bright, almost fully illuminated as it hung above Veronica. The beauty of it annoyed the hell out of her. She craved a gloomy back-drop, something dark and unforgiving. She wanted to feel happy about the love she was experiencing, but instead it was beginning to torment her.

She felt her phone vibrate in her jeans pocket. She pulled it out and glared down at a text message. She returned the phone to her pocket, then shut her eyes and listened for him. He was still in the shower. He had wanted her to join him, but she was struggling to control her mood so he wouldn't detect her angst. She brought her fingers up to her mouth and ran them along her lower lip. She could still taste him.

She remained on the balcony, wallowing in her melancholy, until she heard him coming downstairs. She inhaled and caught his freshly cleansed scent. She took a few deep breaths, allowing it to saturate her. She hoped it would expel her heartache.

Jude came up behind her and swept her hair off her shoulder. His lips softly tickled her neck as he snuggled up against her.

"What is it?" he asked.

She positively sucked at hiding her feelings from him. She shrugged and rested her head back on his shoulder.

"It's the song, isn't it?" He sighed. "Too soon?"

She shifted around in his arms. "No, I love the song. I love it." She looked into his eyes. "You have no idea how much I love it. It's the most beautiful song I've ever heard. Where did you find it?"

"iTunes. I was checking out the Stereophonics and came across it. I thought it was perfect."

"It is."

He lifted her chin. "Everything okay?" he asked.

"More than okay."

He laid his cool lips on her mouth, hovering momentarily until she quivered in anticipation, then kissed her.

All better.

He didn't want to harp on about her mood so he just held her, which is exactly what she wanted him to do. She faded away in his arms, listening to his heartbeat and breathing him in. She could've stood there all night.

"It's freezing out here. There's some wine left over from dinner. Want some?" he asked.

"Sure."

Jude took her by the hand and brought her inside. She flipped off her shoes and settled back against the arm of the couch while stretching her legs out across the cushions. He returned with two glasses of a crisp Riesling and cozied up across from her, extending his legs beside hers.

"What were you thinking about out there?" he asked.

"I was remembering something a friend once told me." She took sip of wine. "He said, when you're in love, forever isn't long enough."

"I like that."

"Honestly, I never believed it. It sounded frivolous, like *love means never having to say you're sorry.*"

"But?" he said, sensing she'd had a change of heart.

"I understand it now. It's like what you said the other night, how before this week the thought of living another twenty-five years would've annoyed you. Forever doesn't seem as eternal anymore."

Jude wondered what was going through that gorgeous head of hers. He couldn't dodge all the emotions she was emitting. He could feel each and every one, but what he couldn't do was get inside her head and know exactly what she was thinking, which is what he desperately wanted to do.

"But for us, it is," he said. "There's no reason we can't spend an eternity together."

Are you fucking kidding me?

He constantly made her feel like she was dreaming.

"Why didn't you ever marry, Jude? I have a hard time believing you never loved anyone enough. You couldn't possibly have kept this bottled up all these years."

"I did. I saved it all for you," he said, nudging her leg.

She smiled and shook her head. "I don't believe you."

He stared at her while taking a deliberate sip.

"Come on, I know you've been in love before. You know you want to tell me," she insisted.

He pursed his lips slightly and squinted at her. He knew she wasn't going to let up.

"Her name was Lena. I met her in Edinburgh right after I got out of France."

Veronica could tell he was wrestling with his words, but she selfishly held back while he figured it out. She wanted to hear this.

"I was laying low on a farm, trying to earn my keep. I knew shit about farming."

"Why a farm then?"

"I was sure the Protectors would be coming after me, so I tried to find the most inconspicuous place."

Jude moved his legs off the couch and sat up. He set his glass down on the coffee table.

"I was so fucking alone," he continued. "You see, I'd never been without one of my brothers. I didn't know what to do with myself, and I knew I couldn't go home. That was the toughest time of my life. I knew it would be a long time before I could even try to go back to Dublin. I decided to settle down and keep busy."

He reclined back, lifting Veronica's legs and putting them on his lap. He stared down and massaged her feet as he told his story.

"I spent a lot of time at a pub in town. That's where I met her. She was the barmaid and, sadly, she watched me get pissed every night. I think she felt sorry for me because we ended up becoming friends, and then more than friends. She quelled the loneliness that was smothering me at the time, and I fell in love with her, but it was different. It wasn't like this."

He looked over at her.

"It wasn't like this," he repeated firmly. "Of course, I didn't know any better. I thought it was real, and I didn't hold back. I got carried away, and when we started talking about getting married, I foolishly decided to tell her about the Condition. I'd never told anyone before. I didn't even know how to explain it, and I'd forgotten how dangerous it was. Needless to say, it didn't go over well. She thought I was fucking insane and accused me of making it up."

He carefully moved her legs aside and got up. He opened the balcony doors again and stepped outside. He lit a cigarette then leaned against the doorframe, dropping his head back.

"Right after that, she said she was pregnant. I told her I still wanted to marry her, but she became unreasonably cross with me. I couldn't convince her I was sincere. She went a bit mad. When her family found out she was pregnant, she told her brothers I had forced myself on her. They came out to the farm and beat the shit out of me, then told everyone I had hurt her. The family I was staying with threw me out. It was brutal."

He took a drag off his cigarette and kept his eyes down.

"I stayed in town a couple more weeks, but then found out she wasn't pregnant after all and had already taken up with someone else. After that, I took off. I disappeared. I gave up on everything and made sure no one would ever find me."

Holy shit.

Veronica wasn't sure how to respond. She walked over and stood against the door opposite him. She had no words. She watched him avert his eyes from her, trying to hide how painful the memory was, but she could see it, and it broke her heart. She was hoping for a romantic tale

where she'd learn how he had come to be such a loving and affectionate man, but instead she was devastated to hear how his heart had been
thrashed.

He finished his cigarette and flicked it onto the balcony. "So yeah, I've
been in love, but not like this, not even close."

Jude walked up to her, took her in his arms, and kissed her. She came
up on her toes as he held her against the door. He wanted to make sure
she knew how much his love for her was unequaled. His passion was fierce
and left little doubt. She clung to him, and the heat between their bodies
intensified.

He took her face in his hands. "I've never loved anyone this much,
ever."

Veronica suddenly felt weak, like she was going to faint. She could feel
her heart beating in her throat, and she couldn't breathe. She pushed him
away.

"Stop, please."

"What's wrong?" he asked.

"Damn it! Why do you have to be like this?" She stepped farther out
onto the balcony.

"Like what?"

"This—it's all so fucking perfect!"

"I'm ... sorry?" He grinned.

"Damn you." She laughed. "I love you so much I can't even think
straight anymore. Could you be an asshole for once, for one minute, one
second? Just bring me back down to earth, please. Say something rude,
something mean."

He put his hands on his hips. "You've got very odd feet."

"Excuse me?"

"Your feet. They're really peculiar—for a woman, that is."

"Oh my God."

She covered her face with her hands and laughed. He came over to her
and moved them away.

"Seriously, I have a problem with your feet. Don't ever ask for a foot
massage, okay?"

She smiled happily. "Thank you."

Hours later, Veronica was sprawled out on the bed, utterly delirious. In an effort to not be so romantic, Jude had fucked her hard. If she had any lingering inhibitions with him, they were gone now. It was late into the night, and he had gone downstairs for a smoke. She was so blissed out she didn't budge until he came back up. He handed her a cool glass of water and eased up next to her as she gulped it down. When she finished, they lay back down and she began rearranging his disheveled hair.

"If I asked you to run away with me, to leave everything behind, would you do it?" she asked.

Jude smiled. "In a heartbeat. Where do you want to go?"

"Somewhere far away."

He brought her hand down from his hair and kissed it. "Why do we have to run away?"

Good question.

"It would be an adventure," she whispered. "We could go somewhere remote and idyllic. We could live untethered and free. Doesn't that sound wonderful?"

"It does."

She could tell he was wondering about the question, so she changed the subject.

"What would you like to do tomorrow? I'm all yours."

"Finally," he said, beaming. "Whatever you want, love. I'm up for anything."

"How about we stay holed up here and never leave. I'm booked through the weekend."

"Absolutely. We can pretend we're somewhere far, far away." He kissed her. "I should swing by my flat at some point tomorrow, though. My phone died and I want to check in on Charlie. He was sleeping when I went by today. I think he's still recovering from dinner." He looked around the room. "I should probably take some of these dirty clothes back home, too. It's starting to look like my bedroom in here."

"Great! I'd love to see where you live."

He scrunched up his nose. "Oh, I don't know about that. It's not very impressive."

"I'm sure it's fine. You don't need to impress me. You're already beyond reproach."

"I think I'd prefer being reproached. I'm far from perfect."

"You are everything I always hoped you would be."

"Now who's waxing poetic?" he quipped.

"Yes, I have a lot of catching up to do."

She curled up in his arms and let herself peacefully drift away.

The fresh air blew hard through Veronica's hair as she drove the convertible on the winding mountain road. It was cool and dry and smelled clean, free of the toxic traces she blocked out in the city. She leaned her head over the door, letting the wind hit her directly and nourish her senses.

She reached down and put her hand on Jude's leg. His red lips curled up. He took her hand, brought it up to his mouth, and kissed it. She kept her eyes on the road but felt her way along his face and into his hair. He settled back as she lulled him with a gentle stroke.

After a few moments, he gazed over at her, and she smiled lovingly at him.

"Watch out!" he yelled when something caught his eye.

Veronica whipped her head forward only to catch a split-second glimpse of a dark-haired man standing in the middle of the road.

She swerved erratically, and the tires skirted dangerously close to the edge of a steep cliff. Jude held onto the dashboard while she desperately tried to regain control. Then, suddenly, the road veered sharply to the left. There was nothing ahead but blue sky. The car hit a large boulder on the driver side and buckled. It tilted to the right, grinded violently along the passenger side, then slid down an embankment. It was about to become airborne when the front end slammed into a portion of the mountain that was jutting out. The car lodged precariously on its side about fifty feet down from the road.

Jude was holding onto the rim of the windshield. "Christ, did that just happen? Are you okay?"

Veronica's fingers were clenched on the steering wheel.

"Yes, I think so."

Jude cracked a timid smile. "Now what?"

Just then, the passenger door burst open with a jolt and knocked Jude from his seat. He fell out of the car, frantically grabbing for anything to stop his momentum. He caught the lower side rail with one hand and was left dangling above a five-hundred-foot drop.

Veronica lunged toward him. "No!" she screamed.

She held onto the steering wheel and secured her legs underneath it.

"Hold on. I'm going to reach down. Swing your other arm up and grab my hand," she instructed.

He peered below.

"Don't look down!" she shouted.

Jude pulled himself up with his left hand, then swung his right hand up and latched onto her. This caused the car to jerk, which made him lose his grip on the rail. They both slid farther down. Jude squeezed her hand as he hung perilously, but he could feel his grip loosening.

Veronica held firm and tried to pull him up, but his full weight was surprisingly too much for her to handle with one hand, and she couldn't let go of the steering wheel or else she would fall out with him.

Their eyes met and locked in as they became aware of their predicament.

He was slipping, but he kept his eyes fixed on her.

"Don't let go of me, Veronica."

"No!" she screamed. She bolted up in bed and lunged forward.

Her shriek startled Jude, and he almost fell out of bed. He found her hunched over, breathing laboriously, and grasping at the sheets.

"Wake up, love, wake up." He sat her up and took her face in his hands. "It was just a dream. Wake up."

Her eyes were wide open, but she didn't see him. Wherever she was moments ago, she was still there.

"Veronica," he said softly.

Gradually, he came into focus. He saw she was back.

"Are you okay?" he asked.

She wasn't, but she nodded.

"Let me get you some water."

She grabbed his forearm and squeezed it, as if she were back in that car holding onto him. She stared into his eyes with such fright.

"It's okay. I'm just going to the bathroom," he said, a little freaked out by her expression.

He gently unclasped her fingers from his arm, placed her hand on her lap, and then brushed her hair from her face.

"I'll be right back. You're awake now; nothing is going to happen."

She watched him closely while he walked away. She didn't want to take her eyes off him for fear she would snap back into the dream and he would disappear from her grip. She struggled to calm herself. Her heart was pounding, and it wouldn't ease up. When he came back, he sat close to her on the edge of the bed as she sipped the water.

"Better?"

"Yes," she said, still staring at him. She handed him the glass, and he put it on the nightstand. When he turned back to her, she reached up and touched his face. She ran her thumb across his stubble, then leaned her forehead on his and sighed. He took her in his arms and held her.

"Do you want to tell me about it?" he asked.

"I'd rather not."

"It might help."

"No, I want to forget it." She put her hands in his hair and stroked it back. "Thank you for being here."

"Always. Come now, lay back down."

He snuggled up next to her and cradled her. "Do you want to go back to sleep or should I turn on the television?"

She shook her head and closed her eyes. "Just hold me."

"I won't let go," he said and kissed her forehead.

Her eyes popped open.

She tried to relax, but it was in vain. She kept picturing the look on his face as he dangled below her. It lingered, and it haunted her. She was prone to wildly vivid dreams, but this was far too real for her. She refused to contemplate the meaning behind it.

When his breathing fell into a steady rhythm, she slid out from his arm and settled back on her pillow. She was profoundly shaken. The sheer terror was still with her. She waited for it to subside, but as visions of the dream swirled around in her head, her breathing became erratic again. She shut her eyes and a tear streamed down along her temple. She wiped it away, then rolled over and buried her face in her pillow.

16

WEDNESDAY—BRISTOL

Charlie spent all of Wednesday recovering from his evening with Jude and Veronica. He liked to think he was a big-time drinker, but in reality, he was not. He was a mild-mannered teacher who lived a humble existence. The only bit of excitement came from his best friend, an eighty-six-year-old man who looked like he was in his thirties because of a condition that prevented him from aging any further. Besides that sci-fi side note, Charlie lived a normal life.

He and Jude had been friends and flatmates for almost seven years, and he thought the world of him. Jude always treated him with respect and never made him feel self-conscious. In fact, he made a point of encouraging Charlie when it came to women and relationships. He taught him a great deal. If it hadn't been for Jude, Charlie would still be frightened of women and, most likely, a virgin. So there was genuine affection for his dear friend.

Jude, in turn, trusted Charlie more than anyone outside his family. When they met, Jude had already spent thirty years away from the Clans. In that time, he never allowed himself to get too close to anyone, especially Regulars, but Charlie was different. There was an instant kinship between them, and Jude knew Charlie was someone he could confide in. So over the years Jude shared a lot with Charlie about his life and the Clans. He knew it could be dangerous for Charlie to know too much, but he made a point of explaining how important it was that he kept this information to himself, under any circumstance. Charlie got a kick out of how clandestine Jude made it all sound.

As Charlie hung around the flat that day, sipping on Alka-Seltzer-infused water and watching television, Jude's new relationship weighed heavy on him. He was fond of Veronica and wholeheartedly approved of her, but there was a double layer of jealousy running through him. Part of him was envious of their relationship. After spending an evening with them, he didn't doubt their affection for each other, but he wanted that for himself. It was kind of depressing hanging out with two people who were that much in love.

On the other hand, he was jealous of Veronica. He hadn't seen much of Jude over the past week and he was beginning to feel neglected. He knew it was rubbish to be hurt by it, but he couldn't help it. Jude was his best friend, his only friend, and now he had a feeling everything was about to change. He tried not to dwell on it because he was genuinely happy for Jude. For as long as he had known him, Jude had never been in a serious relationship. Casual hookups were easy for him, but he never spoke of marriage or commitment. Charlie knew he carried a lot of baggage. He knew how unhappy and lonely Jude really was underneath his lighthearted disposition. Jude was a good guy and he deserved to be happy, but it still made Charlie a little sad.

It was late afternoon when Charlie awoke from a much-needed, coma-like nap. He was horribly groggy as he stumbled downstairs to the kitchen. He opened the fridge, hoping there was an ice-cold Coke with his name on it, and there was—literally. A Post-it note was attached to the can. He grabbed the drink and peeled off the note. It was from Jude. Apparently, Jude had been home earlier but hadn't wanted to wake him. *Damn.* The note said Jude would try to meet up with him tomorrow. Charlie was disappointed he'd missed him. He popped the lid and chugged the Coke as he went back upstairs for a shower.

When evening set in, he mustered up the strength to make dinner for himself. He was back in the kitchen, rummaging through the refrigerator and cabinets for something easy to make, when he heard a knock at the back door. He approached the window and saw a pale, wiry man in a gray suit standing oddly close to the door.

"Can I help you?" he asked through the window.

"Yes, I need to speak with you, Charlie."

"Do I know you?"

"It's about Jude," the man said.

This piqued Charlie's curiosity. No one ever came around asking about Jude, especially at the back door at night. He carefully opened the door.

"He's not here," Charlie stated.

"I know."

"You know? What's this about? Is Jude all right?"

"For now, but I need you to step outside and hear what I have to say. Jude's life is in danger."

Charlie invited the man inside, but he refused, so Charlie sat on the cold steps on their back patio, nervously anticipating what this ghost of a man had to say. He looked around and half expected to spot hidden cameras filming this unusual scene. He thought a presenter was going to jump out at any moment from behind the fence and shove a microphone in his face, but that never happened.

The man spoke in a hushed tone. First, he asked Charlie how much he knew of Jude's past. Charlie remembered Jude's warning and claimed he didn't know much. The man didn't believe him and told him it was okay if he knew more because it would only help him understand the situation better. Reluctantly, Charlie admitted to knowing about the Condition and the Clans.

"Good," the man said. "Then you should be able to grasp what I'm about to tell you. I'm part of an organization associated with the Clans."

Charlie began to feel uneasy. "What kind of organization?"

"Have you heard of the Protectors?" the man asked.

Charlie had, but he shook his head.

"They're similar to the police within the Clans. They are supposed to protect the Clans' existence."

"Supposed to?" Charlie asked.

"Yes, supposed to, but they don't do that as much anymore. These days they're more interested in killing those of us who defy their authority. The people I work for, the Insurgents, have been in conflict with the Protectors for years."

Charlie couldn't believe what he was hearing. It sounded very medieval. He had never given much credence to the stories Jude had told him. They always seemed farfetched, but he enjoyed imagining they were true. Now, it was freaking him out.

"Jude's life is in danger because of the woman he has become involved with," the man said.

"Veronica?"

The man appeared surprised. He didn't expect Charlie to know her real name.

"Yes, Veronica. She's a Protector. We believe she is purposely getting close to Jude in order to penetrate our organization."

"That doesn't make sense. Jude hasn't had anything to do with the Clans for decades. I know this to be true," Charlie replied.

"That is true but, you see, Jude has influential relatives who have kept an eye on him all these years. We believe the Protectors discovered this and are now using him."

"But Veronica and Jude have a history."

"We know, and that's why we believe she was assigned to him."

Assigned to him?

Charlie thought about this. "What are you saying? Is she a spy?"

"More like an assassin."

Charlie gasped and immediately started to panic. He got up and paced along the cramped patio. He didn't want to believe it.

"It can't be. I just spent a lovely evening with her."

"Trust me, she's far more dangerous than anyone would suspect."

"You don't think she'd hurt him, do you?"

"It's a possibility. If she doesn't get what she wants from him, she might."

"What does she want from him?"

"Information."

Charlie fought with the notion. What if this man was lying, he thought. What if *he* was a threat to Jude? How could he know? Why was he being dragged into this? He began to hyperventilate. He sat back down and put his head between his knees.

The man waited for him to calm down.

"Why are you telling me this?" Charlie said sadly.

"Because we need you to tell Jude."

"Why don't you tell him yourself?"

"He won't believe me, and I highly doubt he would willingly go anywhere with me to discuss it. This has to come from you."

The man pulled out a card from his breast pocket and handed it to Charlie.

"Give him this and tell him to call this number as soon as possible from a secure line, not his cellphone or home phone. Do you understand?"

Charlie took the card and looked it over.

"Charlie, do you understand? This is very important. We need you to warn Jude. When do you expect him?"

"I don't know, maybe in the morning. Why a secure line?"

"Everything may be bugged. That's why we're outside."

Charlie's jaw dropped.

"I know this is a lot to take in, but we have to be careful," the man continued. "We need to talk to Jude before he gets in too deep with Veronica. She can be extremely persuasive."

"He's in love with her," Charlie explained. "He has been for quite some time. I'm not sure I'm going to be able to convince him."

"You have to try. His life is at stake."

The man began to get anxious. He peeked over the fence toward the front of the house.

"I need to leave. Please tell your friend to call that number as soon as possible."

"What are you looking at?" Charlie asked.

"There are two men in a car watching your house."

Charlie fell back onto the steps.

When Jude arrived home the next morning, Charlie was on the couch in the living room. The curtains were drawn, the TV was off, and it looked like he had been sitting there all night.

"What are you doing?" Jude said as he took his jacket off.

"I tried to reach you last night," Charlie answered solemnly.

"Yeah, sorry, my phone died. Is everything all right?" he asked while walking into the kitchen.

"A man came to the back door last night asking about you."

He could hear Jude going through the refrigerator.

"The back door? What did he want?"

Charlie stood up and hollered, "He said Veronica is a Protector and your life is in danger!"

There was no reply, only silence. Charlie focused intently on the kitchen entryway. Jude walked into his sight with a bottle of milk in his hand.

"What did you say?"

Charlie was about to elaborate when he remembered what the man told him about everything being bugged. He had scoured their flat throughout the night but hadn't found anything suspicious; still, he was so unnerved he decided to play it safe. He went over to Jude and mumbled for him to follow him. Jude looked at him like he was crazy. Charlie opened the back door and stepped out, then motioned for Jude to join him. Jude put the milk on the table and went outside.

"A man came by last night and told me Veronica is an assassin who is using you to get to the Insurgents," Charlie explained excitedly.

"What the fuck are you talking about? What do you know of the Insurgents?" Jude said.

"I don't know anything about them. What I do know is this man came to see me, and he told me Veronica is dangerous."

Charlie pulled out the card. "He gave me this and said to tell you to call this number on a secure line. I didn't know what the hell to make of it. I've been going crazy waiting for you to get home."

"This is bullshit," Jude said angrily, snatching the card from Charlie. There was a phone number and the letters *MDM* printed on it.

"You said he came to see *you*?" Jude said.

"He knew you weren't home. He also said it's possible our flat is bugged and that two men in a car out front have been watching us."

Jude was stunned. He walked over to the fence and looked over but didn't see anything unusual.

"They were there all night," Charlie assured him.

"Who was this man?"

"He said he was with the Insurgents."

"The Insurgents? No way."

"You know about them?"

"Of course I know about the Insurgents, Charlie. It's the fucking Clans all over again. They finally found me."

Jude headed back into the kitchen, flinging the door open as Charlie followed him.

"They found you because of Veronica," Charlie exclaimed. "Because she's a Protector. It wasn't a coincidence she was at the hotel that day."

"No!" Jude lashed out, but then immediately stepped back and calmed himself. "No, Charlie, that's not true. She's an Elder, an important one. The Clans are so up in everyone's business they must be monitoring her and saw us together. I should've known this could happen."

He went into the living room.

"Jude, why would he say such a thing about her? What motive would he have to say she was a killer who is a threat to you?"

"They all have ulterior motives. It's a fucking chess match. That's why I stayed away from it." He sat down on the couch and slumped back. "And now I'm back in it again. Shit."

"So, you don't believe it?"

"Of course I don't, Charlie. Veronica isn't a killer, and she's no longer with the Protectors."

Charlie paused. "She *used* to be a Protector?"

"She was with them back in France, but that was forty years ago. She's a real estate solicitor now. I know she's connected with the Clans, but she's no killer."

"How can you be sure?" Charlie asked hesitantly.

"Because I know! She's not going to kill me. It's the Clans' bullshit again. That's all it is. I have to let her know." He got up and hurried toward the stairs. "I'm sure she can straighten this all out with the G.O."

"Wait!"

Jude stopped and turned back to his friend. Charlie looked absolutely shell-shocked. Jude was suddenly overcome by Charlie's fear. He sat down on the stairs and took a moment to catch his breath.

"I'm sorry they involved you in this, Charlie. I know it must sound ludicrous."

"It doesn't feel real," Charlie muttered.

"I know, but it is. Now you know why I never went back, but don't worry. I'll take care of it. It's going to be okay."

Jude got up and hugged his friend, then went upstairs to his room.

17

1994—BELFAST, IRELAND

"You need to promise me something," Evie declared as she loaded bullets into her gun clip. "Promise me we can go somewhere warm when we're finished here. I am done with this wretched weather. My hair is shit."

Veronica laughed from the driver's seat. They were on their way to Belfast to remove some Clan members from the civil war brewing there. The members had been told to leave, but they had ignored the order. Veronica and Evie were instructed to meet up with Noah and a few other Protectors and bring the violators back to Dublin.

Despite the circumstances, Evie was her usual jovial self. She loved going on assignments with Veronica. They had grown very close during the ten years since Evie had joined the Protectors. Veronica had trained her and, in that time, they bonded like sisters. They worked well together and enjoyed each other's company.

Evie was forty-five years old and a second-generation Clan member. She had an extremely privileged upbringing in one of the more upper-class Clans south of London. For this reason, she and Veronica differed wildly in personality and disposition. Evie was a free spirit, uninhibited, emotional, and trusting. She wasn't overly paranoid or concerned with the consequences of the Condition. She loved the authority and adventure that came with being a Protector. Evie was everything Veronica wasn't, which is why Veronica adored her so much and kept an eye on her.

"Where do you want to go?" Veronica asked.

"I've been thinking about Mexico lately."

"Mexico? Seriously? That has to be at least a ten-hour flight. How about Greece?"

"Seriously yourself. We were in Athens just last year."

"Actually, that was three years ago, but who's counting."

"Three? Huh. Time is flying by lately. Will it slow down when I get to be your age?"

Veronica side-eyed her. "That's nice."

"Anyway, I was watching a show on the telly and they were talking about where to find the best Mexican food. The dishes looked amazing. I have to have some Mexican food now. I can't stop thinking about it."

"There are some decent restaurants in London."

"No, I want real Mexican food. You know, made by Mexicans. We could go to America! They said the Mexican food is excellent in the south part."

"The south part?" Veronica said, laughing. "You mean the Southwest."

"Yes! That was it. Arizona and Texas, I think. Come on, let's go!"

"We'll see. Did you bring your extra clip?"

"Yes, it's in my bag." She bent down to check. "Do you really think these wankers are going to resist?"

"I have a feeling they might. When the G.O. gives an order, you follow it, and they didn't. They're probably expecting us, which means we may not be able to find them right away. Colin would've called us off by now if they'd had a change of heart."

"Damn, I'm definitely not in the mood to go all Terminator today," Evie whined. "I hate this fucking weather."

Veronica and Evie arrived in Belfast in the early evening. Noah and the others were waiting for them at their safe house. As soon as they walked in, Veronica could feel the tension.

"What is it?" Veronica asked Noah as she placed her bag on the couch. She went to the table where he was sitting and sat down in front of him.

"It's Marshall. He's here."

"Again?"

"Yes, again. He arrived two days ago. Colin said he spoke to him this morning and told him we were coming. He told him to leave with us. Of course, Marshall said no. He said he was here to support the IRA and that we should be joining him. Our whole world depends on it."

"Good God, he's really lost it."

Evie handed Veronica a glass of bourbon and sat down next to her.

"Who's with him?" Evie asked.

"Gabriel and Tim. He wouldn't tell Colin where they were staying."

"So what do we do?" said Veronica.

"Colin is livid. He said he's had it. Marshall has become a liability like the rest of them, maybe even worse. He said if they refuse to leave with us," he paused and made eye contact with both women, "then we should take them out."

"Jesus," Veronica said as she slammed her glass down.

Colin had assumed control of the Protectors four years earlier. Marshall had strayed from the main objective. He kept running off to Northern Ireland or Scotland, but it was more than that. He simply lost his game. It was as if his passion for protecting the Clans had run its course. He had been going full speed since he was a teenager, which was fifty years ago, and he just lost the will for it.

"Do you think you can kill him?" Evie asked both of them.

"I can," Noah said without hesitating.

What a shock, Veronica thought. Noah never cared for Marshall, even after all these years.

"I'm not sure," she answered. "Let's hope it doesn't come to that."

The unruly Clan members were not hard to find. Veronica had given them too much credit. They weren't hiding at all. The following morning they were out in the open mixing with the protesters on the streets of Belfast. After all this time and all the preaching, she was still dumbfounded when Clan members put themselves in precarious situations like this. They knew full well if they were arrested they would be fingerprinted, and then there'd be some explaining to do. She felt like a disappointed mother whenever she had to deal with these kinds of circumstances.

Veronica and Noah grabbed two of the Clan members when they were on their way to a pub. Noah hogtied one of them and threw him in the trunk of their car. The other tried to fight off Veronica, who wasted no time and snapped his neck. They laid him on the floor beneath the backseat.

Evie was watching the third member when they met up with her. He was with a raucous crowd that was forming downtown.

"He's right there," she pointed, "in the red and green shirt. We need to get him now. This shit is growing fast out here."

Noah and Veronica moved in on him. Noah stepped in front of him as Veronica came up from behind and put a gun to his ribs.

"Hi honey, what are you doing out here causing all this trouble?" she said sarcastically. "We need to go home now. Come on."

The member stiffened up, and Noah stared him down. "Time to go," Noah said.

The member slowly turned around.

"That's it, nice and easy," Veronica instructed. "Follow the woman in the purple jacket."

Noah walked behind them, making sure no one took notice.

As they approached the car, Evie unlocked the back door and opened it. Veronica guided the man, then swung him around to help him get in. When he came face to face with her, she looked down and saw he had a pocket-knife in his hand. At once, he tried to plunge it into her gut. She dropped her gun and grabbed his hand right before the knife penetrated her skin. She struggled with him, pushing him down into the backseat of the car. Noah tried to help, but she was lying on top of the man while they fought with the knife. Slowly, she overpowered him and pushed his hand with the knife into his own neck. She held it there, pressing as hard as she could.

"All right, V, you got him. Let up," Noah called out. He leaned over from the front seat, tugging at her arm.

She let go and pulled herself off him and out of the car. Evie pushed in the member's legs and slammed the door.

"You've got blood all over you, V. Get in the car," Evie ordered.

Noah jumped in the driver's seat.

"I'll meet you guys at the house," Evie said and ran toward her car.

Noah hauled ass out of there until he was sure no one was following them. Then he slowed down and drove steadily to the safe house.

"Are you okay?" he asked Veronica, who was wiping blood from her neck and chin with some napkins she found on the floor beneath her. "Did he stab you?"

"No, I'm fine. I hate getting their blood on me."

"I know you do." He reached over and patted her leg. "You think the other one is going to make it back to Dublin in one piece?" he said, referring to the Clan member in the trunk.

"I doubt it. If these two put up a fight, I expect he'll react the same way if he gets the chance. I say we leave him in the trunk until we get to Dublin."

"Right," Noah answered, thinking she was joking. "We still have to find Marshall. It could be another day or so."

"Even better. It'll make him weak, less likely to struggle."

Noah never understood how she could be so ruthless. Away from the Clan bullshit, she was still the woman he fell in love with back in New York, but she could flick that switch so quick it disturbed him sometimes.

When the three of them returned to the safe house, Evie insisted they bring in the member who was in the trunk. She practically carried him herself and put him in a back bedroom. Veronica and Noah put the dead members in the trunk.

While they were reorganizing and making a plan to find Marshall, one of the Protectors who was already out scouring the city phoned in and said he found him at a hotel. Veronica told him to stay back and keep an eye on him.

When Noah and Veronica arrived, Marshall and the Protectors were having lunch in the hotel restaurant. Marshall was unfazed when he saw his colleagues approach the table.

"And here they are. Hello, my friends," he said pleasantly. "Come, join us."

"Marshall, why do you have to keep doing this?" Veronica said as they stood over him. "This has got to stop."

"No, V, you've got to stop coming after me. When are *you* going to learn? Sit down now," he motioned. "Have a meal with me. How long has it been since we talked?"

"We have to go," she said evenly.

"I'm not going anywhere, especially with you," he said, looking up at Noah.

"Marshall, we're not going to make a scene here," she said. "You need to get up and come with us."

He stared at her for a few seconds and then returned to his lunch and continued eating.

Noah was about to knock the table out from under him, but Veronica put her hand on his arm and calmly restrained him.

"All right, if that's the way you want to do this," she said.

She took a seat next to the younger Protector and put her arm over his shoulders. She glared at Marshall.

"Get up or Gabriel here isn't going to see his mother next Christmas."

Marshall squinted at her. He knew she never made idle threats. He put his fork down and sat back, holding her gaze. He took a drink of his wine, wiped his mouth with his napkin, and then, very deliberately, got up and motioned to the other two to do the same. Peacefully, and without any resistance, they left the hotel in one car.

Marshall sat up front with Noah, who was driving, and Veronica was in the back with the Protectors. At first, no one spoke, but it didn't take long for Marshall to begin scheming.

"Gabriel, do you realize you are sitting next to one of the most notorious Protectors of my generation?" he said.

No one replied.

"She is, unquestionably, the loveliest person you will ever meet, but don't let that fool you. If your time has come, she will show no mercy."

Noah looked over at him then glanced back at Veronica. She shook her head, letting him know not to engage him.

"Noah, on the other hand," Marshall continued, "didn't have what it takes to keep a woman like her satisfied."

With that, Noah punched him in the face, knocking him into the passenger window and cracking it. Marshall came up and massaged his jaw. He laughed to himself then remained silent the rest of the way.

By the time they reached the safe house, Marshall was fuming. He marched around the room rambling senselessly.

"This is bullshit! Who do you think you are? You can't hold me here. This is treason."

"Calm down," Noah said.

"Fuck off, Noah. You don't know what you're doing. This country is going to shit. Before we know it, we'll all be wearing Union Jack shirts and singing 'God Save the fucking Queen.' "

"You can't participate in this," Veronica said. "You know that. It's dangerous. What if you get arrested or injured? You know the consequences."

"Fuck the bloody consequences! I'm Irish and nothing more. I can't sit by and watch this happen."

"You are more than Irish, much more," Veronica countered. "Where is this coming from? Protecting the Clans is your cause. It always has been. I don't understand why you've forsaken it."

He put his hands on his face and started rubbing his temples. "I can't control the Clans any longer. They don't care anymore, so why should I?"

"Why do you think they don't care?" Evie asked.

Marshall abruptly spun toward her, as if he was unaware she was standing there.

"Why are you here, Evie?" he sneered. "Shouldn't you be back in London sucking Colin's dick?"

Evie was horrified, as was everyone else.

Noah stepped toward him. "That's enough!"

"Stay away from me, Noah. If Ireland falls, the Clans in Dublin will be exposed and none of this will matter."

Veronica was aghast at how irrational he had become. Colin had confided in her his concerns about Marshall's mental health, but up until now she hadn't seen how far he had slipped away.

"Marshall, please, come back to Dublin with me," she begged. "You can stay with me, and we can monitor this situation together. Okay?"

When he looked at her, his taut expression softened some. She suspected he remembered how much he cared for her, how important she was to him. But then, almost immediately, his eyes flared up and he advanced aggressively toward her. Noah swiftly jumped in front of him and grabbed him. He tried to take him down, but Marshall was very strong. They started wrestling, knocking things over and slamming against the wall. When Veronica tried to help, Marshall picked up a piece of broken glass and heaved it at her. He threw it so hard it struck her in the abdomen and lodged right next to her belly button. She pulled it out and charged at him. Everyone else backed away while Noah and Veronica tried to get him under control. He pushed Noah off him and fell back over a chair, knocking Evie's purse to the ground and spilling its contents, one of which was a gun. Marshall quickly grabbed it, flung around, and pulled the trigger. The gun went off three times, and everyone ducked for cover. Veronica lunged at him and knocked the gun away. She hit him across the forehead with a bottle of gin that was on the floor next to him and he slumped over.

Suddenly, Evie screamed out.

Veronica turned around and saw Noah upright on his knees. He was staring down at his chest where blood was seeping through his shirt.

"No!" Veronica shrieked as she ran over to him.

"Oh my God, Noah! You're okay! You're okay!"

She touched his chest in an attempt to find where exactly the blood was coming from and found two wounds near his heart.

Noah looked down at her. "I never liked him. He was always such a dick." Then he fell back onto the floor.

Veronica grabbed his hand. "Please don't leave me, Noah. Please."

His eyes rolled back then closed. She laid her head on his shoulder, and Evie fell to her knees next to him.

He was gone.

Veronica squeezed his hand and brought it up to her heart and cried out, "No!"

Tears welled up in her eyes as she breathed him in, then she heard Marshall fussing.

She sat up and looked over at him. He was still on the ground writhing in pain from the hit to his head. She jumped up and pounced on him. She grabbed him by the shirt and jerked him up.

"V, don't!" Evie shouted.

"Too late. This is over. Stay here and watch the others."

She dragged Marshall to the front door and out to the car, then threw him in the front seat. When he tried to speak, she slammed his head into the dashboard to shut him up. He didn't say another word as she drove through town and into the country. She didn't know where she was going. She just wanted to get as far away from the safe house as she could. It was as if she were trying to remove herself from what had happened, but she couldn't escape it. All she could think about was Noah.

Veronica drove for about forty minutes until abruptly pulling off the road into a secluded, wooded area. It was late afternoon and gloomy from the heavy cloud cover hanging low in the sky. She stopped the car and ordered Marshall out at gunpoint. He laughed when he realized they were in the middle of nowhere.

Veronica paced furiously a few yards away as he propped himself up against the car, still reeling from the head wound that was now layered in dried blood along his left temple.

"So, what, are you going to kill me now? Is that it?" he said.

"You've become a liability," she answered sharply.

She stopped and faced him, then lifted her weapon and pointed it at him.

"Your services are no longer needed."

"I don't think you have it in you, V, to kill me. I know you're cold-hearted when it comes to these situations, but to revenge kill me. No way. That's not you."

"I kill to protect the Condition, Marshall. That's all it's ever been about."

"And now you're protecting it from me?"

She looked upon him with disdain. He had changed so much over the past decade. She used to admire and respect him, but now he was far from that person she once knew. He even looked different. He had grown a beard and kept his blond hair cut short, taking on a tough biker image with tattoos and leather clothing. She didn't know him at all anymore.

"Yes. You've made your choice, and now you have to face the consequences," she said.

"Bullshit! This isn't about the Clans. This is about Noah and Colin. I'm sorry I shot Noah, but we wouldn't be here if Colin hadn't sent you after me."

"You still don't get it. It's not about you."

She pulled the trigger and hit him in the chest, knocking him back against the car. Marshall stayed standing, shocked that she actually shot him. He put his hand over his wound and then looked up at her.

"It's all for the greater good, my friend, my mentor," she said. "That's what you always preached. That's what you always believed in, the greater good. I'm sorry you lost your way."

Veronica pulled the trigger again, this time hitting him between the eyes.

Marshall slid down against the car. He descended listlessly until he came to rest on the rough terrain. She lowered her arm and let the gun hang from her hand.

What's happening?!

Veronica's legs went numb and she fell to her knees. She sensed everything crashing down around her.

She reached up and grasped the pendant on her necklace—the one Noah gave her when they first arrived in Ireland. The one she always wore. She started to tremble. Noah was her touchstone. He kept her grounded and true to herself. It was too much to bear. She crouched over and sobbed.

She looked over at Marshall, who was on the ground, bloody and lifeless. The two most important men in her life were gone, just like that. Her heart was broken.

When she finally picked herself up, she wrapped Marshall in a tarp and placed him in the backseat. She couldn't bring herself to put him in the trunk. It was a long and painful drive back to the safe house. She tried not to think about Noah, but it was impossible. She gritted her teeth, furious at how senselessly he had died. An emptiness began to swell inside her.

She rolled down the window and let the crisp Irish air hit her face. She had to stay focused; now was not the time to grieve. She took slow, even breaths while she searched deep down for the strength to steady herself.

Find it, V.

She kept her eyes on the road and concentrated on how she was going to get all the bodies back to Dublin.

It was dusk when she arrived back at the safe house. She pulled into the long driveway and saw the front door was open. She slowed down, coming to a stop several yards way. She had a strange feeling as she waited for any sign of the Protectors. Everything was still.

Something's wrong.

Veronica grabbed her guns from the passenger seat and took a quick inventory of bullets. She knew it wasn't enough. She got out of the car and walked cautiously over the graveled pavement toward the door. She tucked one of her guns behind her and kept the other concealed under her jacket until she came up to the door, then entered the house with it aimed in front of her. She stepped into the entryway and saw Noah's body still on the floor in the middle of the room, but then she noticed two other bodies, one by the table and the other by the hallway. It was Gabriel and Tim, the other Protectors. She stopped in her tracks when she heard a male voice coming toward her from the bedroom. She stood her ground and zeroed in, waiting for a target to appear.

James McNair entered the room with a mobile phone to his ear and a gun pointed directly at her. She didn't recognize him, but there was something familiar about him. His short black hair shined under the ceiling lamp, while his thick eyebrows hovered dangerously close to his smallish black eyes. He was sharply dressed in a dark gray tailored suit. He reeked of money and self-importance. A smirk lingered on his little mouth as he hung up the phone and placed it on the table.

"Who are you?" Veronica demanded while still holding her aim. "Where is everyone?"

"By everyone, do you mean all the dead Protectors?" he said, switching his gun to his other hand.

She took a step toward him.

He shook his finger at her. "Don't," he warned.

She repeated slowly and sternly, "Who are you?"

"It doesn't matter who I am. This war has begun," he said in a thick southern Irish accent. "The Protectors' time is running out."

"You're an Insurgent. How did you get here?"

"Enough with the questions. We're at a standstill here. What next?"

Veronica scoured the room for Evie's body but didn't see it, and she couldn't smell her either.

"You tell me," she said, looking back at him. "If we lose our heads, maybe one of us could make it out of here alive. Maybe."

She took a step to the side, her weapon still pointed at him.

"On the other hand," she continued, "we could both walk out of here and meet up another time."

She lowered her chin and glared up at him.

He broke his stare to get a better look at her.

"You okay there?" he said, pointing to the bloodstain on her abdomen.

"I'm fine."

"Yes, you are," he leered. "I know who you are. You're Marshall's Girl Friday. I think I would enjoy meeting up with you at a different time. Who knows what could happen?"

She smiled dismissively.

"Let's do that," he said, lowering his gun and motioning for her to lower hers.

She complied.

"There now," he said with a sly grin. He looked around the room. "It appears you've lost your team."

She didn't say anything but kept her eyes fixed on him.

"You know, if you keep killing Clan members, you're going to end up dead yourself," he said.

"But killing Protectors is okay?" she replied curtly.

"That's called justice."

"Oh, and you're the judge and jury?"

He smiled. "Aye, maybe I am."

"So, what now?" she asked.

"Maybe you should go."

"Aren't you going to kill me, too?"

"In time, love," he said and winked at her.

This puzzled her. She wasn't sure if it was a trap.

"I'm taking him with me," she said, pointing down at Noah's body while keeping her eyes on McNair.

"Just that one?"

"Unless you have a girl lying around here somewhere."

"No, she got away."

Sigh.

She couldn't take her eyes off him. She had no idea who he was, but she was very curious. Her intuition was fired up, and yet she couldn't figure out what was so intriguing about him.

Veronica was so engrossed in the moment that she didn't hear two men approaching from behind her. When they entered the front door, she swung her gun around at them. They immediately took cover and aimed their weapons at her.

"Whoa! Hold on there!" McNair yelled out.

Veronica turned back to him and pulled out her other gun and directed it at him. She stood between the men with her guns pointed in both directions.

"Fucking hell!" McNair shouted. "Stop! I'm letting her go!"

The men relented and put their hands up. She lowered her guns.

"Damn, that was exciting. You are something else, aye. Help her with this body," McNair commanded and pointed to Noah.

Veronica was burning up inside having to yield to this man, but she knew it was her best chance to get out of there alive.

The men picked up Noah's body and stepped outside.

She scowled at McNair. "This is far from over."

"I know. I'm sure we'll see each other again."

They looked each other over one last time, then she backed out the door.

18

THURSDAY—BRISTOL

Jude sat on his bed staring at his cellphone while it charged. His head was spinning after what Charlie had told him. He knew it was a bigger deal than what he led Charlie to believe, but he didn't know what to make of it. When his phone finally restarted, he saw she had called. He scrolled his contact list until he came to her name. He stopped, glued to the digits. He put the phone down next to him and lay back.

Why would the Insurgents try to contact me through Charlie?

It didn't make any sense. He looked at the card Charlie gave him. Something isn't right about this, he thought. He picked up his phone and skimmed through his text messages and voice mails.

Nothing.

No, this definitely isn't right. Unless...

He flicked the card onto the floor.

Fuck.

Jude patted his pockets for his cigarettes then realized they were in his jacket downstairs. He started going through his clothes that were strewn on the floor until he saw a half-smoked stick on his nightstand. He settled back onto his bed and lit his habit.

It can't be true. It can't.

At that moment, he had the urge to hear her voice. He opened up his phone and called her.

"Hey, there you are. Why did you leave without me?" Veronica said, sounding hurt.

"I'm sorry. You were sound asleep. I couldn't bring myself to disturb you, especially since you had such a restless night."

"Oh. I was looking forward to seeing your place."

"Trust me, you don't want to see this mess, and, honestly, you looked so peaceful. I was hoping to return before you woke up."

"Are you on your way?"

"Just about. I'm letting my phone charge a bit."

"Well, hurry back. I'm missing you."

He didn't reply.

"Is everything okay?" she asked.

"Yeah." He paused. "Veronica?"

"Yes."

"I love you."

"You really do, don't you?"

"I do."

"I love you, too, very much."

"Good," he said sweetly, then hung up.

He tossed his phone onto the bed.

No way.

He went to the closet and pulled down his duffel bag. He wasn't exaggerating when he said his room was a mess. He was glad she hadn't come with him. He was shamefully untidy, and she didn't need to see it. He sifted through his clothes in an attempt to find some clean items, but he wasn't having much luck. He picked out a few T-shirts and another pair of jeans and threw them in his bag. While he was collecting his things, he could feel his body tensing up. He tried to ignore it, but it persisted.

What am I doing?

He dropped his bag and sat down on his bed again. He pulled his shoulders back to stretch out the tension, but it was no use. It was gnawing at him.

What if she is a Protector?

He didn't want to consider it.

Then what?

His feelings with regard to the Clans were painful at best. He didn't single out the Protectors when it came to his contempt. He lumped them all together: the Protectors, the Governing Order, and the Clans themselves. He blamed them all for what happened to his family.

Yet, in his heart, he had already accepted the fact that she was part of it all, and he was even grateful for it. The way he saw it, if she wasn't involved, they never would've found each other again, and he truly believed it was fate. He knew they were meant to be together.

Besides, he had always known it was possible she was a Protector since she was with them that night in France. During the past forty years, he had convinced himself there was a reasonable explanation, and maybe there still was, he wondered, but did it matter?

Could I still love her?

He didn't have to think long about it. He knew the answer.

Yes.

He would love her no matter what. He grabbed his pillow, covered his face, and screamed into it. He didn't want it to be so complicated. He just wanted to love her. He didn't want to deal with the Clans and everything that came with it. He wanted to run away with her, far from all of it. He wanted to wake up with her every morning and go to sleep with her every night, but now he knew it wasn't going to be that simple.

He threw the pillow off the bed and stared up at the ceiling. He had made a point of avoiding entanglements and confrontations in his life, so he wasn't in the habit of dealing with such an arduous dilemma. Being the youngest sibling, his brothers had shielded him from stressful situations when he was young, partly because he was passive by nature but mostly because of his extraordinary empathy for those he came in contact with. Kelly was particularly overprotective, which was why Jude retreated within himself after his brother was gone.

He suddenly longed for his brother. Kelly always made sense of things and guided him through the sea of emotions he would sometimes find himself drowning in. He clutched the sheets with his fists, wishing his brother were with him now.

Relax.

Jude took a deep breath and unclenched his fists. He rolled over, reached under his bed, and pulled out a handsome antique silver-plated lockbox. He had picked it up at a market in India back in 1969 and used it to hold all his cherished possessions. He grabbed his keys from the nightstand and unlocked it, then moved off the bed and onto the ground, shoving a pile of clothes from beneath him. He took another deep breath and settled down.

A familiar scent wafted up from the box as he opened it. He breathed it in and picked up a handful of papers and photographs. On top was a photo of him and Kelly in front of the Arc de Triomphe in 1963. Paris was Kelly's favorite place in the world. They spent so much time there it felt like home. He sorted through more photos and mementos from their various adventures. Rome, Athens, Morocco—there were keepsakes from everywhere he'd ever been. He and Kelly had lived a lifetime during the eighteen years they traveled together. Jude sat back against the bed and shut his eyes. He could picture Kelly as if he were standing in front of him with that dazzling smile he wore so proudly. Kelly would often boast that it was his golden ticket. He was very aware of the effect it had on women. Jude remembered how hard Kelly tried to instill a certain swagger in him, but it never stuck. Even though Jude had all the same physical characteristics as his brother, he wasn't that guy. Kelly was the one with all the bravado. Jude was happy following two steps behind and watching his brother shine.

For such a long time Kelly was his only companion. His brother would fall in love frequently and a young girl would tag along with them for a period of time, but it never lasted more than a few months, and then they would continue on their own. Jude had his share of romantic encounters, but his intentions were purely sexual. He never yearned for a relationship. He was content with the life he lived with his brother, and he had never met a woman who made him feel otherwise.

During this time, they lived off a trust fund their father had set up for them. Despite that, Kelly brought in a sizable income as a master chef. A sophisticated palate was his special gift from the Condition. He never had trouble finding a restaurant at which to apply his talents, and it was the ideal setting for his personality. Jude, on the other hand, was able to do what he loved best: experience the world around him. Wherever they took up residence, he would spend his days wandering the city and exploring its intricacies. He would immerse himself in its culture and learn the language and customs. That's what pleased him, and he knew why. He never forgot about Mark and how badly his brother wanted to live that life. He had hoped someday he would be able to share it all with him.

Jude searched through some more photos until he found one of Mark and his family. The kids were still really young and Mark looked happy. It was hard for him to think about his oldest brother. In his memories there were two Marks: the one before the escape and the one after. It was difficult to put them together because they were vastly different. Even in the photo he held, Mark was smiling, but Jude could see it in his face. His pain and regret were obvious. Jude wished he had a photo of Mark before he ran away, but he didn't.

Right underneath that photo was the last letter they received from Mark. As he reread it, the desperation in his brother's tone sent a chill through him. Mark described how the Protectors were throwing their weight around in their community and making life difficult for anyone who didn't concede to their authority. He feared for his children, who were growing up in such a rigid environment. He told his brothers not to return, to keep a low profile and live freely beyond the reach of the Protectors. He said it was only a matter of time before it got out of hand and Clan members started dying because of it. It was dated July 15, 1971.

Jude had forgotten about this letter and how it affected them when they received it. He tensed up again as the memories came flooding back. He had wanted to go home, but Kelly knew it was in their best interest to stay away, like Mark suggested. They hadn't been back to Dublin since they left in 1954. Early on, it was because they were having too much fun, but then, as the years passed, they avoided going back because they worried they might not be allowed to leave again. Kelly argued if there was that much unrest going on it was the last place they should be. Jude knew he was right. The Clans' bullshit was a distant memory. They both had forgotten the stress that came with it.

Unfortunately, they were reminded of that anxiety the day they found out Mark had died. Their parents were reluctant to give them too many details, most likely out of fear. They were told Mark had taken his own life. Kelly and Jude were appalled and refused to believe it. Kelly took it the hardest; it ate away at him. He never accepted that Mark committed suicide and was fraught with regret and resentment over it. He contacted other people in their Clan for more information, but no one was willing to tell him anything more than what he already knew. Deep down, though, he believed the Protectors had something to do with it.

Over the next couple of months, Kelly changed dramatically. His spirit and passion for life dimmed. His mood gradually grew darker. He became obsessed with the Protectors and, in particular, Marshall. Jude tried to reason with him, but Kelly was determined to find out what really happened to Mark. He vowed to get back at those he was sure were responsible.

Jude sat quietly in his bedroom and remembered the conversation that set everything in motion.

"We don't know what happened, Kelly. It's irrational to make assumptions. We don't know if anyone had anything to do with it. Mark sounded hopeless in that last letter, you know that."

"God, you're so naïve," Kelly fumed. "Of course Marshall had something to do with it. He always had it out for Mark, even before the incident. Why do you think he volunteered to go after him? You remember how fucking smug he acted when he brought him home. I've never been so sure of anything in my life."

Jude didn't want to believe it. "You said yourself we can't go home. What's the point in getting worked up? We can't do anything about it," he argued.

"We don't have to go home to avenge Mark."

Jude recalled with perfect clarity how much that remark frightened him. He knew whatever Kelly was planning wouldn't end well. He tried to warn him but, despite his efforts, he was never able to dissuade Kelly from enacting revenge. His brother's dazzling smile and wicked charm had been replaced with righteous indignation.

Jude followed Kelly to Marseille, where he had arranged to meet up with a group of Clan members who were making brazen attempts to expose the Condition. Kelly's intention was never that extreme. Both brothers understood the necessity of keeping the Condition hidden, but Kelly was so impressed with their audacity he was sure it would cause Marshall and his thugs to find them, and that's what he wanted. He wanted Marshall to come to him.

Jude placed the lockbox on the ground next to him and groaned. It had been a while since he thought back to that time. He got up and went downstairs to get his cigarettes. When he stepped into the hallway, he heard the shower going and was relieved he didn't have to face Charlie again. He grabbed his jacket and hurried back upstairs. He opened his bedroom window all the way, leaned back against the window frame, and lit a cigarette. The cool breeze blew in around him and washed away the stale air in his room.

Fucking Grenoble.

The events in Grenoble were always a blur to him. It all happened so fast he had trouble connecting one incident to the other—the ambush, the chase, the accident, and Kelly dead in his arms.

Jude rocked back and forth, lightly tapping the back of his head against the window as he recalled that fateful night.

He remembered they were caught off guard by the attack at the house. They didn't expect the Protectors to show up and start firing on them. He and Kelly didn't even have guns. They were in the back bedroom when the onslaught began. He still wasn't sure how the hell they got out of there, but they did. They managed to take off on their motorcycle.

Kelly tried to maneuver the dark, wet road as Jude held on, shielding his face from the bitingly cold air, but it was in vain. The Protectors were on their tail within minutes. Jude didn't know if Kelly lost control or if the car hit them from behind, but, either way, they went flying. The next thing he remembered was seeing Marshall step out from the car a ways back. Jude had landed in a ditch filled with mud and water. He wasn't badly injured, but he was disoriented and in shock. He saw his brother sprawled out on the pavement. Kelly was dead, half his head smashed in from the impact. Jude crawled over to him and tried to pick him up, but he was too unsteady. When he saw Marshall approaching him, he managed to stand up. He was prepared to confront him when, out of nowhere, a pickup truck pulled up next to him and a man offered him assistance. Without hesitating, Jude jumped in and told the guy to drive off. It was devastating to leave Kelly behind, but he knew his brother would've wanted him to get away.

Jude flicked his cigarette butt out the window and went back to his bed. He rubbed his temples and remembered how he ended up in that deserted building where he saw her.

Did she lie about what happened there?

He never saw her at the house or on the road, so he couldn't be sure. He didn't want to believe it.

"Jesus, I'm a fucking cliché," he said out loud, falling back onto the bed. He could see the red flags, and yet his heart refused to give in to them. He spent half his life wanting to love her, wanting to feel loved and be loved by her. During the past week, she satisfied every hope and expectation he had of her. She filled the void he had carried with him all those years.

I have to give her the benefit of the doubt. I want to trust her.

After gathering his things, Jude went downstairs, ready to go back to the hotel. He found Charlie on the couch clicking through channels on the TV. He looked over at Jude with the saddest expression. Jude couldn't help but feel sorry for him. Even though Charlie was thirty-two years old, Jude was very protective of him, like a parent. It was hard to see Charlie so beat up about what had happened.

"Are you going back to the hotel?" Charlie asked.

"Yeah."

"Don't you have to work?"

"I quit."

Charlie shook his head. "Of course you did. Let me guess, it's just a job."

Jude dropped his bag and sat next to him on the couch.

"I'm sorry you got mixed up in this," he said. "I should've known something could happen. It's always a shit storm when the Clans are involved. Are you okay?"

Charlie frowned at him. "No, I'm not okay. What are you going to do?"

"I'm going to tell her what happened. I'm sure we can figure this out."

"And the card?"

"Never mind the card."

"Do you honestly think she'll admit to it all?" Charlie questioned. "I know you think I'm naïve, but who's really lacking judgment here?"

Jude sat back and shrugged. "I love her, man. More than I can even say. She's touched something I didn't even know existed in me anymore. I've got to hear her out. Can you understand that? I fucking love her."

"No, I don't understand. It's barely been a week. How can you be that much in love with her already?"

Jude stood up.

"It's been more than a week, Charlie. It's been forty-two years, longer than you've been alive. Wrap your head around that while you sit here trying to make sense of it."

He picked up his duffel bag and flung it over his shoulder.

"The Clans don't follow the same rules," he continued. "What may seem absurd and illogical to you may not look that way where I come from. I'll find out what's going on, okay?"

He extended his hand to Charlie, who quickly got up and accepted it. Charlie was very emotional, and he gave Jude a big hug.

"Please, keep in touch. You know I won't be able to let this go."

"Okay, I'll try to remember," Jude teased.

Charlie stepped back.

"Relax, Charlie. I'll ring. I promise."

Jude went toward the door, but before leaving, he looked back at his friend and smiled, and then he was gone.

Charlie couldn't shake the feeling he might never see his friend again.

Jude sat wistfully on the train while staring out the window. His hair was slicked back behind his ears; a gray cotton scarf was bundled around his neck and tucked into his black peacoat. His mood was intense, and he couldn't hide it. He reached into his coat pocket for the card. He studied it, flipping it over and over. He knew who would be on the other end of that number, and he wondered if he should call it. Maybe he can help, he thought. *Maybe not.* He put it back and leaned his head against the window. He missed her.

When Jude arrived at the hotel, Veronica was in the living area waiting for him. The sight of her overwhelmed him, and it was too powerful to resist. Without saying a word, he walked up to her and kissed her the way he knew she loved to be kissed, with unyielding vigor. This surprised her. She willingly surrendered and squeezed him tight as if doing so would make his kiss even deeper. It did.

He held her in his arms, not wanting to cease. She tasted sweet and smelled of spearmint ChapStick. She was delicious. Slowly, he softened his kiss and pulled back. He placed his forehead on hers and steadied her as she regained her poise.

"There's something I need to ask you," he said.

"You can ask me anything," she sighed, feeling wonderfully gratified.

Jude held her face and gazed over every inch of it. He gave her a tender peck and then looked directly into her eyes.

"Are you a Protector?"

She stared back at him without flinching.

"Yes, I am," she said softly, but with conviction.

Jude stepped back from her. His hands slipped down from her neck, brushing by her breasts and coming to rest by his sides.

"You lied," he said.

"Of course I did. I've never admitted that to anyone, ever, much less someone I just met."

He tried not to appear bothered by it, but he was. "Were you ever planning on telling me?"

"Eventually, but not until I absolutely had to," she admitted. "It's going to complicate everything."

His eyes zeroed in on her, waiting for more. She averted their grip and moved away from him.

"This has been like a dream. I didn't want to ruin everything with talk of it," she uttered, making her way to the bar.

Jude was motionless, not sure what to do or say now. He had spent the whole morning refusing to believe it could be true.

"How did you find out?" she asked.

"A man came to my flat last night and told Charlie."

Jude saw her stiffen up as soon as the last word left his lips. She turned around.

"A stranger told Charlie I was a Protector? Is that what you're telling me?"

"Yeah. Why would he do that?"

"Don't you know? Are you that unaware of what is happening within the Clans?"

Jude wasn't exactly sure what she meant, but he felt her concern. She went over to him and put her hands on his shoulders.

"Jude, you're telling me someone identified me as a Protector and told Charlie. Charlie's a Regular." She stepped back. "I'm fucked."

She picked up her phone from the coffee table and rushed up to the bedroom.

Jude didn't budge. He was confused. It took a minute for him to understand what just happened.

She's in danger.

He knew what was going on between the Protectors and the Insurgents, but that hadn't entered his mind. All he had thought about was what the Insurgent told Charlie, that *he* was the one in danger. He never considered it could be a ploy to get to *her.*

Of course she couldn't tell him. It made sense, he thought. How could she, knowing his background with the Protectors? But the Insurgents wanted him to know. *Why?*

The anxiety he associated with the Clans was growing inside him again. It was uncomfortably familiar, and he couldn't let it go. The thought of her being threatened suddenly scared the hell out of him. It reminded him of when Mark ran away, and he couldn't bear it. He went upstairs. When he stepped into the room, she was on her cellphone, pacing back and forth. As soon as she saw him, she stopped and stared at him while she finished her conversation. When she hung up the phone, she stayed fixed on him.

"What's going on?" he asked.

"I need to leave, tonight," she said and sat down on the bed. "I shouldn't have stayed here this long."

"I thought you were working. I thought you were a solicitor."

"I am. I could've finished this transaction days ago. I've been dragging it out—you know that." She tried to smile, but Jude could see her struggle with it. He went over and bent down on one knee in front of her.

"You really think they'll try to harm you?" he said.

Her smile easily broke through this time. "You absolutely have no idea, do you?" She untangled a curl on his temple. "Yes, they want to harm me. They'll kill me if they get the chance."

"Can we leave right now?" he asked innocently.

"No, you can't come with me. It's too dangerous."

He balked and stood up. "You're going to leave me? Where will you go?"

She sighed. "I can't tell you. It's for your own good."

His eyebrows came down low, fully expressing his disappointment.

"Jude, this isn't a game. The Insurgents shoot to kill."

"Just like you?" he snapped.

Her face tightened up. "Yes, just like me."

She stood up and brushed by him as she left the room.

Jude put his hands on his face, roughly dragging them over his head and pulling his hair back.

Shit.

When he went downstairs, she was at the bar facing away from him.

"I can't imagine what you think of me now," she whispered, knowing he could hear her. "This is exactly why I didn't tell you sooner. I knew this wouldn't last."

He gently put his hands on her shoulders and turned her around.

"Don't say that," he said.

He touched her face and stared into her eyes. Then he kissed her like he did when he first arrived, which let her know how much he still loved her. She brought her hands up into his hair and kissed him back.

"I'm not letting you leave here without me," he said. "I know this is fucked, but let's get you somewhere safe, and then we'll sort out the rest, okay?"

She fondled his curls and gazed up at him. She knew he wasn't going to take no for an answer. She nodded.

"Now, where are we going?" he said, smiling.

19

TWO WEEKS EARLIER

Veronica stepped into the nondescript office building in north London somewhat irritated for having been summoned by Colin earlier that morning. She had only arrived back in town the previous day and hadn't yet settled in. She was looking forward to a quiet day, but the call came in right after she'd had her first cup of coffee.

When she arrived, the office was stirring. She was accustomed to the hum of chatter and computer keys tapping, but today the staff was scattered and moving around purposefully. As she made her way to Colin's office, those who streamed by her greeted her respectfully; the others discreetly glanced her way. She wasn't a stranger to this base of operations, but she also didn't make a habit of coming in. It was too risky for her to show up anywhere on a regular basis, so when she did make an appearance, the staff would always get a little fired up. It usually meant something exciting was happening, and today was no different.

"I can't believe you couldn't give me at least a few days to relax before ringing," she moaned when she entered the room. Colin was standing by an oval mahogany meeting table near his desk. His face lit up when saw her. He walked over and gave her a big hug.

"I missed you." He laughed. "Nice work in Brussels."

"Please tell me you called me in for something other than a pat on the back."

"All right, I know you're tired but, trust me, you won't be disappointed."

He went back to the table and started organizing a bevy of papers.

"Sit," he said nicely, pointing to the chair pulled out near him. His assistant, Vince, handed her a folder as she made herself comfortable.

"We've got a line on McNair," Colin said, matter of fact.

Veronica shot a deadly serious look at him.

"Yes, you heard me," he said.

After Belfast, Veronica tried to find out who the intriguing Insurgent was that she had unfinished business with, but she was never able to put a face to a name. He was as elusive as Jude, and it bothered her just as much. She became adept at scanning people's faces, always on the lookout for these two men who had crossed her path and affected her in their own unique way.

The difference with McNair was that he always seemed to be near. There were times over the years when she thought she saw him. She would find herself chasing a shadow or tracking a vehicle only to discover he wasn't there. Some days she worried her fixation on finding him was spilling over into her psyche and causing her imagination to run wild. On other days, she knew she was being followed. She wasn't sure if it was McNair, but the possibility was always on her mind.

Once it became clear that the Insurgents were more than just a group of disgruntled Clan members but an organized faction, Colin began his own inquiry into who was backing them. He formed a team of Protectors to go through the files of the Governing Order and identify any Clan members who could possibly be involved. Names would come up, and they would investigate. They would find out where these people were living and what they were doing. It was a tedious task since Clan members changed their identities like they changed their clothes, but this was where James McNair was flagged as a possible participant. When they tried to track him down, he came up unaccounted for after 1982. This wasn't unusual. There were Clan members who had gone deep underground, and as long as they stayed that way, the Protectors let them be, but McNair was different. He had a history of making formal complaints to the G.O. about the Protectors. When it was determined he was a likely Insurgent, Veronica identified him as the man in Belfast and he became her number one target.

McNair's involvement in Belfast confirmed his association with the Insurgents, but they didn't know whether he was leading them. Colin instructed his investigators to find out everything they could about him. Most of the information in his file pertained to his childhood. It was noted that his father was an Elder who committed suicide when McNair was a teenager. Beyond that, there was little else they knew about his current situation or where he was now.

Colin suspected McNair was a key player, but he wanted proof. He went to the G.O. and informed them a descendent of Original Scott McNair was most likely an Insurgent. Scott was contacted, but he refused to provide any information. Colin realized he would have to dig deeper to find out the truth about McNair, and he knew exactly how far he would need to go.

Colin was familiar with the McNair Clan from Dublin. He knew something that wasn't in McNair's file—something only he and Marshall knew. He told his investigators McNair's father had two brothers who were involved in the Grenoble incident in 1972, the very first time Clan members were killed. One brother died, but the other got away. Marshall had informed the G.O. that both McNair brothers had been killed and then he spent years trying to find the other brother, but to no avail. Colin ordered his Protectors to find the other brother who was living underground.

"You know where McNair is?" Veronica asked excitedly.

"No, but we've come across someone who might be able to help us find him."

Colin slid a photo over to her. It stopped directly in front of her.

She gasped. It was the man.

Colin always suspected she let him go that night, but until that moment, he was never sure. Her expression gave it all away.

"Yes, the one that got away," he said smugly.

She couldn't take her eyes off the photo. She hadn't seen his face since that night. All she had was her memory of him and now there he was, in a photo, and he looked exactly the same.

"Who is he?" she asked.

"He's McNair's uncle. He's been living away from the Clans all this time."

She was stunned. "What's his name?"

"His birth name is Alexander McNair, but these days he goes by Jude Xavier. From what we can determine he has worked menial jobs over the years and moved around quite a bit. That's why it took so long to track him down. He has been living in Bristol for the past eight years."

Bristol!

He'd been less than two hundred miles from her for the past eight years, she thought frantically. There's so much she wanted to know, but she could tell Colin was watching her closely, so she composed herself.

"I'm assuming you want me to handle this?" she said.

"If you're up for it."

"What do you want me to do?"

"I want you to get close to him and find out if he's involved with the Insurgents and if he's in contact with McNair."

"You think he might be working with them?"

"Not likely, but we need to be sure. I want to know if he's communicating with his nephew. We'll be monitoring everything by the time you get there."

"Well, if you're going to infiltrate his life, then why do you need me? If he's in contact with McNair, you'll find that out pretty easily if you bug everything."

Colin didn't say anything. He could tell she wasn't thinking strategically as she normally would. He knew the photo of Jude had rattled her.

He set down the papers he was holding and went to the nook console where he had a selection of liquor handy. Casually, he poured a glass of bourbon and waited patiently for her to catch up.

When she finally did, she took a deep breath.

"I'm bait," she exhaled.

Colin came back to her and set the glass of bourbon in front of her. "Exactly."

Friday

When Benedict pulled up to the safe house, Veronica was still trying to come to grips with the incredible evening she had shared with Jude. When she accepted the assignment, she didn't know what to expect. She read very little about him beforehand so she wouldn't have to feign too much. She had her own preconceived notions, based on her many fantasies over the years, and she hoped he would live up to those expectations, but she prepared herself in case he turned out to be a jerk or, even worse, an Insurgent.

Now, she was so emotional over what actually happened she couldn't process it. She wasn't used to feeling excited over a man, but he wasn't just any man and she knew it, which made it all the more confusing. Her feelings were real. She was giddy just thinking about him, and that was not normal for her. She bent over and hugged her knees.

What the fuck!

She stayed in that position until Benedict opened the door and peeked in.

"You all right in there?" he asked in his deep Brummie accent.

"Yes, I'm fine."

She reached for his hand and he helped her out of the car. Simply put, Benedict was her bodyguard. He was a strong, brawny man from Birmingham, much more intimidating than what his chauffeur disguise would lead one to believe. During the past five years, he rarely left her side. And even though she was confident in her abilities to take on anyone who challenged her, she trusted him and knew it was wise to have an extra set of eyes at all times.

The safe house was buzzing when she walked in. The dining area was set up as a control room with computers, listening devices, and maps along one side of the room. The Protectors were monitoring Jude's every move. She had placed a tracking device in his wallet when he was asleep, and a digital map showed him on his way home.

Veronica passed through and continued into the master bedroom, which was set up as an office for her. She tossed her bag onto the couch and went to the desk and logged into the computer. Moments later, Colin appeared on-screen.

"How did it go?" he asked.

"I don't think he's involved."

"Why?" he said, surprised by her immediate assumption.

"He seems very content living quietly among the Regulars. I didn't sense any apprehension at all."

"Did he mention his family?"

"I brought it up, but he didn't engage. I got the feeling he wasn't close with them. He did admit to being underground all these years, mainly because the Protectors were after him, but I don't know." She paused. "My gut is telling me he has nothing to do with the Insurgents."

Colin couldn't help but be skeptical.

"Did you sleep with him?" he asked, knowing that Jude had spent the night at the hotel.

Veronica sat back and folded her arms.

"Are you implying that I'm not capable of being impartial?"

"Hey, you barely spent an evening with the guy and you've made up your mind already. He could be just as adept at hiding his true nature as you are. Let's not jump to any conclusions yet."

"I'm not jumping to conclusions," she said. "I'm giving you my opinion. I spent several hours with the man, and he gave no indication that he had extreme opinions either way. It was actually quite the opposite. He didn't want to talk about the Clans. He was uncomfortable with the fact that I worked for the G.O. If you're not going to trust my opinion, then what am I doing?"

"I'm sorry," he answered. "That was out of line. I do trust your opinion."

"What do you want me to do now?" she said sternly.

Colin smiled. "Keep on it. I want you to stay close to him. That's not going to be a problem, is it?"

"No. He's meeting me back at the hotel for the weekend."

"Good. Just keep the conversation flowing. See if you can get any information out of him about McNair or anything else."

"Fine," she answered.

"V, relax. There's about a dozen of us in and around the hotel. If there's any sign of the Insurgents or trouble, we'll contact you."

"Should I come in over the weekend?"

"No, but check in at some point. Let me know everything is cool. I don't know how you talked me out of tapping into that hotel room."

"That was easy," she said with a smirk. "I said I wouldn't do it if you did. I'll see you Monday."

She logged out.

Colin moved away from his monitor. "Vince, where's Evie right now?"

Vince checked his iPad. "Liverpool."

"Send for her. I have a feeling we're going to need her on this."

Veronica went to the window. It was a beautiful day. She propped up against the window frame and closed her eyes. She thought about his scent, his voice, his touch and became instantly aroused. She wrapped her arms around herself.

Damn.

She stepped back into the room and fell onto the couch. She pulled out her phone and scrolled down to his number, then hit call.

Monday

Veronica enjoyed the drive to the safe house. It was several miles south of the city centre so there was ample time for her to get back in Protector mode before arriving.

Since Friday, she had allowed herself to pretend that part of her life didn't exist, and it was exhilarating. She was a Protector to the core, and it consumed everything about her. She had to be vigilant at all times. Her life depended on it. However, when she was with Jude in that hotel room, she didn't feel that weight on her shoulders. From the moment she laid eyes on him in France, she never saw him as a threat, and she knew after their first night together that he wasn't working with the Insurgents. She didn't know yet if he was communicating with McNair, but she was confident he wasn't a danger to her or the Protectors. Therefore, secured in the hotel and surrounded by her associates, she was able to let her guard down and relax, and she loved every second of it.

Veronica settled back into the plush leather seat and increased the volume on her iPod. One of her favorite Stereophonics songs had just begun.

As she walked up the pathway to the front door, she could feel the anxiety building.

Protector mode.

Before entering, she stopped and stretched her neck to one side then the other. She flipped her inner switch and opened the door.

She immediately saw Evie chatting up a handsome Protector near the control center. When she walked by, Evie winked at her. Veronica shook her head and snickered.

"Is he home yet?" she asked Stuart, who was seated in front of the monitors.

"Almost," he answered.

Veronica handed her bag to the handsome Protector, who took it from her and went into the master bedroom.

"Come on, you've missed me, haven't you?" Evie teased.

"Did you enjoy that? You do know the hotel room isn't bugged."

"It isn't?"

"Nope, your performance was for naught, but I enjoyed it," she said and kissed her on the cheek.

Oh yes, there's the Veronica I know and love, Evie thought.

"Now, answer the question," Veronica changed her tone. "What the fuck are you doing here?"

"Colin asked me to pop in, scope out the place, make sure you were on point," she said as she picked up her cigarettes. "I'll be honest with you, V. I wasn't so sure when I left there. You were a bit out of sorts."

She lit her cigarette. "You seem better now. Tell me," she lowered her voice, "is he that good?"

Veronica was about to get into it with her when they heard Jude arrive home. The room became silent as everyone tuned in. He was in the kitchen with Charlie talking about her.

Veronica listened in, but as the conversation unfolded she began to feel uncomfortable. She tried to disregard it, but it was no use. All of a sudden, she had a desperate urge to leave the room. Quietly, she backed away and went into the kitchen. She grabbed a bottle of water from the refrigerator then nonchalantly walked into the bedroom.

This was unfamiliar territory for her. She'd never experienced regret or remorse for anything she'd ever done. She wasn't impulsive. She was calculating. She weighed and measured every decision she'd ever made. She wasn't exactly sure what she was feeling, but she knew it was some form of weakness. She sat down at the desk and downed half the water bottle, as if trying to quench a feverish thirst. She tried to relax, but she could still hear the conversation going on in the other room.

Evie observed Veronica's stealthy exit and thought it was unusual. When Colin had expressed his concerns to her, she'd derided the notion Veronica could be compromised. But now, she worried something was amiss.

"Well done, V. You've got him wrapped around your little finger already," Evie remarked as she strolled into the bedroom after the conversation had ended. She shut the door behind her.

Veronica straightened up but didn't respond.

Evie stood on the other side of the desk and surveyed her friend. She recognized the same look in her eyes that she had noticed at the hotel.

"You know, when Colin told me who he sent you to look after, I was very surprised." She walked over to the window and peeked out. "Does he know who this man is to you?"

"I doubt it," Veronica answered. "He knows I let him go in France, and he may know I searched for him afterward, but that was a long time ago."

"So, he doesn't know you've been pining after him all these years?"

"What's your point?" Veronica said. "Are you trying to say something? Because if you are, please, do me the courtesy and just fucking say it."

Evie went back to the desk, placed her hands on it, and looked Veronica squarely in the eyes.

"I believe you've had earth-shattering sex. Am I right?"

The grin on Evie's face expressed her absolute delight at the thought.

Veronica reclined back into the chair. "For fuck's sake, Evie."

"You can't hide it from me." She turned around and sat facing away from Veronica on the edge of the desk. She took the last drag on her cigarette.

"It's so obvious." She looked back over her shoulder. "Can I get details?"

Veronica glared at her. "No."

Evie pouted just as the alert chimed on the computer.

"No need to share this info with Colin," Veronica said as her hand hovered over the mouse. "I've got it under control."

Evie wasn't so sure.

"Ah, you're alive," Colin said sarcastically as soon as he appeared.

"Why did you send Evie?" she asked.

"For backup."

"I don't need backup on this, Colin."

"I thought you might, and then I didn't hear from you over the weekend. Just covering all the bases, V."

"There was nothing to report. I couldn't get anything out of him about his family, and he doesn't give a shit about the Clans. He's just a fucking bloke living in Bristol."

"Let's hope you're right about that."

"Have you come up with anything on your end?" she asked.

"Nothing. Absolutely nothing."

"Well, that should say a lot."

"It says he's not being monitored. That's all."

"So what do we do now?"

"We shake the tree and see what falls out."

Veronica glanced over at Evie, who was sitting on the arm of the couch listening in.

"I want a photo of you two together," he said.

"What do you mean? You want me to take a selfie with him?"

"No, something more than that. Go out to dinner tonight. When you're leaving, wait outside for the car. Benedict will take his time pulling up to the curb and we'll shoot some pictures."

She tried not to react, casually rubbing her fingers along her chin. "Okay."

"And V, I want you to look cozy with him. Can you do that?"

"Sure," she said.

Tuesday

Marshall knew him.

Veronica couldn't believe it. Marshall grew up with Jude, which meant he knew who Jude was in Grenoble.

Why would Marshall keep that from me?

It didn't make any sense, or at least she couldn't think of any reason for it. What bothered her even more was that she'd never know why he did it. That is, unless Colin knew. Which he probably did, she imagined. She seethed at the thought.

Did they purposefully keep me from finding him? Why the fuck would they do that?

She could feel her temples throbbing as her anger grew.

Assholes.

She sighed, knowing she had to let it go for now. She was on her way to the safe house and had to focus. She put her earbuds in but, right away, drifted back to the hotel. Whereas before the Stereophonics always calmed her down and settled any lingering annoyances she was dealing with, now they only reminded her of Jude.

Veronica knew she was falling in love with him and, for a moment, she allowed herself to feel like a normal human being, like nothing else mattered but what she was feeling. Unfortunately, it didn't take long before the sting of reality brought her back to who she really was and the circumstances that brought them together. She was aware her feelings were spiraling out of control. She had let herself indulge in all its beautiful glory when she was with him, and now it was spilling over into her reality. She was becoming conflicted. Her emotions had never played a part in anything to do with being a Protector. She had trained herself as soon as she committed to Marshall and his Irish Protectors. She never allowed herself to be the weak link.

She yanked the earbuds out and shoved the iPod off her lap.

Fuck.

She rolled down the window and let the cool breeze flow over her as she tilted her head back and breathed in the fresh air. She began to wonder if there was a way she could get through this without losing him. She was positive now that he wasn't involved with either the Insurgents or McNair, and it wasn't her love for him or the phenomenal sex that brought her to this conclusion. She knew he wasn't capable of that kind of deception. No, that was her expertise, she thought. Their time together was exceptionally intimate. She felt very close to him already, so close she was afraid he might be sensing her dishonesty.

There's got to be a way.

Evie was in the kitchen making tea with the handsome Protector when she arrived. Veronica walked past them and straight into the bedroom. She took a seat at the desk, logged in on the computer, and waited for Colin to answer.

"Great photo, love. Exactly what I wanted," he said.

"Why didn't you tell me he was from Marshall's Clan?" she said bitterly.

"You said you didn't want to know too much about him going into this, that you wanted it to be as real as possible."

"Yes, but I think that would've been an important detail to divulge."

"You knew he was from one of the Clans in Dublin. You should've put the two together. Don't get angry with me because you went into this with your eyes shut."

"That's not the point I'm making, Colin," she said.

"What is it then? Did something happen?"

Evie entered the room and handed her a cup of tea, which she took and set down next to the computer. She realized now was not the time to start making accusations.

"No, nothing happened. I just wasn't prepared when it came up."

"How did Marshall enter into this?" he asked.

"Jude saw us that night in Grenoble, in front of the building. He casually mentioned it, but I managed to smooth over it. No harm done. What are you going to do with the photo?" she said, wisely changing the subject.

"We attached McNair's name to it and posted it onto some of the sites we know the Insurgents troll. It's bound to cause a stir once someone recognizes either you or his name, and then, hopefully, it'll reach him. Now, we wait and see what happens."

"What do you think *could* happen?" she asked.

"If McNair is one of their leaders, I would expect some kind of reaction because his uncle is consorting with a Protector, and not just any Protector. He knows you. I would imagine the Insurgents would get involved. If we're lucky, he'll try to contact him. If nothing happens, then we know McNair isn't high up on the food chain."

"If there is movement, then what?" Evie asked.

"Then we figure a way to draw him out."

"Draw him out?" Veronica scoffed. "There's no way McNair is going to expose himself over this, not after all these years of living behind the Insurgents. If anything, he'll send someone to take me out. Then at least we'll get confirmation he's a major player, but I wouldn't count on him showing up, especially if he's one of their leaders."

"We don't know that," Colin snapped. "We're still trying to figure this out, V." He sounded frustrated. "This is the closest we've ever been to a possible leader, and we've got his relative in our clutches. We have to step lightly or else it could all blow up in our faces and we could lose him again, and I know you don't want that."

"No, I don't," she fumed. "I told you, he's mine if we ever do find him."

"I know, V. You've made that perfectly clear."

Evie saw that fierce look in Veronica's eyes when she spoke of McNair and realized she hadn't seen that familiar expression recently. A softer, more distracted Veronica had shown up the past two days. Great sex can do that to you, she thought—but so can love.

Oh no.

Wednesday

The song.

Unbelievable.

It was the most beautiful song she'd ever heard. She was so touched that he went to the trouble to copy it for her. She listened to it over and over on the way to the safe house and felt his love in every note. It was wonderful and yet painful at the same time. As it played on, the events of the past week unfolded in her mind. Her mission, her deception, her love for him—it was all coming together like some bad spy flick. She envisioned a crappy ending where the woman kills herself to save the man she loves, and then this song would play over the end credits.

Good God.

Veronica thought back to what she told him that morning about her parents. It wasn't difficult for her to stretch the truth; she'd been doing it her whole life. But the more she distorted the truth to him, the more uncertain she was about whether they could have a future together. She knew she was digging a very deep hole, and she wasn't sure if she would be able to pull herself out of it.

She switched off the CD player when she saw they were approaching the safe house. She suddenly became flustered. She couldn't deny it any longer. She was definitely compromised, but she knew she had to stay on point. She had to finish this mission despite not knowing where it could lead. She reminded herself it was about McNair. Everything she was doing was to get that bastard from Belfast.

She sat back and took a deep breath. She realized it came down to one question—how far was she willing to go to get McNair?

When she stepped out of the car, she saw Evie standing in the doorway. A feeling of dread shot through her. Evie's usually chipper countenance was nowhere to be seen.

"There's movement," Evie said in a monotone voice. She stepped back and allowed Veronica to enter.

There was an air of urgency from the Protectors as Veronica walked up to the control desk.

"What's happening?" she asked.

"Nothing yet here in Bristol, but the Internet is blowing up," Stuart answered.

Evie motioned for Veronica to follow her into the bedroom.

"The boards are going crazy over the photo," Evie explained. "There's lots of speculation, but no one has nailed it yet."

"Do we know if it's made its way to McNair?"

"Not yet. Everyone's trying to figure out the significance of the photo, and who James McNair is. If anything, the man's going to be pissed we put his name out there."

Evie waited while Veronica settled in. "This is going to make it difficult for you to get around," she said.

"It'll pass," Veronica assured her. "I'll lay low for a while after this."

"Mexico?" Evie said eagerly.

"Stop it."

"Ladies, it appears we've caused quite a stir," Colin happily declared when he appeared on-screen. "I'm positive now we're going to uncover the truth about McNair. The dialogue online is proving extremely fruitful. We've got Insurgent sympathizers posting from all over Europe."

"Any word on McNair?" Veronica said.

"Not yet, but I'm confident now something is going to pop up. Any new info from Jude?" he asked, with low expectations.

He had believed her when she decided early on that he wasn't involved. Her instincts were usually spot on despite her emotional attachment, which he was mindful of. What he needed from her now was to stand guard over Jude and wait for McNair to make a move.

"Nothing pertinent," she answered. "He talked briefly about his family, but no mention of McNair."

Just then, Stuart came running in. "Insurgents have been spotted near Jude's home!"

"That's it!" Colin shouted.

"Holy hell, it worked," Veronica mumbled, and then she quickly stood up. "Where's Jude?"

"He's at the corner shop a few blocks down from his flat. We've got two Protectors following him," Stuart reported. "The Insurgents know we're there."

"Get two more on him," Colin instructed. "If they know we're monitoring him, they may not try anything. They would certainly know the risk."

Evie left the room with Stuart.

"I'll call him and send Benedict to pick him up," Veronica said nervously. "We can't leave him out there."

"No, you can't do that. We need to watch him and see what they do. Listen to me, V. It's going to get serious now. I need to know your head is in this."

Colin knew her so well. Sometimes it was a blessing; he was always one step ahead of her. They had always worked well together, starting back when he trained her at their facility in Dublin. Other times, it annoyed the hell out of her. He was like an overprotective brother, hovering over her but also goading her into doing things he knew could lead to trouble. She realized right then that he knew she was compromised.

Damn him.

"Was this all part of a sordid plan, Colin? I'm starting to wonder how much of a pawn I am in this."

"No, you got it wrong. I knew you might have feelings for him. What I didn't know is how far you would take it. How far are you taking it, V?"

Evie walked back in, aware of the conversation taking place. She leaned up against the door.

"I'll take it as far as is needed to get the job done," Veronica stated. "After that, it's my business."

Evie smiled suspiciously.

"McNair is my target," Veronica continued. "He always has been, and I'm not going to stop until I get him. What's going on between Jude and me in that hotel room has nothing to do with him."

Evie laughed out loud. "How can you say that? It has everything to do with him. If you kill McNair, don't you think that's going to affect what you have with Jude? Or are you going to keep that from him as well and base your entire relationship on lies?"

"Evie, we're Protectors. All of our relationships are based on some form of deception," Veronica said snidely.

"That's beside the point. You're going to have to make a choice here pretty soon," Evie snapped back. "You know that, right? Jude might not make it out of this alive if you think you're both going to move on from this unscathed."

"V, you've got a huge target on your back now and the Insurgents are circling. I need you focused," Colin said.

Veronica slapped her hand on the desk.

"Have I ever done anything to make either of you doubt me? My head is in this. This assignment is my priority, and if McNair shows up anywhere near here, I will take him out! Understood?"

That's exactly what Colin wanted to hear. "Yes, love, understood."

"It's gone!" Stuart shouted from the other room. "The photo has been deleted from all the sites!"

"This is it, V," Colin said. "If they're in the city centre already, they'll be on you as soon as you arrive at the hotel. You can't come back to the safe house now. Evie, have Stuart secure a laptop for her. They won't try anything out in the open so we'll have the hotel locked down. If Jude makes it back to you, stay in tonight and stay alert. We don't know what they're going to do. Just be sure to keep Jude with you at all times from now on."

"All right," Veronica said.

"If McNair shows up, we'll contact you. Please V, be careful," he said before logging out.

Veronica looked over at Evie, who was still standing at the door.

"You're completely in love with him, aren't you?" Evie said.

Veronica didn't want to talk about it, but she knew there was no avoiding it.

"I don't know what to say. I've never experienced anything like this, Evie. Noah was always closest to my heart, but Jude has surpassed that more than I ever thought possible."

Veronica got up and went over to the couch. Evie followed her and sat down next to her.

"You had to know it was a possibility when you took the assignment. Jesus, you've been fantasizing about this guy for forty years."

"He could've been an asshole. I thought *that* was a possibility."

Evie laughed but then got serious again. "You've got to stay focused on the bigger picture, V. This is too important."

"I know, but it's getting harder the more time I spend with him."

Evie leaned back and crossed her legs. "Do you remember that guy in Athens who tried to rip us off?"

"That's not the same."

"Well, it is, sort of. I had just slept with him, and then I had to kill him. It was kind of fucked up."

"Please, you didn't love him. You didn't think about him for years. You didn't spend six of the most incredible days of your life with him. Not the same."

"I'm only saying," Evie muttered.

"What are you saying?"

Evie sat up and took Veronica's hand in hers.

"We're programmed differently, love. We can shut that off. You know that. You taught me. You know what you have to do."

Veronica was comforted knowing her friend was right. She did know how to suppress it. Unfortunately, the problem was she didn't want to.

Thursday

Veronica was sound asleep when she heard her phone vibrating. She fumbled for it on the nightstand, knocking it to the ground. She hung her hand down and picked it up.

"Yes," she grumbled.

"Veronica!" Evie yelled. "Why is Jude leaving the hotel on his own?"

"What?"

She sprang up and looked around the room. He wasn't there. She jumped out of bed and ran down to the living area. He wasn't there either.

"Fuck! He left?"

She was disoriented. She had slept so soundly that he slipped out of the hotel without waking her.

"It looks like he's on his way home," Evie said angrily. "We've got Protectors scrambling to follow him. We weren't expecting him to leave. Jesus, V, there's Insurgents everywhere. What the fuck happened?"

"I don't know. We were up all night talking," she tried to explain while on her way back upstairs. "We were supposed to go by his flat together this morning to get some of his things for the weekend. Wait," she stopped when she reached the bed. "He left a note. His phone is dead. He didn't want to wake me. Be back soon with breakfast."

She couldn't believe it. She sat down on the bed.

"What the hell," Evie sighed. "This could get nasty if they try to grab him. I've got to let Colin know and see what he wants us to do. Hang on."

Veronica hurried and got dressed, then set up the laptop on the desk in the living area.

"Is he home yet?" she asked Evie when she appeared on-screen.

"Almost. He took a taxi. I'll have Stuart connect you to the flat. Colin is en route to his office. He said to wait and see what they do. He doesn't think they'll engage since they're aware of our presence. But if they do—"

A satellite map opened up, and a flashing red dot showed Jude's exact location.

"He's home," Stuart interrupted. "The Insurgents saw him but haven't moved."

"Oh no," Evie said a moment later.

As soon as the audio synced, Veronica heard Charlie yell, "*He said Veronica is a Protector and your life is in danger.*"

"Holy shit," Veronica blurted out.

Jude replied, and then there was nothing.

"What happened?" she and Evie both shrieked.

"They went outside," Stuart answered.

"Outside! What the fuck is going on?" Veronica yelled.

She could hear Evie hollering in the background, trying to find out what happened.

"You told him your real name? Why would you do that?" Evie scolded her when she returned.

Veronica didn't answer. She was paralyzed. Evie continued to rail the other Protectors until they heard Charlie again. He and Jude were back in the kitchen.

"They found you because of Veronica; because she's a Protector. It wasn't a coincidence she was at the hotel that day."

Veronica keeled over in her chair, the air knocked out of her as if she had been punched in the stomach. She put her face in her hands trying to subdue the shock. She got up and started pacing as the conversation continued.

"He doesn't believe it," Evie said.

"I know."

When Jude went upstairs, chaos erupted at the safe house. Everyone scrambled to find out how someone got to Charlie.

Veronica grit her teeth, "Unbelievable."

"I'll find out how this happened," Evie said, trying to remain calm.

"It doesn't matter. It's out there now."

"What do you think he'll do? Do you think he'll come back to you?"

"I don't know."

Suddenly, her phone rang. It was Jude. She became flustered as she stared at his name on the phone.

"I guess we'll find out," she said.

She stepped away from the computer and answered it. She could tell he was laboring over what Charlie had told him, but he didn't mention it.

"Veronica?" he said.

"Yes."

"I love you."

She tried to hold back her emotions. "You really do, don't you?"

"I do."

"I love you, too, very much."

"Good."

She kept the phone to her ear and let his last word linger. She felt hollow, and her heart hurt. She knew it was going to be different if he made it back to the hotel. A conversation she did not want to have was going to happen.

What to do?

"You can't tell him," Evie said when Veronica appeared on-screen again.

"I think I should."

"Why?"

"I can't lie about this. He'll know."

"Is that why you told him your real name?"

"He'll know," Veronica repeated.

"How can you be sure? He hasn't figured it out so far."

"Why would he? He's not like us. He's been away from the Clans for so long. I've watched him. He's very complacent in the Regulars' world. He's no longer suspicious or paranoid. He's—"

"Gullible," Evie said bitingly.

"Virtuous. I know it's hard to fathom in our fucked-up little world, but it's not normal to always assume the worst in people. I doubt he grasps the severity of the situation. I can play on that. If I tell him a variation of the truth, his senses are less likely to set him off."

"And then what?"

"I get him out of here."

Evie knew what that meant.

The alert went off on the computer. It was Colin.

"How the hell did this happen?" he shouted. "I told you to stay with him! And I thought we had someone watching his flat!"

"We're not sure how it happened. Someone may have snuck in the back," Evie tried to explain.

"It doesn't matter; you can deal with that later," Veronica interrupted. "You have to make sure he arrives back at the hotel."

"Are you sure he's going back? If they let him, that is," Colin said.

"Yes. He's coming back. Evie, just make sure he gets here."

"How are you planning on handling it then?" Colin asked her.

"I think we should leave."

"Leave? Why?"

"McNair's not going to make a move here in Bristol. I think that's obvious now. Look what he did: He snuck someone into Jude's flat and reached out to Charlie. If he were planning on pulling Jude out, he would've done so. He knows we have Jude covered. If he tries something, Jude could get hurt. I think we know who we're dealing with now. He's no scrapper in this organization. He's right up there."

"She's right," Evie said. "He knew we were watching his flat and that it could be bugged. He might be waiting for us to show our hand, or to get a shot at Veronica. It might be a good thing you didn't go with him this morning, V."

"Yes, agreed," Colin said.

"I think if we disappear, McNair may overreact and make a mistake," Veronica said. "He's too smart to call or show up now. It's already a fucking war zone downstairs. If we can get out of here, he might come after us."

"I don't know," Colin hesitated. "Where are you thinking?"

"Denmark."

"Do you still have a place there?"

"Yes, in Copenhagen, but not there. It should be somewhere more remote. There are some small towns on the islands to the west. The Begley Clan relocated to Odense about seven years ago—maybe somewhere near there."

"And you think Jude will go with you after you admit to being a Protector?" Evie asked.

"You're going to admit to it?" Colin said, sounding surprised.

"I can't deny it. And yes, he'll come with me."

They were both visibly skeptical.

"Trust me," she assured them. "I know what I'm doing."

"Give me a minute." Colin stepped away from the computer.

"Are you sure about this?" Evie asked her.

"Yes. This escalated too fast. I'm positive McNair won't show up now. I wouldn't. Let's put him in panic mode and see what happens."

"If you vanish, it's going to take a while for him to find you."

"I know."

"You're buying time, aren't you? You want more time with Jude."

"This is about McNair, Evie! I'm trying to figure out how best to draw him out."

"Say whatever you want, but I know what you're doing. I'm not saying it's wrong; I'm saying don't bullshit me."

"Okay," Colin returned. "We can have a place set up in Denmark by tonight. We're going to need a distraction to get you guys out of there. Evie, that's you."

"Got it," she said.

"I'll send the jet to Bristol now, and it'll be waiting for you." He paused. "V, this better work. It's our only shot."

"Actually, there is one other option."

20

TUESDAY—LONDON

"They've got Alex!" James McNair shouted as he stood over his desk, gauging the surveillance photo of Jude and Veronica.

Martin Pitts, who was on the speakerphone, knew who "they" were, but what McNair said seemed unfounded.

"What are you talking about? How do you know?" he replied.

"I'm looking at a photo of him with Veronica Farrell. Daniel is forwarding it over to you right now."

"Farrell? What the hell is he doing with *her*?"

"I don't fucking know!"

"I thought you were keeping an eye on him."

"I was up until about a year ago. He hadn't given me any reason to keep checking in regularly."

"Until now," Pitts said curtly. "Son of a bitch," he called out upon receiving the photo. "They look rather comfortable with each other. Is this recent?"

"I have no idea. It could be."

"How did you get this?"

"It was posted online with my name on it."

"This photo is viral with your name attached to it?"

"Yes. I think it's from her."

"Oh, you think this is a threat?"

"I'm not sure. If it's not from her, why would my name be on it?"

"Maybe someone wants you to know he's keeping company with a Protector? Maybe that's what this is about."

"No, absolutely not. It's from her. I know it."

"James, if that's true, then they know who you are."

"I know. Grandfather told me a few years ago they were getting close to figuring it out, but nothing ever came of it."

A moment passed without a word as they both realized the consequences of the Protectors knowing his identity.

"I'm still not convinced," Pitts spoke up. "It could mean a number of things. When was the last time you had eyes on Farrell?"

"Eight months ago. She was in Limerick dealing with the Rhys Clan. I trailed her for about two weeks before she dropped out of sight."

"Why is that? You've been tracking her since Belfast and you can't seem to keep a steady beat on her for more than a few weeks at a time?"

That was true. McNair had spent the past twenty years keeping tabs on the Protectors' preeminent agent. When he encountered her in Belfast, he knew exactly who she was, and their confrontation impressed him so much he became obsessed with her after that. He wanted to know where she was at all times. It was a difficult task because she was a master at disappearing without a trace, especially after the Insurgents became known and the Protectors became targets, but he had a few Insurgents on the lookout for her at all times under the order that if she was found he was to be contacted and she wasn't to be touched. When the time came to take her down, he insisted it would be at his hand. Pitts worried about McNair's preoccupation with her, but he trusted McNair knew what he was doing.

"Tracking her has given us loads of information on the Protectors over the years," McNair explained. "We always find her again, eventually."

"Ah yes, eventually, and here we are again. Well, it could definitely be a threat from the Protectors. You and Alex are far removed from each other. Who else would've put you two together? If they want you aware of whatever this is, the question raises again, what the hell is he doing with her?"

McNair couldn't stop staring at the photo. Clearly, they were intimate. Jude held her close as she rested her head on his cheek. McNair examined every inch of their embrace, trying to discern whether they were lovers. He pursed his lips at the thought.

"She figured it out, and now she's provoking me," he said.

"You really do hold her in an incredibly high regard. Tell me then, what is she after?"

"Me."

Pitts remained silent, curiously waiting for McNair to elaborate.

"If she discovered my name, then it wouldn't take her long to find Alex. Somehow I've always thought she must know I've been following her. Sometimes I've thought she was intentionally putting on the chase. I have a feeling she's doing this to let me know she knows who I am."

"Is it a feeling or are you being hopeful?" Pitts remarked. He knew McNair's obsession wavered between his desire to kill her and his desire to have her.

"Martin, she put Alex in the middle of this! I would never fucking hope for that."

"Don't you think it's possible they got your name from *him*?"

"No. He knows better. They must've got my name first, then found him."

"You don't think she could turn him? You know how conniving she is."

"He has no interest in the Clans," McNair explained. "Remember, I tried to get him back in after Belfast, but he refused. He said he never wanted to be a part of it again."

McNair got up and went to the window. The thought of his beloved uncle in danger stirred up feelings from his childhood and made him think of his father.

"It doesn't make any sense," Pitts questioned. "You'd think he'd remember her from Grenoble."

"Unless he never saw her," McNair said. "He may have no idea. I can't imagine he'd be involved with her if he knew who she was."

"Then maybe it's not a threat. Maybe it's just a coincidence."

"You don't really believe that, do you? That would be a fucking incredible twist of fate. It's deliberate. It has to be. I have to find out."

"Do not contact him, James."

"I have to! He's got to know who he's dealing with," he said and returned to his desk.

"No, it could be a trap," Pitts demanded. "That's what this could be about. They could be trying to lure you into exposing yourself. I'm sure Colin has many of his Protectors trying to figure out who we are. It looks like they finally put it together."

"That's possible, but if they're using Alex as bait, then it's too dangerous for him. He's extremely vulnerable. You know that."

"Then maybe you should've kept a closer eye on him."

"What are you saying? That this is my fucking fault?"

"I'm not saying it's anyone's fault, but you yourself have said on numerous occasions that it wasn't wise for him to be so unfettered by the Clans, especially because of his association with you. You knew something like this could happen."

"I've got to find out what this is about. If she's manipulating him, he could be in real danger."

"Do you think she'd kill him?" Pitts asked.

"Not if she thinks he's useful. If she's using him to get to me, then he stands a better chance if I make her think it's working. She obviously knows who I am so there's no point in being discreet about it."

"How so?"

"First, I need eyes on him. I have to find out where he's at and what he's doing."

"Do you know where this photo was taken?"

"I'm assuming Bristol. He's still living there with Charlie."

He motioned to Daniel, who was sitting on the other side of his desk. Daniel flipped open his laptop and started tapping away.

"I'll send out a team to locate him and find out if she's with him and if there are Protectors in the area," McNair said. "At the very least, I'll have someone close by in case something happens."

"Good, but do not make contact with him and do not engage the Protectors if they're there," Pitts insisted. "That could be exactly what they want. They have the same capabilities we do, maybe even more. Do you understand me? There's too much at stake."

McNair groaned and sat back down at his desk. "I can't leave him out there, Martin," he said angrily.

"Why don't you just have her killed then?" Pitts blurted out. "You've been putting it off for years now. You're no longer under any obligation. She's messing with your family again. I can't think of a better reason to finally get rid of her."

"No, if I make an attempt on her life it could get Alex killed as well."

"You don't even know if he's at risk. You have to at least consider that possibility, James!"

"There is no fucking way he is working with her! He hates the Protectors almost as much as I do. And besides, he doesn't know how intense this situation has gotten. We haven't talked about it in years. All he cares about is my mum and our family. That's all he ever asks about. He's clueless about everything else."

"Then all the more reason to tread carefully. I know how much he means to you. I need you to remain calm and handle this rationally. He is right in the thick of it now. You've got to be careful, for his sake. Let me know when you find him, then hang back and see what you can determine and we'll go from there. I doubt they'll harm him without provocation."

McNair grimaced, knowing Pitts' passive course of action was the right one, just not the one he wanted to follow.

"And have that photo removed from everywhere it's posted. Wipe it out. We don't need that stirring up any conspiracy theories—or worse," Pitts added.

"Yes, all right. I'll let you know when we find him."

"I need you to stay focused," Pitts said calmly. "This couldn't have happened at a worse time. We're so close to putting our plan in motion. I need you with me."

"I'm with you, Martin."

By the next morning, Jude still hadn't been located. McNair had sent a dozen Insurgents to the Bristol area, but there was no sign of him. He wasn't at home or at work. McNair started to feel uneasy. He put in a call to have Jude's cellphone traced, but that was going to take some time. He paced furiously in his office, waiting anxiously with his son, Dominic, for any news. Dominic worked closely with his father as an Insurgent, so he was aware of how much this turn of events was affecting him. It wasn't until mid-morning that McNair finally got a call from one of the Insurgents.

"There are Protectors watching his flat, sir."

"How many?"

"I see two in a parked car, but no sign of Alex."

"And you're sure he's not home?"

"Yes, we rang, but no one answered."

"Okay, if the Protectors are there, then they must be expecting him. Let me know if you spot either him or Farrell."

McNair tried to be cool, but it was getting more difficult as the hours passed. He hadn't slept, choosing instead to stay at his office while trying to make sense of it all. Mostly, he spent the time absorbed in the photo. There were all sorts of ways to interpret it and he tried to figure out as many as he could, but he kept coming back to his original thought, that she was challenging him. Despite his fears for his uncle, the notion of her coming after him excited him much more than he wanted to admit.

"Any word?" Daniel asked as he walked into the office with more coffee.

"Protectors have been spotted near his home," Dominic answered.

"That's a good sign. That means he should be close. They wouldn't be monitoring it if he wasn't around."

"Unless they're hoping that I show up," McNair said.

Just then, another call came in.

"We've got him, sir. He just arrived home."

"Is she with him?"

"No, sir. He's alone. Well, sort of."

"What do you mean?"

"There were two Protectors following him, and I think they've spotted us."

"Okay, stay back. Do not engage them. Do you understand?"

"Right, sir. What then?"

"Wait and see if she shows up."

"Okay, this should be interesting," said the Insurgent hesitantly.

McNair hung up, feeling somewhat relieved.

"He's home, but she wasn't with him. The Protectors are following him."

"That's peculiar. She's not with him?" Dominic said.

"They want me to reach out to him. I'm sure of it now."

"What are you going to do?" Daniel asked.

"Nothing yet. I want to know where she is."

About an hour later, McNair got word that Jude was on the move again. He instructed the Insurgents to stay close but not to make contact with him. They followed him back to the city centre and watched him enter the hotel.

"The city centre is crawling with Protectors, sir. They're everywhere," the Insurgent told McNair. "They think they're so goddamn inconspicuous. I'm looking at three of them right now. I could easily take them out."

"Settle down. Don't do anything, especially in public," McNair instructed.

"It doesn't have to be out in the open, sir."

"Enough!" McNair shouted. "For every three you see, there's probably four or five others looking at you as we speak. Any sign of Farrell?"

"No, sir. He took the train into town alone and walked over to the Radisson."

"She's got to be in there. I want eyes in that hotel. Find out if she's there." McNair slammed his phone down.

"So?" Dominic asked.

"I've got to talk to him."

"You can't contact him."

"I know," he said sternly. "There's got to be something I can do. If only I could get a message to him."

"That could be exactly what they want you to do. Martin specifically said not to contact him."

McNair angrily shoved his chair away from his desk.

"Damn it! I can't simply wait for something to happen!"

"I'm sorry, but are you absolutely sure he's not working with them?" Daniel said, calmly returning the chair back to the desk. "He appears to be moving about normally."

"He's not working with them," McNair said, trying not to lose it. "He's walking around without a care because he has no idea who she is or what the hell is going on around him. It makes perfect sense."

McNair sat back down, then hunched over his desk and placed his head in his hands. Then, it dawned on him and he sprang up again.

"Charlie!"

"James, no." Daniel said.

"We can contact Charlie and have him get a message to Alex. Where's he teaching these days?"

"He's not, at the moment. I already checked. The schools are on holiday this week."

"So, he's at home?" McNair started devising a plan in his head.

"I suppose so."

"We can get someone in there," McNair announced.

"You said they're watching his flat."

"We can get someone in there," Dominic concurred and nodded at his father.

"Martin said—"

"I know what Martin said. Martin doesn't need to know," McNair replied harshly.

Daniel shook his head.

McNair leaned over his desk and glared at him. "Are we going to have a problem?"

Daniel looked up at him defiantly.

"No, sir."

21

THURSDAY—BRISTOL

Veronica spent the remainder of the morning on the phone planning their getaway. Jude waited patiently, pacing the room, listening in and taking smoke breaks out on the balcony. He peered over the railing and wondered if there were Insurgents down below waiting for the opportunity to kill her. The thought of her as a target made him feel sick. He knew it was something she was probably used to, but it disturbed him. That kind of stress was why he distanced himself from the Clans. He hated to think of her mixed up in it.

"We're set," she said when she joined him outside. "We'll leave this evening, after dark."

Veronica came up behind him and put her arms around him. He kissed her softly over his shoulder as she cuddled up against him.

"Where are we going?" he said.

"Denmark."

"Why Denmark?" He turned around, keeping her close.

"It's quiet and isolated, and not too far away. We'll be able to monitor the area easily." She nestled into his neck.

"How long do you think we'll be gone?" he asked.

"I have no idea. Until everything settles down, I suppose." She looked up at him. "Are you sure about this, about coming with me?"

"Yes, it'll kill me not knowing you're safe." He kissed her forehead and then held her in his arms.

Evie was right. She was prolonging her time with him. When he held her, she felt cherished in a way she had never felt with anyone else, not even Noah. The love he so willingly gave her made her yearn for a normal life, a Regular's life, something she had never desired before. She knew she would do whatever she could to keep him with her for as long as possible.

"I remember living like this, constantly on the go, fearing for my life," he said. "I don't know how you do it."

"It's not usually like this, not anymore. I try to keep a low profile. I'm generally a lot more cautious."

"Can I ask you something?"

"Of course."

"Have you killed a lot of Clan members?"

Fuck.

She'd hoped he wouldn't go there. She had thought about what she would say if it came up, but she knew now was not the time to open up about it.

"Jude, my past is complicated at best. I've lived a life I'm not sure you could comprehend. I don't think I'm ready to share all my sins yet."

"So, it's in your past? You're no longer doing that, right?"

She stepped away from him. "No, I'm not."

Right away, he regretted putting her on the spot. He pulled her back.

"I'm sorry," he said. "I haven't had a chance to process all this yet." He brushed her hair from her face. "Listen, it doesn't change the way I feel. I don't think anything could. I know that now."

He raised his eyebrows, smiled knowingly, and nodded. He did love her, no matter what.

"How do you do that?" she said softly. "Make me feel so loved just by the way you look at me."

"It's a gift, darling. Just for you." He nuzzled her nose.

"There you go again," she said with a laugh. "Promise me you'll never stop being grossly romantic."

"Oh, now you like it?"

"Definitely." She clutched his shirt, pulled him in, and kissed him passionately.

They spent the next few hours joyfully expressing their love for each other. They acknowledged how young and spirited it made them feel, and how grateful they were for it. They talked about their future, but not so much their past. When Jude asked her questions about being a Protector, she skirted around the subject enough to keep him at bay. Instead, they discussed their trip. Jude wanted to know more about Denmark. He had never been there, so Veronica filled him in on everything she loved about it. She spoke of it with such enthusiasm he was genuinely excited about going, totally dismissing the reason for their sudden departure.

"Shit, my passport," he exclaimed. "It's at home."

In the frenzy to set up their plans, it had slipped her mind to ask if he had it with him.

"Can we swing by there on the way to the airport?" he asked. "I should probably pick up some more things and let Charlie know I'm leaving town."

Veronica knew that wasn't going to happen. "No, it would be better if I sent someone over there."

She started to get out of bed.

"Wait, I should go," Jude stopped her. "Charlie might come unglued if another stranger shows up at our flat."

"I don't think that's a good idea."

"Why?"

She chose her words precisely. "They might try to stop you from coming back to me."

He was surprised she would even think that was possible. "No one is going to keep me from coming back to you."

"Maybe Charlie can bring it to you?" she suggested.

He stared into her eyes and could see her concern. "Okay, let me see if he's home."

When he left the room to find his phone, she got out of bed. Once dressed, she went to the window and looked out over the city. Bristol had become the backdrop to this unlikely chapter in her life, and she knew it would forever hold a special place in her heart. She looked down at the harbor below and thought about all the Insurgents and Protectors who were stalking each other, nervously anticipating a showdown of some kind. She hoped it wouldn't come to that.

"He's not answering," Jude said when he came back up to the room.

"Good, then I'll send someone."

"No, I want to go. If we're going to be gone for some time, there are some things I'd like to bring."

"Jude, it's dangerous. I'm not exaggerating."

"No one is going to bother me. I won't be long—I promise. I'll be all right."

She walked up to him and tucked a stray curl back in place, then ran her hand down along his face. "I'll have Benedict drive you. It'll be faster. Hang on."

Veronica went downstairs, and Jude listened in as she explained the situation over the phone. She sounded terse at first, having to admit she had forgotten about his passport. She argued about letting him go on his own, making a case for him by saying he was being stubborn and wasn't going to allow a stranger into his flat. He liked hearing her defend him. Her voice calmed down once she suggested that Benedict drive him. There was a back and forth about it not being a good idea, but finally it sounded like there was an agreement.

"Okay, but you have to go now," she said when she returned to him.

He was already dressed and ready to go. She lovingly pulled his chin down and kissed him.

"Make it quick. And Jude, if you talk to Charlie don't tell him where we're going. Don't leave him a note or anything. Okay? He can't know, for his own safety."

Jude lost himself in her eyes until he heard a knock at the door. He agreed and kissed her good-bye.

The door had barely closed behind him when Evie showed up.

"His passport, eh? I guess that's an important detail we failed to account for," she joked.

Veronica put her hands up. "I guess not everyone carries several with them at all times. Are you sure he's covered?"

"Absolutely. Benedict won't let anything happen."

She knew he was in good hands, but she also knew she was going to be on edge until he returned.

Evie placed her bag on the coffee table and made herself comfortable. "I'm assuming everything went well since the plan is still a go."

"Yes, he's completely in."

"Completely?" Evie said sarcastically.

"He says he loves me no matter what."

"Damn, I didn't think he'd go for it."

"Ye of so little faith," Veronica sneered. She held up a bottle of bourbon from the bar.

"Pass. You know I can't stand that crap."

"Oh, my apologies. I left my $1,500 bottle of Pappy Van Winkle at home." Veronica reached around and pulled out a bottle of Smirnoff. "Better?"

"Much. So, are you okay?"

"Yes. Do you have the details of the plan set?"

She handed Evie her drink and sat across from her at the desk.

"I do. It'll be noisy and chaotic, my favorite."

"Let me guess, you're going to blow something up."

"You know it. I think the situation calls for it. There are about fifteen Insurgents down there. Maybe we can take a couple out while we're at it."

"Don't jest. Colin said no casualties. Just tell me the plan."

"At precisely 7:45, a car explosion out front, immediately followed by the fire alarm in the hotel. Take the stairs down to the ground floor and go left when you come out. You'll see an employee-only door. Go through there and follow the hallway down to the first emergency exit. There will be three vehicles in the alley. Benedict and I will be in one of them. Pile in and stay low. The other cars will be decoys so we should be able to get out of there."

"Are you sure it's the first emergency door? Remember Oslo?"

Evie squinted at her. "There's no need to bring that up."

Veronica laughed and sipped her drink.

"I'll come up beforehand and pick up your luggage," Evie continued. "I'm looking forward to finally meeting him. I want to see what all the fuss is about."

"What about the Insurgents?" Veronica asked, ignoring her comment.

"Everyone has been instructed to keep them distracted but not to provoke them. We don't want any altercations in public. I doubt they'll try anything. We number just as many. Everyone has a target to engage in case it does escalate."

"Jesus, all I can picture is that shoot-out scene in *True Romance*. I hope it doesn't come to that," Veronica said.

"Oh, I haven't watched that movie in so long. Remember my cat, Alabama? She was so sweet. Don't worry, love. Everyone is on point with the plan."

"Where is he now?" Veronica asked.

Evie pulled out her iPad. "He's almost there. I hope you told him not to dawdle. I'm ready to get out of here. It's very tense downstairs. I've never seen anything like it." She downed the rest of her vodka. "It really does say something, though. No one has attempted to get physical with us. They've obviously been instructed to stand down, just as we have. It's extremely unnerving."

"Colin was right. He knew if McNair was a powerful Insurgent it would lead to something significant."

"And so it did, but will it bring him to us? That's the question. I hope this works. The rumors are growing that they're up to something big. I don't want to say it frightens me but—"

Evie's phone chimed.

"He's home."

Jude returned to the hotel carrying three shopping bags. He walked in and raised them up.

"Benny made me use these. I feel like a transient."

Veronica laughed and walked over to him. "He didn't want it to appear as if you were packed for a trip. He's a smart man, that Benny. I'm glad you're back," she whispered.

He dropped the bags, picked her up, and kissed her as if he hadn't seen her in days. He started for the bedroom, but she stopped him.

"No, we don't have time."

"Aw, come on, just a little bit," he said playfully.

"Baby, we can't. It's going to get crazy here pretty quick."

Jude placed her down and continued to lavish her with kisses. He tried his best to coax her into submitting, but she pulled away from him. She was aroused and breathless, and yet amused with his efforts. She collected herself.

"Nice try, but, really, we need to prepare."

He shrugged. "It was worth a shot." He kissed her on the cheek then journeyed toward the living area.

Veronica shook herself, then followed him. She found her drink, finished what was left, and sat next to him to explain the plan.

From his expression, she could tell the details upset him. For someone unaccustomed to the turbulent conflict within the Clans, a plan like this would seem extreme, but it was par for the course for the Protectors. She tried to ease his apprehension by explaining the need for such a diversion, but when he got up and poured himself a shot of vodka, she had a feeling he wasn't at all comfortable with it.

"Are you all right?" she asked.

He nodded. "Yeah. I didn't expect it to be so violent and frantic. I thought we would just sneak out of here."

"I know, but it's necessary. Apparently, there are quite a few Insurgents downstairs."

"There are? I didn't notice. But, then again, I suppose I wouldn't." He drank another shot.

"No. They're hard to spot if you don't know what to look for," she said. "It's going to be fine. I promise you."

She went up to him and gave him a peck on the cheek, hoping to reassure him.

He put his forehead on hers. "Okay, I trust you," he said.

She swallowed hard as his words pierced her heart.

Over the next hour, they packed up their belongings and prepared for their escape. After spending a full week together in that hotel room, Jude was a little sad about leaving it behind. It had become their sanctuary, the place where they got to know each other, where they fell in love. He went out on the balcony to take in the view one last time. The sun was setting on Bristol's horizon, and he wondered what it would be like in Denmark. He was curious if it would feel different. At once, he shook it off. He wanted to spend the rest of his life with her. It didn't matter where they ended up.

When he went back inside, there was a knock at the door. Veronica knew it was Evie so she asked Jude to answer it. He opened the door and was surprised to see a vibrant redhead leaning provocatively against the doorframe.

"Hello, love. Is your luggage ready?" Evie said cheerfully.

"Let me guess, you're the porter?" he answered.

Veronica tried not to laugh as she came down the staircase.

"She doesn't look like a porter," he said, giving her a once-over.

"Because I'm not," Evie replied. She winked at him and sauntered in.

"Jude, this is Audrey. She's an associate."

"An associate? You're a Protector?"

Evie batted her eyelashes and flashed her sexy grin at him.

"Stop it," Veronica said while handing her their bags.

"These will be downstairs in the car," Evie explained to Jude. "That way you don't have to deal with them while you're rushing out of the building. Got it, love?"

"Got it." Jude smiled and winked back at her.

Evie turned away from him and gaped enthusiastically at Veronica, demonstrating her overwhelming approval. Veronica folded her arms.

"Thank you, Audrey. That'll be all."

"Right. I'll see you all in a bit."

And with that, she left.

"I've been away a long time. Do most Protectors these days look like you two?" Jude asked curiously.

"No," Veronica said as she cuddled up to him. "They look more like Professor Snape. We're the exception."

"I bet you are."

Veronica scanned the room one last time. Like Jude, there was a twinge of sadness for her about leaving the hotel. In her heart, she worried about what might happen outside those walls. She hoped for the best, but as a Protector she knew to never count on that.

She leaned back against the door and waited for the chaos to begin. Jude pressed up against her, kissing her on the neck and touching her all over. He was making it difficult for her to stay focused, but she let him have his fun while she played with his hair and listened for the blast.

"Can we do it on the plane?" he whispered in her ear.

Good Lord.

Her knees buckled. "I wish, but we won't be alone. Benedict and Audrey will be there."

Right then, the explosion went off. Despite being seventeen floors up, it shook the windows and knocked a frame off one of the walls.

Veronica sighed.

Too much, Evie.

"Christ!" Jude yelled.

The fire alarm triggered, and they bolted out the door. Veronica led Jude down the hallway to the stairs. People started running out of their rooms, and the scene escalated. They swiftly managed the first few floors, but it became harder to maneuver with each passing level as more people streamed in. Many were panicking, and it soon became claustrophobic.

Perfect.

They approached the third floor when Veronica got that familiar feeling that someone had eyes on her. She glanced around, trying not to lose her balance on the steps. As she rounded one of the corners, she saw him. There were about a dozen people between them, but she could see he was fixed on her.

Insurgent.

She squeezed Jude's hand as they hustled down to the ground floor. When they exited, they could hear the pandemonium in the lobby. Veronica took a sharp left and moved quickly toward the employee door. Jude was running beside her when she peered over her shoulder and saw the man following them. She flung open the door and pushed Jude through.

"Keep going," she insisted. He stumbled but kept moving.

She turned back to the door and waited for the man to come through. As soon as he entered, she kicked him in the gut and threw him against the wall. Before he could react, she clocked him in the face with her elbow and stepped back as he fell to the ground. She kicked him in the head, and blood began streaming out of his nose and mouth. He was out.

Jude stood a few feet away with his mouth open. He couldn't believe what he had just witnessed.

"Come on," she shouted, grabbing his arm and pulling him with her. When they reached the first emergency door, she put her hand on his chest to calm him down.

"We're almost out. Let me check," she said.

Veronica opened the door, which set off an alarm that blended in with the fire alarm that was still ringing. Sure enough, there was a set of vehicles right where they were supposed to be. The door to the SUV in the middle flung open, and she pulled Jude out and jumped in the back.

"Get down and stay there until I say so," Evie commanded from the passenger seat. She waited until they cleared the alleyway before giving the order over the radio for the Protectors to evacuate and scatter.

Jude was stretched out over his lap, staring at Veronica, who was seated beside him in the same position. His heart was beating fast and he couldn't catch his breath. He closed his eyes, but the sight of her taking down that guy flashed before him. He felt numb.

It was several minutes before Evie told them they could sit up. They had managed to get away without anyone following them.

"Are you okay?" Veronica asked Jude, who looked understandably traumatized.

"Yeah, I'm good."

The women looked at each other and doubted his admission. Veronica scooted closer to him and took his hand.

"I'm sorry you had to see that," she whispered.

"It's okay, really."

He gave her a kiss, then put his arm around her and brought her in close.

"Do you have GPS activated on your phone?" Evie asked him.

"I don't know."

"Not likely," Veronica answered.

"May I see it?"

Jude handed it to her. It was an old-school Motorola flip phone.

"Wow," she said.

"Told you." Veronica grinned.

"I know, I know. It's an old piece of shit, but I don't use it much."

"I can see why," Evie teased.

She fixed his settings, disabling everything, then turned it off and handed it back to him.

"I'd prefer you keep it off. If you need to make a call or text, I can give you a phone to use. Okay?"

"Yeah, thanks."

Not much was said on the way to the airport. Jude's and Veronica's ears were still ringing from the alarms. When they arrived, Benedict pulled the car right up to the private jet on the tarmac. They all climbed out and Benedict tossed the car keys to a man who had stepped out of the plane. Jude noticed that Benedict seemed to have a bit more authority than your typical chauffeur. Evie spoke to the man, and then they all entered the aircraft.

As they settled in for the three-hour flight, Jude was still struggling to unwind. The mental image of Veronica in that hallway was haunting him. He had refused to imagine her as a Protector, but now he had a video playback running in his mind that he couldn't shut off.

"Do you need a drink?" Veronica asked him.

"Sure."

She went to the back of the plane where Benedict and Evie were sitting.

"Is everything okay?" Evie asked.

"He's shaken up," she said quietly while grabbing a beer from the mini fridge.

"Because of the explosion?"

"I took down an Insurgent on the way out."

"He saw you? Uh-oh."

"Shhh. There's no uh-oh. It was nothing."

"Good luck with that," Evie mumbled as Veronica headed back to her seat.

Veronica peered back over her shoulder and gave Evie the evil eye.

When she returned, Jude was staring rigidly at the reflection on the window.

"Here you go, love."

She handed him the beer, and he promptly chugged almost all of it.

Uh-oh.

"Oh my God, Jude. Talk to me."

"I'm sorry. That was really intense. Do you think anyone was hurt at the hotel?"

"By the explosion? No. Precautions were taken. It was done as a diversion. No one was injured, I assure you."

"And that man, he was an Insurgent?"

"Yes. I recognized him."

He ran his finger along the lip of his nearly empty bottle.

"What is it?" she asked.

"I don't want to think of you in that way."

"Then don't. I'm sorry, but I had to stop him."

"I suppose," he whispered.

"Think of it like this: Your girlfriend has mad ninja skills. That isn't such a bad thing, is it?" she said with a smile.

Jude laughed and pulled her over onto his lap. She ran her fingers through his hair, which soothed him. He laid his head on her shoulder and placed his arms around her waist. He thought about the sadness in her eyes. He wanted to see if it was still there, but instead he closed his eyes and kissed her. She grabbed the lapel on his coat and tugged at it, holding him against her as she reciprocated. They didn't let up until the pilot called for them to prepare for takeoff. She slid over to her seat, buckled in, and then snuggled up to him.

"I promise that was the worst of it," she said. "Once we get settled, it'll be like it was at the hotel again."

"Where will they be?" he asked, motioning over to Evie and Benedict.

"They'll be monitoring the area at a nearby inn. They won't bother us. You won't even know they're around."

"I'm sure." He kissed her hand and laid his head back.

Veronica felt certain she had subdued his anxiety—at least for the time being. She regretted what had happened. She knew he was going to have that image of her in his mind forever. All she could do, all she wanted to do, was continue to love him and make him feel comfortable again. She leaned on his shoulder and hoped that once they got to the townhouse in Denmark everything would be as tranquil as it was at the hotel.

The remainder of the flight was uneventful. She stayed close to him, keeping his mind off the events in Bristol. Before long, she had him laughing and excited again about their journey, and once their casual rapport had resumed, so did their fervent passion. They were both eager to be alone again.

When they touched down at Billund Airport in southern Denmark, Veronica went to the back of the plane to talk to Evie. As Jude sat alone, the images from Bristol came rushing back to him, and then he remembered Charlie. If Charlie heard what happened at the hotel he was probably losing his mind. Jude pulled out his phone to check his messages, but he remembered what Evie had told him. He looked over his shoulder and saw the three of them talking. He flipped open his phone and turned it on. When it restarted, it began vibrating from all the notifications. There were several missed calls and six text messages. Four of the texts were from Charlie. He was frantic. But it was the next two texts that startled him. Both messages were identical: *911 MDM.*

It was the same initials that were on the card Charlie had given him, and he knew what they stood for—*Mark David McNair,* his brother and James' father.

Jude had forgotten about the card. He searched his pockets until he found it, then ran his thumb over the number. He knew he had to call it, but he couldn't tell her. When he heard her coming back, he shut his phone off and shoved it back in his pocket along with the card.

"We have to wait for a customs agent, and then we'll be off," she said.

"Okay. I need to phone Charlie. He probably heard what happened at the hotel."

"Can it wait until we get to the house?"

"It's getting late. He had a rough day of it already and as far as he knows I'm at the hotel. I want to let him know I'm all right."

She thought about it, then got up and went to the back again. A few minutes later she returned with a cellphone.

"Here, use this one. It's untraceable. But whatever you do, don't tell him where we are. Don't even tell him we left the city. He can't know."

"Okay."

He saw that the door was open on the plane.

"Can I step outside for a smoke?"

"Sure, but stay close."

After one ring, the phone picked up.

"Alex!" McNair shouted.

"James."

"Where the hell are you?"

"I can't tell you, but I'm okay."

"No, you're not okay. You're in extreme danger. Didn't Charlie tell you?"

"Yes, he told me, but you've got it wrong. I'm not the one in danger."

"Bloody hell!" McNair shouted. "You have no idea what you've got yourself mixed up in. She's using you to get to me."

"That's ridiculous. What's going on between us has nothing to do with you or the Clans."

"Alex, listen to me. It has everything to do with the Clans. They've made a threat, and you're the pawn. You are right in the thick of it."

Jude paused. "What kind of threat?"

"They posted a photo online of the two of you together with my name attached to it, my real name. They're trying to get me to expose myself so they can kill me. I don't know how they found you, but they did, and now they're using you to get to me."

"What kind of photo? Are you sure it was us?"

"Yes, absolutely. You were in each other's arms, standing outside somewhere, maybe in front of a restaurant."

Jude became very still, and he was barely breathing.

"She's ruthless, Alex. Veronica Farrell is a high-ranking Protector. I know. I've been tracking her for years. She will kill anyone she thinks is a threat. She's not whoever she says she is."

"I know she's a Protector."

"Do you know she was there when Kelly died? Do you know she killed her parents? I'm pretty sure she knows what really happened to my dad. She was in Belfast. I confronted her there. This isn't bullshit. She is notorious, and she has you in her crosshairs. For fuck's sake, this is why I've been trying to contact you."

A sudden tightness filled Jude's chest. He trusted his nephew. He knew James was telling him the truth. He knew it.

The fucking sadness.

"Now, tell me where you are!" McNair demanded.

"Why? So you can come kill her? No. I don't want her harmed, no matter what she has done. I'll take care of this."

"I'm not going to kill her! If I wanted her dead I would've done it years ago. This is about you. I want you as far away from her as possible. I don't know what she'll fucking do if she thinks you're no longer useful to her."

"No," he said harshly, trying to keep his voice down so he couldn't be heard from the plane. "I understand you see her as a vicious Protector, but she's more than that to me. There's something between us that you couldn't possibly understand. I'll deal with this and fly back to Bristol as soon as I can."

"You're not in Bristol?" McNair hollered. "Where are you? Tell me! I can send someone to pick you up!"

"I'll call you as soon as I'm away from her. I'm sorry I didn't get in touch with you sooner, James. Honestly, I'm so sorry."

"Alex, no!"

"Good-bye."

22

THURSDAY—DENMARK

The pain was excruciating. Jude bent over and put his hands on his knees. He squeezed his eyes shut and tried to catch his breath. As preposterous as it sounded, he knew it was possible. After seeing her beat the crap out of that Insurgent, he was sure she wasn't telling him everything, but he never imagined it could be this bad.

When he finally calmed down, he looked around. He had no idea where he was. From the blackness surrounding it, the airport appeared to be in the middle of nowhere. Just then, Veronica stuck her head out of the plane and called out to him. The agent was there to check their passports.

He felt his coat and realized he had his passport on him. He could see the main terminal a short distance away and contemplated taking off toward it. He was sure he could make it, but then he remembered his duffel bag was on the plane, and in it was his lockbox.

No!

He knew he couldn't leave it behind. Everything it held was precious and irreplaceable. Immediately, he regretted bringing it. He had wanted to share it with her—in his own way giving a piece of himself to her, something he'd never done before with anyone.

Dumb fuck.

He nervously headed back to the plane.

It was a forty-five-minute drive from the airport to the island of Funen, where they had secured a townhouse along a peaceful harbor. Evie entertained them on the way with a lively discussion about the ways of the Danish, but Veronica could tell Jude was still preoccupied with what she assumed was the evening's earlier events. She held his hand, occasionally giving an affectionate squeeze to reassure him.

When they arrived, everyone went in to make sure the place was in order. It was a modest two-story home, neatly furnished and roomier than the upscale hotel room. The light-colored hardwood floors and matching countertops made it feel more like a country cottage than a townhouse nestled in the heart of a small historic town, but it was cozy and exactly what Veronica had requested. Once everything checked out, Evie and Benedict left.

"Alone at last," Veronica said. She started to put her arms around Jude, but he backed away from her.

"What is it?" she asked, surprised by his rebuff.

He glared at her without saying a word, which alarmed her.

"Is it Charlie? Is everything okay?"

"I didn't call Charlie. I called James."

Veronica felt all the blood flow out of her face as the name echoed in her head.

James.

"What?" She staggered back from him.

"I know everything," he said.

Without hesitation, her mind clicked into defensive mode, and she quickly assessed what was happening.

How much does he actually know?

"Everything? Are you sure about that?" she replied coolly.

Veronica tried to hold it together, but she wasn't prepared for this. She had been so thrilled she had gotten him out of Bristol that she had assumed the threat of McNair contacting him was gone, at least for a while. It had failed to cross her mind that Jude would reach out to him. Her heart rate accelerated, and she measured her options.

"Why did you do it?" he asked. "Was it because of Grenoble? Because of me?"

"Yes, that was part of it," she said carefully.

"Is this really about James?"

She wasn't sure what to say. It was obvious his opinion of her had been drastically affected. His eyes were filled with pain and contempt. She could see she was losing him.

"I've been looking for your nephew for twenty years. I still can't believe you two are related. I never understood my obsession with him, until I found out two weeks ago you were his uncle, and then it all made sense."

"What made sense?"

Veronica tried to remain still, but she began fidgeting. She wasn't sure how much to divulge.

"I crossed paths with him in Belfast years ago, and there was something about him that was familiar to me. I couldn't place it, but I was sure there was something significant about him." She kept her eyes fixed on him, hoping he would know she was telling him the truth. "You've been in my heart for so long, Jude. He reminded me of you. I know that now."

"And yet you still want to kill him, knowing he's my blood?"

She took a deep breath and let it out slowly.

"The Insurgents are threatening the very existence of the Clans. They want the Protectors to relinquish their power, and if that happens, it's only a matter of time until the Condition becomes known."

"And that would be a bad thing?" he smirked, knowing it would provoke her.

She bit her lip. "Yes. It would be a very bad thing. Think end of the world as we know it."

"That's a tad dramatic."

"Good Lord, Jude. How would you know? You've been living like a Regular all these years. If the Condition were to be discovered, we would all be exposed and we'd be left defenseless for society to judge us."

She sighed, exasperated at having to explain herself once again. She desperately scoped out the premises for any sign of liquor and spotted a bottle of bourbon on the kitchen counter.

Thank you, Evie!

She went over to it, poured herself a shot, and downed it.

"Were you there when my brother was killed?" he said under his breath, almost as if he were afraid to ask.

Her hand began to tremble as she set the glass down. She poured another shot and then turned back to him. He was standing in the same place with his hands firmly in his coat pockets, his gray cotton scarf wrapped casually around his neck. Even under the current circumstances, she found him irresistible. She'd never seen him angry, and it favored him.

"I didn't see it happen," she admitted. "I was back at the house."

He winced and tried to remain calm.

"And your parents? Did *you* kill them?" he said more pointedly.

"My parents? I told you what happened with my parents."

"Yes, but now I don't know what was the bloody truth and what was a load of shit!" He raised his voice, angrily shoving his hands deeper into his pockets.

"I never lied about my feelings, Jude," she answered sharply but instantly relented. "I accepted this assignment because of you. I searched everywhere for you. I was constantly looking for your face. When I found out you were McNair's uncle, I was devastated, but I couldn't pass up the opportunity to finally meet you. I had no idea I would fall so in love with you."

Jude averted his eyes. "I was an assignment," he whispered.

"Stop it. You know this is real," she pleaded. "I know you know it. I'm not a fucking sociopath. That was the real me in that hotel room. I've never, *ever*, opened myself up like that before. I know who I am, Jude, and I trust myself, but the way you make me feel, it's something I've never experienced. And I know, *I know*, you feel the same way."

Veronica put her glass down and went back over to him. She approached slowly and stood in front of him.

"I'm usually very cautious," she said. "I've had to be to survive this long, but I didn't hesitate with you, not at all. That's why it scared me at first. I'm not accustomed to expressing my emotions as I did with you."

He put his head down. He couldn't bear to look at her. His heart was breaking.

"The Protectors and the Clans, they destroyed my family," he said in a cracked voice. "I wanted to let that go, put it behind me and move forward with you. I wouldn't let myself think of you as a killer, a manipulative, deceitful Protector. But now, I come to find out you are all those things. It's too much. I can't accept it."

"Don't dismiss me, please. Look at me, Jude."

He mustered up the strength to face her. His eyes were red and swelling up from the tears he was trying desperately to hold back. He shook his head.

"I can't do it. I can't go back knowing what I know now."

He wasn't sure if that was entirely true, but it was how he felt at that moment, and it shattered her.

"Please, don't do this." She put her hands on his face and was startled at how cold his skin felt. "Don't leave me. We can work through this."

He reached up, took her by the wrists, and brought her hands down.

"I don't see how. You stand for everything I hate about the Clans. I lost the most precious people in my life because of the things you believe are worth killing for, and you're still doing it. You want to kill my brother's son, and for what? How could we go on together?"

Veronica closed her eyes, and everything inside of her gave way. He was right. Evie was right. She had been fooling herself all this time thinking she could work it out. It took all her strength not to completely fall apart. She clenched her eyes, pushed it down, and then looked up at him. She knew she wasn't going to be able to change his mind, but she couldn't let him think it was all for nothing. He didn't share her pessimistic view of the Condition, which is why she felt the need to explain herself. She wanted him to know why she did it.

She stepped back but kept her eyes locked in on him.

"Everything I do is for our survival, so we can live somewhat normal lives in this callous, ignorant world. That's what it's for, Jude. It's for the greater good for all of us. Otherwise, all that's left is despair."

"Despair? You truly believe there's no hope for us if the Condition is exposed?"

"I do, with everything that I am."

She tried to swallow, but her mouth was dry. She wanted to grab the bottle of bourbon and chug it, but she held firm in place.

"As soon as I was told about our affliction, I knew we were doomed," she said. "And the way the Originals instilled fear in us only fueled my hopelessness. I was always so scared. I couldn't sleep. I was anxious and overwrought with thoughts of how to keep it secret. I was terribly uncertain about my future, the Clans' future. I didn't think we could survive it."

Jude wasn't sure whether to believe anything she had to say, but he wanted to hear her out, so he let her continue.

"When we started receiving Marshall's newsletter, I understood everything he was saying. I was relieved I wasn't the only one who could see how badly this could all end up. Even still, I didn't think it was possible to keep it hidden forever. I always knew the day would come when we would be found out, but Marshall was incredibly determined to keep it under control. I had no choice but to join him. I never saw any other path for myself. I had to do everything in my power to keep us safe."

She took a slow, shaky breath.

"McNair and the Insurgents are on the verge of destroying everything I've worked so hard to protect. This world we live in is not in any way prepared to deal with the Condition. We're talking about millions of people being affected by this. They won't be able to control it or contain it. I don't understand how the Insurgents can't see that, how you can't see that. Everything we know will change, and not for the better. I can't let it happen. I won't."

Jude could feel her pain, and he could see it in her eyes. They were wide open and teary. It wasn't sadness. It was panic and desperation. His heart ached for her, but he couldn't trust himself anymore. She had made him question everything he believed in. He knew it wasn't enough.

"I hear you, I do," he said, "but right now, I don't care about the Condition and its consequences. I don't care about James or the Protectors and the Insurgents. I loved you. I trusted you, and you betrayed me. That's all I feel."

Jude stared at her exactly the way he had that night in Grenoble. He soaked in as much of her as he could, then turned away.

He picked up his duffel bag and walked to the door. He grabbed the handle but didn't open it. Instead, he gently placed his forehead on the door.

"This is so fucked," he whispered. "I was meant to love you. I know it. I feel it in my bones and in my soul. It wasn't supposed to be like this."

He softly banged his head against the hard wood.

"What a cruel fucking joke."

He opened the door and walked out.

23

1989—PHILADELPHIA

Veronica stepped back into the house without knocking. Her parents were still in the living room.

"Please, you must stop," she implored.

Her mother looked away, shaking her head.

"The time has come, Veronica," her father said. "This was bound to happen. The Clans are growing. You won't be able to keep it hidden much longer."

"Why can't you see how devastating this will be?"

"Devastating? We'll be free—that's what I see," her mother said.

"Why are you doing this?" Veronica pleaded. "You were there from the beginning. You raised me to fear the consequences. How can you be so flippant about it? And don't tell me this is about me; I don't believe that."

"We've lived a lifetime avoiding the consequences. We're done with it," her father said.

"And it is about you," her mother asserted. "We wanted so much more for you than this."

"Please, get over it! It's been fifty years. I have devoted my life to protecting the Clans. You cannot put this on me. You have to stop."

"It's too late," her father said. He turned away, picked up a poker, and began tending the fire.

"Listen to me. This isn't only about us," she tried to explain. "If the Condition is exposed, they'll want the serum. And if the serum is released, it could conceivably alter the human race. Can't you see that? You can't inflict this on people under the false pretense that this is a cure-all and everyone will live forever healthy and unimpaired. It's a lie. It's been almost seventy years and we still don't know everything about it. Are you aware of the side effects that are developing now?"

They both showed no interest, callously averting their eyes from her.

"The G.O. has documentation of abnormalities in second- and third-generation members, not to mention the mental deterioration that is showing up in Originals and Elders, which is clearly evident in both of you. We have no idea what could happen. Twenty or forty years from now we could all be dead."

"Stop!" her mother snapped. "This is a gift. We are very fortunate."

"You still believe that? Maybe for you and the other Originals who chose to do this to themselves, but for the rest of us, there was no choice. You took the serum and then procreated, essentially creating guinea pigs, and you expect me to rejoice in it. I'm a lab rat, and I have you to thank for that."

"That's enough!" her father shouted.

"You were right, Chris," her mother said as she put her hand on his shoulder. "She's gone. There's no hope for her."

"Your mother hoped there was a small part of you still in there, that the Protectors hadn't destroyed your soul. But by coming back here and spouting all this nonsense, you've shown us you are no longer the person we knew and loved."

"The Protectors didn't rob me of my soul. You did this to me, and I won't let you continue to do it to anyone else."

Veronica pulled a gun from behind her and shot her father between the eyes. She then turned the gun on her mother and put a bullet in her heart.

Her arm dropped to her side as they fell to the ground. A few seconds passed before she gasped for a breath. She squeezed her eyes shut and breathed in again, slowly this time, but the familiar scents from her childhood stung as they flowed through her. She opened her eyes and turned away.

She felt lightheaded when she reached the entryway. She leaned up against the wood column and held onto it, trying to suppress the emotions that were flooding her senses. She swallowed hard and concentrated on collecting herself. Once she had, she put her gun back behind her, straightened up, and walked out.

When she opened the door, Noah was standing there waiting for her. She stared into his eyes, and he looked back at her solemnly. He reached out for her hand, but she gave a slight shake of her head and walked on toward the car.

She climbed into the backseat.

"It's done," she said.

24

THURSDAY—DENMARK

Veronica was motionless, still staring at the door. She couldn't take her eyes off it.

What the fuck just happened?

The sight of him walking out played over and over in her head. She was stunned by how suddenly he slipped away from her. She stumbled back until she felt the arm of the couch. As she steadied herself on it a tear streamed down her cheek.

He's gone.

She couldn't believe it. She felt ill. She actually thought she may get sick, but then her phone vibrated and she was jolted back into the moment. It was a text from Evie asking why Jude was on the move. Veronica phoned her back.

"I lost him," she said.

"What do you mean you lost him?"

"At the airport, he didn't call Charlie. He called McNair."

"Oh my God."

Veronica didn't reply.

"I'll be right there," Evie said frantically.

Veronica tossed the phone onto the coffee table and looked around the room. Her luggage was still sitting untouched by the door. They had only just arrived. How the hell did everything fall apart? It came out of nowhere. She manically thought back over the past week and tried to figure out how she missed it.

Fuck!

She wrapped her arms around herself and bent over. Her anguish was unbearable. She closed her eyes, inhaled slowly, and held it in.

Find it, V. Find it.

She tried not to faint while she searched for her strength, her core. When she exhaled, she could feel it growing. She took another deep breath and held it even longer. With all her might, she quelled her emotions.

Veronica opened her eyes, sat up, and stretched her neck from one side to the other. She took another breath, then wiped her eyes and brushed her hair back. Carefully, she stood up, went over to her bags, picked one up, and placed it on the couch. She pulled out her black overcoat and scarf, then grabbed her toiletry bag and headed to the bathroom.

Standing in front of the mirror, the light from the incandescent bulb shined a pale yellow glow over her. She studied her face. She knew full well what she was about to do was going to scar her. She fought off the apprehension that was pounding inside of her, trying to weaken her stance. She held her ground. This was the last thing she wanted to do. She had tried so hard to avoid it, but she knew she couldn't fail now. McNair was her target. She couldn't lose him, too.

Veronica cleared her mind and opened her bag. She picked out a black elastic hair tie and pulled her hair back into a tight ponytail. It sat high on the back of her head, her thick hair cascading down like a horsetail brushing against the base of her neck. She reached down again and felt around the side pouch until she found her necklace. She hooked the clasp behind her neck, and the Irish trinity-knot pendant slid down over her chest. She picked it up, held it in her hand, and tightly gripped it. She placed it underneath her shirt and felt the hard metal slip between her breasts. She was back on point. She bent down and splashed cool water on her face. When she came up, she heard Evie arrive. She dried herself and returned to the living room.

Evie was surprised at the change in her demeanor.

"V, don't do it. You'll regret it."

"What other choice do I have?"

She went to the couch and put on her overcoat and wound her scarf around her neck.

"There's got to be another way," Evie pleaded.

"There isn't. You were right. I was stupid for thinking we could be together. Once I realized McNair wasn't going to show up, I knew it might come to this."

"Why did he call him?"

"I don't know."

"You didn't ask him?"

"I was caught off guard! I don't know what the hell I said."

"Do you think he was communicating with him the entire time?"

"No, it was the first time since we'd been together. He had no idea what was going on—until now."

Evie watched as Veronica methodically moved around gathering her things. She went into the kitchen for a few moments and then came back out.

"Let's sit and think this through, V." Evie was struggling to catch up. "Are you even sure this will work? You have no idea how McNair will react."

"I know exactly what he'll do," Veronica replied firmly.

"Let me do it then."

"No. I have to do it. You know that."

Evie stepped in front of Veronica and took her face in her hands.

"Veronica, you don't have to do this."

Veronica stared at her. She desperately wanted to hug her friend and cry, and Evie knew it.

"I can do this," Veronica uttered.

"I know you can. I just don't want you to."

Veronica stepped away from her and pulled out her black gloves from her coat and put them on.

"Where is he?" she asked.

Reluctantly, Evie opened up her iPad.

"He's about half a mile down the street. I don't know where he thinks he's going. It's the middle of the night. It's deserted out there."

"Is there anything in that direction?"

"Not anything open. The inn is back the other way. Wait, there's a park on the other side of the town square, a deer park. What the hell is a deer park?"

"It's a park with deer in it. It's more akin to a forest." Veronica walked toward the door.

"V, wait."

She looked back at Evie for a long second.

"Stay close behind," Veronica said. She opened the door and walked out.

Jude wandered aimlessly down the cobbled sidewalk of the seaside town. He was so consumed with grief he didn't notice how beautifully the full moon lit up the multicolored buildings along the medieval street.

Instead, he fought back images from the past week that were flashing in his mind. He pictured her on the balcony as the breeze tousled her hair, and listening attentively to him when he spoke. He could see her lying across from him in bed while playing with his hair, and gazing up at him while he loved her. He stopped and braced himself against a building as tears filled his eyes again. He wiped them away and continued on.

Eventually, he reached the harbor and the town square. It opened up into a wide area of shops and local businesses. Unfortunately, everything was dark and closed up. He didn't see anywhere he could retreat. The cold, wet sea air sent a chill through him. He knew it was unlikely he would find somewhere to stay the night. He set his duffel bag down and pulled out a knit beanie and a pair of leather gloves. As he bundled up, he glanced ahead and saw a path near the waterfront heading in the direction of a large bridge in the distance. He didn't care where it would lead him. He just wanted to keep moving. He flung his bag over his shoulder, dug his hands into his coat pockets, and marched on. A short distance later, a lighted path veering off to the left caught his eye. It led into a darkened forest. He stopped and read the sign.

A deer park?

He imagined a cozy spot beneath the trees and, suddenly, the thought sounded incredibly appealing. He realized it was too late and he was too exhausted to keep walking in hopes of finding somewhere more agreeable. He decided it was his best bet at getting some rest before figuring out how to get back to England in the morning.

The moonlight illuminated the dimly lit path enough that with his extraordinary vision it was like early dawn. He entered the park hopeful he'd find an appropriate place to settle for the night. He trekked along the trail lined with tall, thick beech trees until he noticed the silhouette of what appeared to be some sort of structure. As he got closer, he saw it was a picnic area, but its design was oddly out of place. It resembled a small house that had been restructured with the windows removed and the interior cleared out to create an open seating area. There was a table and bench alongside it, as well as underneath the covering, all of which were made from the very trees that walled it in. There was thick moss on the gable roof that fell off the sides like tassels hanging from a Christmas tree. Strangely, it reminded him of the farmhouses he and Kelly would see when they traveled to Dublin on their day trips. He felt compelled to take refuge in it.

Jude set his bag on the table and pulled out his cigarettes. He sat on the wooden ledge as the weight of the evening's drama set firmly on his shoulders. Her betrayal left him drained and empty. He hung his head down, trying to stop the images. He wanted nothing more than to disappear and fade into the background again.

He was beginning to calm down when, all of a sudden, he felt a presence behind him. He looked over his shoulder and was shocked to see Veronica standing there. He jumped back around as she walked up to the structure.

"Here we are again in an old building," she said. She ambled around the picnic table while running her finger across it as if she were inspecting it.

It was dark underneath the covered shelter, but the moonlight rippled through and he could see her plainly. She looked different. Her hair was pulled back from her face, a black scarf wrapped all the way up to her chin, but it was the cold stare in her eyes that concerned him.

He stayed silent as she drew nearer.

Veronica stopped a few feet from him, in awe of his appearance. His hair was tucked beneath a beanie but she could see strands of curls trying to escape. His eyebrows loomed disturbingly over his black eyes, which shot through her. He was not happy to see her, and it pained her to see him like that.

"I wish I could make you understand, Jude," she said as she peered deep into his eyes, "or should I call you Alex?"

He clenched his teeth. "It was all bullshit, wasn't it?" he said.

"No, absolutely not. It was quite the opposite. It couldn't have been more real. That's what makes this so tragic."

"Tragic? Is that what you call this?"

She dropped her head, taking in the cold air and breathing it out slowly, trying to will herself to carry on. She came back up with a solemn expression.

"I'm so sorry. I didn't mean for this to happen."

"I'm curious. What exactly are you sorry for, manipulating me, lying to me, crushing my soul?"

"All of it," she said, pulling her shoulders back and standing stoically in front of him.

Jude tried to look away but she held his gaze and, once again, they were locked in. It was obvious their bond remained intact despite the unpleasant and tense situation.

"I love you so much," she whispered.

"Don't."

"It's true. I've never loved anyone this much, and I know I never will again."

"It doesn't matter." He broke away from her stare and flicked his cigarette over the ledge.

"It matters to me, that you know that," she said.

She took a step closer, and he instinctively stepped back. He felt for the wall behind him. He was wary of standing too close to her. He didn't trust himself not to grab her and kiss her one last time.

It was a futile effort because she continued forward until he was up against the wall. When she reached up and touched one of his curls, he looked into her eyes. It was gone. The sadness was gone. There was nothing there.

She ran her fingers down his cheek, across his stubble to his lips, and then tenderly kissed him. She came up on her toes, put her forehead on his, and breathed him in.

Jude shut his eyes. He wanted her to stop. He put his hands on her but couldn't bring himself to push her away.

"I never intended to hurt you," she said softly. "I wanted to love you, but it wasn't meant to be."

She revealed the knife in her right hand and plunged it into his chest.

Jude's eyes shot open as the blade cut into him. The pain confused him until he clutched his chest and saw his hand covered in blood. His mouth gaped opened as he raised his eyes to her in disbelief. The shock paralyzed him.

Veronica closed her eyes, kissed him on the cheek, and then stabbed him again.

She pulled out the knife and stepped away from him, her left hand following his arm down until she grasped his hand. She kept a hold of it as he leaned his head back against the wall, all the while keeping his eyes fixed on her. The moonlight streaked across her face, and he could see her breathing heavily in the cold air. He squeezed her hand and felt himself losing consciousness.

Slowly, he slid down the wall, holding onto her until his fingertips slipped away and he came to rest on the ground. He took a few shallow breaths and then closed his eyes.

Veronica was numb and detached as she stood over him, watching him take his last breath. She wanted to feel something, but she knew the wretchedness that lay beneath her defenses would surge uncontrollably if she let it.

Evie ran in and came up next to her. For a moment, they both watched over him.

"I can't believe you did it," Evie said. She knelt in front of him. "You stabbed him?"

She looked up at Veronica and was startled at how pale and stricken she appeared. Immediately, Evie stood up in front of her and cut off her view of Jude.

"V," she snapped.

Veronica brought her focus up to her.

"You should go," Evie said.

Veronica nodded. "Make him disappear," she said calmly and handed Evie the knife.

Veronica turned around, picked up Jude's duffel bag, and stepped out into the darkness.

It was cold, severely cold. She pulled her collar up and tightened the scarf around her neck, then continued on toward the park entrance.

When she reached the harbor, she set his bag down and dug deep into her pocket. She pulled out an unopened pack of cigarettes. She unwrapped it, tapped one out and lit it, and then took a long drag while scanning the empty square in front of her.

A set of headlights caught her eye, and a black sedan appeared. It drove up to the curb where she stood. Benedict came around, put Jude's duffle bag in the backseat, and opened the front passenger door for her. She took one more smoke off her cigarette, then tossed it into the street and got in. The steady hum of the engine faded as the car receded into the night.

Defender
Coming soon

The Condition Series Vol. 1
The accompanying short stories collection that introduces the world
inside the pages of *Protector*.
Available now

ABOUT THE AUTHOR

Elaine Gonzales graduated from the University of Arizona with a journalism degree and worked at The Arizona Republic for 17 years. She's an insane sports enthusiast, pop culture/news junkie and an unapologetic fan girl. *Protector* is her first novel.

You can connect with her here: **@MsLaineyG** (Twitter), **mslaineyg** (Instagram), **facebook.com/mslaineyg**, and **elainegonzales.com**.

Made in the USA
Charleston, SC
12 April 2016